Elijah Hael

The Genetic Code

by Steve Goodwin

© 2013 Steve Goodwin
ISBN: Paperback 978-0-9873784-3-9
ISBN: eBook 978-0-9873784-4-6

Published by Software Development Pty Ltd
Brisbane, Queensland, Australia

Acknowledgements

Warm thanks go to Val and Bruce Perkins for once again helping with the manuscript, contributing their thoughts, and providing some initial editing to my sometimes crazy writing style – which I understand, but maybe others wouldn't. Andrew Argent, I extend to you my warmest regards for your invaluable advice that helped this novel come to fruition in many respects.

To my wife: Many thanks for putting up with the countless times she probably said something to me and I ignored her while deep in thought, lost in Elijah Hael's world.

Maryanne D'Costa, thank you for your constant support and assistance while I was recovering from illness and after my mountain biking accident. In many ways, your appearance in my life during a time of need was as if God himself sent you to fuel my faith for a speedy recovery.

And to the many readers of my blogs, social media pages, and other novels who leave their encouraging comments: Your comments and reviews go a long way in motivating me to write and wanting to bring more exciting adventures to you.

Thanks also to the people who have spent time leaving reviews on my novels at Amazon and other online bookseller sites. These reviews help others in deciding what to read, and I understand the effort it takes to make them. You have my deepest thanks.

Finally, I thank Scott Stewart for his expertise and diligent editing of the novel. I have been fortunate enough to be able to secure Scott's services for my novels to date. Not only does Scott produce brilliant edits, he takes the manuscript up a notch. I feel blessed to have found such a terrific editor, who seamlessly gels with my writing.

To the memory of

Andrew Todd
1969-2003

God sheds a tear for those who have passed away,
not because they have died but because they are coming home.

Author's Foreword

Firstly, if you have just picked up this novel and have not read *Elijah Hael & The Last Judgement*, fear not, for this novel is a standalone piece of work. When I began writing this novel, I was conscious of the fact that some readers would pick up the book without having first read *Elijah Hael & the Last Judgement*. I wanted them to be able to start with *Elijah Hael & The Genetic Code* and still enjoy the novel to the fullest.

So, if you're new to Elijah Hael, welcome to Elijah Hael's world. If not, welcome back to enjoy Elijah's second adventure.

The idea behind *Elijah Hael & The Genetic Code* was spawned from two main sources – my background in software engineering (hence, *The Genetic Code* part) and my faith. You needn't worry about the software part getting too nerdy or techno-geeky, for while it plays a role in the story, you certainly don't need to be up on computers to understand the concepts as they are intertwined with the novel's plot.

Although the story is fictional, some parts are based on real struggles that real people go through. As I did in *Elijah Hael & The Last Judgement*, I try to bring understanding to difficult real-life circumstances that many of us face.

Those who read *Elijah Hael & The Last Judgement* will see a return of Frank, Araton, Nemamiah, Sophia, Castiel, Gunthor, and, of course, *Elijah Hael in Elijah Hael & The Genetic Code*.

After finishing this novel, I moved directly on to the third Elijah Hael book, which will also be a standalone novel set within the Elijah Hael universe. The story is focused on Sophia, a character some will first come to know in this story or meet again from Elijah Hael & The Last Judgement. The third book is set before Elijah Hael, but you will see some familiar characters, including Elijah, and various touch points with the other two novels.

Chapter 1 - Nya

Nya, lying on her queen-size bed in the early hours of the morning, in silky maroon pajamas, whispered into the mobile phone held gently against her ear in her native Irish brogue: "Take your right hand and start undoing your shirt buttons from the top down – slowly: one button at a time."

Isaac, an ocean away in Australia, replied, "I would rather this be *your* hand undoing these buttons." He started to undo the top button of his white cotton crinkly shirt and proceeded, slowly and methodically, down to the bottom button. All the while he imagined Nya's soft hands doing the work. "But since we are apart, this will have to do."

Just then Nya heard several short high-pitched beeps sounding from the adjacent living room. Her blue eyes sparkled like sapphires and a wide smile parted her lips. "I've done it!" she shouted.

Isaac jerked the phone away from his ear as an instinctive reaction to Nya's shout. He furled his eyebrows and fumbled to get control of the phone. "Wait, what did I miss? I haven't even gotten started yet, Nya."

"It's not *that*," she said, her rich voice so playful. "I have to go, Isaac. I'll call you later." She punched the end call button and raced into the living room of her modest two-bedroom flat. The little speaker on the ultra-light 13" Ultrabook she had recently purchased continued to sound successive beeps. She sat down in the black leather lounge in front of the coffee table and studied the text scrolling down the Ultrabook's screen. The genetic code unraveled line by line into readable English instructions. She shook her head, struggling to comprehend her accomplishment. Nearly a decade's work was all coming together. She closed her eyes and drew in a long breath. This was her moment, her Nobel Prize in the making. She knew that this was a true game-changer that would change scientific knowledge on life forever.

The smell of day-old coffee wafting up from a coffee mug stamped with a bright-red heart that Isaac had given her last Valentine's day fired her senses. Anxious for a caffeine hit despite the fact that she was high on adrenalin, Nya picked up the half-full mug with a shaky hand and took a sip. The taste of the bitter cold coffee raced across her tongue. She screwed up her nose and gulped down the remaining coffee. She set the mug on the table and leaned back waiting for the caffeine hit she was chasing to course through her veins and give her mind a kick-start.

Her mobile phone emitted a high-pitched beep-beep. She read the SMS message that popped up on the display: "Get out of the apartment now. You have 60 seconds." Each sentence caused her eyebrows to raise more than the previous. She read the message again and wondered why. Another text appeared: "They will be at your front door in 50 seconds. Take your Ultrabook and go out through the bedroom door."

Nya chewed at the fingernail of her left forefinger and tapped the SMS message to bring up the details about the sender. *Anonymous.* No profile, no return number, no particulars. She didn't need that caffeine now. Her heart rate spiked as a number of thoughts raced through her mind. *What should I do? Is this believable? Who is coming to the front door?*

A new SMS message: "10 seconds."

She heard the sound of the front door handle being jiggled. She spun around and saw the door handle rocking back and forth. Her heart pounded. She snatched up the Ultrabook, slammed the screen shut, and bolted for the bedroom door. The apartment began trembling violently and she stumbled as she juggled the Ultrabook and mobile phone in an attempt to shield her ears from the thunderous boom of an explosion. Through the high-pitch ringing in her ears, she heard a masculine voice bellowing, commanding: "Move, move, move!"

Nya slid open the glass bedroom door and hurried out onto the balcony. The rusty fire escape ladder provided a method of descent from her second-story flat. She unhooked the holding catch and the metal rungs lowered, clunking and rattling, until the bottom rung was four feet above the ground. With the Ultrabook wedged under her armpit and the mobile phone clenched between her teeth, Nya clambered down the ladder as fast as her legs would go.

She glanced over her shoulder and saw a man wearing a balaclava and dressed in all black standing at the rail of her balcony with a machine gun slung over his shoulder. Now covered in sweat and nearly breathless, Nya dropped down from the final rung of the ladder onto the cold pavement below. She landed so hard her knees buckled. She pulled the mobile phone out of her mouth and took off sprinting, barefooted and in only her silk pajamas, as fast as she could down the street. In the distance, in front of her, a white BMW sedan came skidding around the corner at the end of the street and speeded toward her.

With nowhere to run, she froze. The BMW's tires bellowed smoke and screeched, clawing for traction as the car lurched to a stop beside her. The driver leant over and flung open the passenger side door. "Get in!" he shouted.

Nya glanced back towards her apartment and saw several men with machine guns strapped to their backs clambering down the fire escape. After weighing her options, she accepted the man's proposal. Before she could even pull the door closed, the driver had grabbed onto her arm tightly as he spun the BMW one 180 degrees. She fought to keep hold of her Ultrabook and mobile phone. Not being able to secure both, she put all her effort into the Ultrabook. Her mobile phone succumbed to gravity and flew out the open door and clinked onto the pavement. At the end of the spin, the driver released her arm and stomped his foot hard down on the accelerator. The passenger side door slammed shut with a slap.

"Hold on," the man said as he pointed the nose of the BMW into an approaching corner. The clapping of gunshots echoed from behind the BMW as it drifted around the modest bend. Nya fought the g-force generated by the turn and tried to stay upright in her seat, but lost. She ended up thrown hard against the passenger door.

The man shifted through the gears as he weaved the BMW in and out of traffic like a seasoned rally car driver. He scanned for obstacles along the road and planned exactly where and when to steer the car to carve an ideal pathway through the traffic. She saw him glance in the rearview mirror and looked through the side-view herself. Two black SUVs were gaining on them.

"Fasten your seatbelt, Nya!"

Nya heard the words. She could see what was going on around her. But she struggled to move. The man's words echoed slowly around in her head like a DVD playing warbled in slow motion. *Am I dreaming?* No. She knew this was reality, although she did not want to believe it.

The man slapped the steering wheel and yelled. "Nya, fasten your seatbelt!"

That snapped her back to the present and her mind began processing her surroundings. She guessed the man was in his early 40s. He had pale skin and short brown kempt hair, piercing blue eyes that were honest and clear, and he appeared to be in great physical shape. She grabbed the seatbelt, pulled the metallic clip over her shoulder, and buckled it.

The deafening sound of metal on metal, shattering glass, and a bone-rattling bang thundered through the rear of the BMW. They both lurched forward. Their seatbelts snapped tight, holding them in their seats. An SUV had rammed the BMW from behind. The BMW swerved wildly as the wheels lost traction from the shunt. Nya screamed, hugging her Ultrabook against her chest, and swayed violently in her seat. The man made a few short steering corrections and regained control of the car.

"Hang on," he said, as they approached a narrow side street of the main road. He downshifted to use the engine to brake while banking the car sharply onto the side road. The SUV's tail end struggled to make the sharp turn and overshot which gave the nimble BMW some leeway. Nya felt as though the car was skating on ice as it accelerated out of the turn. Fast-tracking back up through the gears, the driver quickly had the BMW blazing way over the local speed limit.

Nya looked behind them anxiously. Once again the SUVs were gaining on them. Ahead in the distance a railroad crossing light started flashing as a freight train approached from the left. The man punched the gas and the car lurched forward. Nya winced, knowing that he wanted to cross the track before the train reached the intersection. The boom gate started to descend blocking the road ahead. The BMW swerved to the opposite side of the road.

The train approached the intersection. It was impossible for the BMW to outrun the train, yet, the man accelerated. Nya's heart boomed. She did not want to die. She felt the blood drain out of her face as she yelled, "What are you doing? Stop! We are going to crash!"

In a soft reassuring voice the man said, "Trust me."

"Trust you?! We're going to die!" She wondered if her father had experienced the same level of anxiety in the moments before his plane crashed. *Did he know he had only seconds to live?*

An endless succession of freight cars was passing by ahead. No way would the train pass the intersection before they ploughed into it. Nya expected that when they hit, it would be over quick, and there would be nothing left of them. She shut her eyes, hugged her Ultrabook tightly, and, believing impact was imminent, whispered a prayer.

The BMW hit a slight incline just before the railroad crossing and launched into the air. The man gripped the steering wheel tightly and gritted his teeth as the BMW slammed into the side of the freight car. The wood of the freight car splintered like matchsticks pummeled by a hammer. Open air greeted the BMW in the middle of the freight car before plunging through the opposite side leaving behind a gaping hole. With a thud, the BMW landed nose first on the other side of the railroad crossing and bounced back and forth a few times before settling.

The man swerved the BMW back onto the correct side of the road and resumed driving at a leisurely speed as though it was all in a day's work.

Nya whimpered. "Is it over?"

"Yes," the man replied.

"Am I dead?"

"Do you *feel* dead?"

Nya opened her eyes and let out a huge breath.

She gazed out the window at the passing countryside and then turned and looked out of the rear window. No sign of any SUVs. Still shaking from the adrenalin running through her veins, and that day-old coffee she hadn't really needed, she locked her eyes onto the man." Who are you?"

"Elijah," he replied. "Elijah Hael."

Chapter 2 - Isaac

Isaac, attempting to continue what Nya started, closed his eyes and tried to conjure the image of her undoing the buttons on his crinkly white cotton shirt. But … thoughts intruded. *Why had Nya hang up so fast? What had so captured her attention that she just dropped him so cold and hard?* Her voice echoed in his mind: "I have to go, Isaac. I'll call you later. I have to go, Isaac. I'll call you later…."

He pressed redial on his mobile phone. "Hey, this is Nya. I'm either on the phone, out of mobile range, or I've switched it off. Please leave a message and I'll get back to you shortly."

"Dammit," Isaac muttered. He hopped off his king-size waterbed and headed for the living room of his two-bedroom house in Caboolture just north of Brisbane. As he did every morning, he grabbed the remote off the top of the mahogany bookshelf and pressed 9 which sparked to life the 60" flat screen TV on the wall opposite the kitchen.

He tossed the remote onto the ash-grey sofa and surveyed his collection of toys – various entertainment appliances in the black wooden cabinet beneath the TV: a Blu-ray player, surround sound amplifier, XBOX 360, PlayStation, and a Wii. His friends often referred to Isaac as an "entertainment addict." If he was not playing video games, he was watching TV or a movie or … talking on his mobile phone … or listening to music on his state-of-the-art stereo system. Nya always told his teasing friends, "Now, now. There are worse addictions. This one's harmless, so leave my Isaac alone." Nya didn't mind Isaac's amusements because they gave her ample time to develop software for ASIO, Australia's Security Intelligence Organization, or to work on decrypting ancient texts and codes for museums and universities.

In the kitchen, Isaac flicked on the stainless steel kettle. He gave a coffee-stained cup in the sink a quick rinse, dumped a spoonful of instant coffee in it, and then placed it on the long breakfast counter that separated the kitchen from the lounge. It was the perfect layout for an entertainment addict. He could watch TV while preparing meals, or better yet, play games with a free hand. He spun around and grabbed a non-stick fry pan out of the cupboard and set it on the stove. He put a little jive in his movements and danced around while preparing his breakfast. He hummed along with the dramatic music as the Channel 9 morning news came on. He sashayed sideways, pulled a couple of eggs out of the fridge, and cracked them into the fry pan. When the kettle whistled he filled his cup with boiling water and let the strong aroma of coffee fill his nostrils. He cradled the cup in his hands and took a long sip that drained the cup. He added another spoonful of coffee into the cup and began pouring the steaming water in for a second round.

A news story drew his attention to the TV. "Armed men invaded a residence at the Green Arbor apartment complex…. Shots were fired…. New Zealand police are currently on the scene." Isaac leaned over the counter for a closer look. The newscast cut from the anchorwoman to footage of the scene of the home invasion. Isaac squinted and looked at the buildings, which were familiar, very similar to the ones near Nya's apartment in New Zealand. A burning sensation licked his toes. He sprang backward. The boiling water had overflowed the cup, run down its side, and off the kitchen counter and onto the floor. "Damn," he said.

As he shook his foot he wondered if the news story had anything to do with Nya. "Nah," he said. "Coincidence."

He grabbed a dishcloth and began cleaning up the overflowed coffee when a rapping came on the front door. *An early morning visit,* he thought as he opened the door to two men – one stern looking and middle-aged, heavy set and dressed in a black suit, and the other a police officer. The heavy set man said, "Are you Isaac?"

Isaac, sheepish, whispered, "Yes."

The man flashed his badge. "I'm detective Senior Sergeant Frank Mercer from the Australian Federal Police, and this is constable Stevens. Sir, we require you to come with us down to the local police station and then accompany me to the AFP headquarters in Brisbane."

Isaac raised an eyebrow. "But, *why?* Has this anything to do with Nya?"

Sergeant Mercer was blunt. "Yes. We don't have much time. Please come now."

"Certainly," Isaac said. "I'll just grab some shoes and lock up." He was not overly surprised. In her work with ASIO Nya sometimes became involved in situations that put her and her loved ones in danger. Truth was, Isaac had no idea what she was working on in New Zealand. Nya was not permitted to tell him about her work. A few years earlier the Australian Federal Police had taken him into protection for safety after Nya had received death threats. He presumed something similar might have happened again … until that news story flashed back into his mind. He winced and shook his head, finding it much more difficult now to dismiss the report as having nothing to with Nya.

After a short search in all the usual places he found his Nike running shoes under his bed. Though Nya always complained about how much they smelt (and demanded that he spray the soles with a deodorizer quite often), Isaac often quipped that he wished the foot odor they gave off was even stronger so he could find them easier. He had to admit that at close proximity the shoes were a bit pungent. He picked up his mobile phone and charger and returned to the front door.

* * *

Meanwhile, Sergeant Frank Mercer scouted the road approaching the house to check for any signs of hostility. Nothing looked unusual and he was not expecting any problems. The tip off he received from Castiel, a stranger but someone he trusted, had informed him that he should take Isaac into protection because Nya was in some kind of trouble and it was possible that the people after her would seize Isaac to get to her. Frank had worked with Nya in the past and knew she was a powerful resource for the AFP when they were lucky enough to drag her away from ASIO. Modern-day technology was all getting to be a bit much for Frank and he found himself having to rely more and more on experts like Nya. Crime was now a high-tech field with Internet scams, credit card fraud, and other techno-robberies. Not like the good old days of bank hold-ups which Frank loved sinking his teeth into. In his 20 years with the Australian Federal Police, Frank had scored over 100 arrests. And he was damn proud of it.

* * *

"Right, I'm ready," Isaac said as he locked the front door behind him.

"This way," Sergeant Frank Mercer said as he led Isaac to the black late-model Holden Commodore sedan parked on the road.

Constable Stevens offered Isaac the front seat, which Isaac accepted. Isaac sat down into the front passenger's seat, eager for the chance to check out the various gadgets that littered the undercover police car. In the center of the dash panel, a sophisticated GPS police computer system displayed a map showing Isaac's house. He scanned the dashboard covered with a bewildering assortment of switches and buttons. Isaac fought the urge to begin flipping the switches and pushing the buttons. *Keep your hands to yourself.* The temptation was strong, but he managed to resist.

Sergeant Mercer called the Caboolture Police Station on the car's radio system and advised them that they were approximately 15 minutes out. Mercer was clearly not familiar with the area and updated the guidance computer's destination to the police station. Then he drove off following the directions delivered by the device's well-spoken female English-accented voice. The route to the precinct took them down a few back roads before merging with the Bruce Highway and then exiting onto King Street, the main road through central Caboolture, to the police station.

Isaac was busy studying all the gadgets in the car as Mercer joined the highway until, suddenly, the sound of shattering glass pierced the calm. Then the ringing sound of a gunshot penetrated Isaac's ears. He looked up to see blood splattering the inside of the windshield. He shot his head around and saw Constable Stevens dangling lifeless in his seatbelt in the backseat. Blood flowed freely from a gaping hole between his open staring eyes. Isaac slapped his hand over his mouth, dry retching as his stomach churned. He had never seen a dead body before – well, in video games, yes, in real life, no. Through the shards of the smashed rear windshield, Isaac saw a black SUV with a man hanging out of the passenger window with a rifle pointed directly at him.

"Get down!" Sergeant Mercer hollered. Isaac ducked just as the sound of bullets spraying into the rear of the Commodore rattled his ears. Frank responded by hitting the gas and jerking the wheel left and then right, doing his best to avoid endangering vehicles on the highway while making it difficult for the gunman to execute a clear shot at either one of them.

He grabbed the mouthpiece and spoke into the two-way radio: "This is Detective Frank Mercer. We have a Code 1 with a 303 and 701 in progress on the Bruce Highway, North of Caboolture. Need immediate backup."

The dispatch operator replied: "Roger that. Backup on its way to your vehicle's current GPS location."

Mercer turned to Isaac. "Can you use a handgun?"

In a weak voice Isaac replied, "I've never tried. Well not in real life, only in video games."

Mercer seemed to consider his options for half an instant before deciding not to give Isaac a piece. "OK."

Isaac was relieved. He knew that the possibility of accidentally gunning down a member of the public was too high for a newbie shooter.

The car suddenly lost traction and veered sharply towards the left side of the road. "Bullet," Mercer said. "Front left tire." He tried his best to regain control, but sparks flew as the front left bumper of the Commodore collided with the guardrail on the side of the road. An instant later the SUV rammed the vehicle from behind causing the front of the police car to dig into the guardrail. The car turned sharply and the right hand tires dug into the tarmac and the vehicle flipped. The vehicle rolled, over and over, crumpling the roof and sides. Isaac and the detective were tossed around like ragdolls in a spin dryer to the extent their seat belts allowed. The car slid down the embankment on its roof before coming to a final sudden stop in a grove of trees.

Dazed, Mercer asked, "Isaac, are you still with us?"

"I, I-, I think so," Isaac stuttered.

Frank unlatched his seatbelt and crawled through the remains of the smashed driver's side window. He stumbled over to the passenger side window, kicked what remained of the broken glass, and pulled Isaac through it. Both men looked as though they had been in a losing street fight. A steady stream of blood was flowing from a large gash on the left side of Mercer's head. Isaac gave himself a once-over and was relieved to find no apparent open wounds.

"Can you walk, Isaac?"

Mentally scanning his body, Isaac replied, "Yes, I think so."

"Quick, let's enter the forest. They will be after us soon. We'll have a better chance in there."

Mercer navigated quickly through the trees with Isaac following closely behind. A rush of adrenalin from the shock circulated throughout Isaac's body, allowing him to move swiftly even though he was in a world of pain.

* * *

Deep in the dense forest Frank noticed a little dried up creek bed. He considered it the best possible position to bunker down and hope backup arrived before whoever was trying to kill them succeeded. They hid behind a bank of large rocks in the creek bed. Frank armed himself with his Glock 22 pistol in anticipation of an attack.

Faint sounds of movement in the distance echoed amongst the trees. Louder and louder it came as the pursuers were closing in. Then: nothing, a moment of silence, until a calm but authoritative voice said: "Get up slowly and drop your gun."

Frank searched out the source of the voice until he fixated on two fit looking men dressed in black business suits and holding 9mm silenced pistols that were trained on him and Isaac from the rear. Frank cut his eyes around to Isaac. "Get up, slowly." He himself rose and turned towards the gunmen keeping his Glock 22 pointed towards the ground.

In a commanding voice, the man bellowed: "Drop your gun! I will not tell you again!"

Frank paused for an instant and considered his options. Too late. A sharp sting above his left breast drew his eyes down. A flow of blood started to extend outwards across his white shirt from the source of the pain under his tattered suit jacket. His knees buckled and he collapsed to the ground. Concerned for Isaac, he attempted to fight off the dizziness flooding his mind. He failed. All went dark.

* * *

The gunman shook his head. "I told the fool I wouldn't tell him again." He shrugged his shoulders. "Why do they never listen?"

Twice today Isaac had seen a person shot. He stood frozen, numb. The second gunman approached him. "Let that be a lesson to you," he said as he grabbed Isaac's arms and secured his wrists behind his back with black duct tape. "You are coming with us, Isaac." Dazed, Isaac stumbled along as they led him by his elbow back to the SUV. After shoving Isaac into the back of the SUV, the man pulled a black cotton bag over Isaac's head and sealed it around his neck with more black duct tape.

Isaac shook violently as if he were standing naked in an ice field. He clamped his chin down on his chest and closed his eyes. Warm urine flowed down the inside of his leg as shock and fear ravaged his body.

Chapter 3 - Cain

Cain, with a look of evil determination on his face, asked his son Enoch, "Well, did you get her?"

Enoch had been dreading this moment. Fearing Cain's reaction to his answer Enoch kept his distance from the man who was seated behind the desk. Cain was a sight. He was a fairly weathered man in his late 40s with a zigzag scar that ran down his face from the base of his left eye to the bottom of his left ear. He had lost the eye and had the empty space filled with a bionic eye implant that his corporation N.O.D. – Nanorobotic Organ Development – had created. His head was hairless, not because he was genetically bald but because he preferred to shave. The man had an issue with body hair, which he believed signified "an un-evolved human," and thus he shaved all traces off his head, face, arms, and legs. With no eyebrows, no hair, that bionic eye, and the angry scar, Cain had quite the menacing appearance.

Enoch took a step back. "Unfortunately, Cain, Nya ... escaped. We did, however, arrest Isaac. Seth's team is bringing him here as we speak." Enoch referred to his father not as Dad but by his first name and had done so for as far back as he could recall.

Cain slammed his fist on the desk. "How can a team of professionals let a girl slip through their fingers?"

"Early reports suggest someone helped her," Enoch said, more calmly than he felt. "A car picked her up after she made it down the fire escape of her apartment."

Cain bored his eyes into Enoch, squinting and clenching his teeth. His cheeks glowed red. "Who?"

"We are not sure. We are looking into several possibilities. We did recover Nya's mobile phone from the scene. The SMS messages in its logs may give us more information."

* * *

Cain spun his chair around and stared through the window at the cloudless sky, contemplating his next move. He wanted Nya. He needed what she had discovered and was prepared to go to any lengths to get it – *any lengths.*

"Will there be anything more?" Enoch asked, his tone cautious.

"No!" Cain shouted. "Just get out!"

Enoch turned and walked softly out of Cain's grand office on the 77th floor, which at one time had been an observation deck in the Q1 Tower, a modern 78-floor skyscraper. The glass walls around Cain's office were six inches thick and afforded a breathtaking view of the ocean and Surfers Paradise on the Gold Coast. Cain had purchased the well-known Queensland landmark and converted it to the headquarters of his global corporation.

The phone on Cain's desk beeped and a voice said, "You have an incoming call from Seth. Should I pass it through?"

"Very well."

Seth's voice boomed through speaker: "Cain, we have Isaac. We are five minutes out."

"Good." He smiled at the good news. "Take him to the interrogation room."

Cain tapped the end call button and then spun back around on his chair, stood up, and strode to the elevator. He wanted to be present for the questioning.

* * *

As Seth removed the sack covering his head, Isaac squinted to shield his eyes from the blinding white shaft of the spotlight trained on his face. His forearms and ankles burned where the white polyester ropes securing them to the metal chair chewed into his flesh. Isaac was thankful that his wrists were bound with duct tape, for the thick material provided some protection against the cutting strands of the rope.

Seth paced around the chair moving in and out of Isaac's view. "So, Isaac, we can do this the easy way or … the *hard* way." He leaned into within inches of Isaac's face, blocking the rays of the spotlight. Isaac grimaced as he felt Seth's hot breath on his face. "All we need to know is where Nya is. If you tell us, you can go. If not, you will experience pain." Seth slapped his palms against the sides of the chair to punctuate his sentence. Isaac jolted upright. "Cain doesn't mess around."

With Seth blocking the blinding spotlight Isaac noticed another man in the room, standing behind and to the left of Seth. He presumed the bald man was none other than the Cain who didn't mess around. When Seth had first tied Isaac to the chair he had introduced himself in a rather cordial manner and advised him to co-operate. It had seemed to Isaac that Seth was trying to befriend him. Now he was not so sure.

Isaac stuttered. "I-, I- I don't know. I spoke to her briefly this morning on the telephone, and that was all."

"Did you know?" he said. "And what was the last thing you talked about?"

Isaac stared down at the floor and replied, "Nothing in particular." He had rather not share the intimate details of his last phone call with Nya. For one, nothing had actually happened, and for another, he would prefer not to have to fess up to a little phone sex.

Cain strode over to a nearby cabinet and retrieved a glass jar. He held it up. "See this, Isaac?"

Isaac gulped at the sight of an eyeball floating inside the jar in some sort of liquid.

"Eyes are always better in pairs," Cain said. "We will add your left eye to this jar and make it an even pair … if you do not tell us."

Isaac leaned back hard into the chair to move his head as far away from the gruesome image as possible. "You see, the problem is," Isaac said, clenching his teeth, "I really don't know."

Cain let out a terrifying evil laugh. "Seth, fetch a knife. Let's add an eye to our collection." Seth turned and left the room.

Isaac grimaced, his bottom lip quivering. "Wait, wait, you have to believe me. I really don't know."

Seth returned, holding a smallish knife that appeared to be a scalpel. He gripped Isaac's head in his large left hand and positioned the blade near the corner of Isaac's left eye. "Stay still. This is going to hurt."

Isaac tried to wrench his head free of the man's hand, but Seth's grip was too strong. He shut his eye hoping to somehow stop the knife. Isaac pleaded. "Please, please…." He began to sob. "I don't know."

Cain spoke up. "Forget it, Seth. He doesn't know anything. Dose him up with GHB and take him to the compound. We might be able to use him later."

Seth slipped the sack back over Isaac's head and secured it with duct tape around his neck. He cut the ropes holding his legs and arms to the chair and then dragged him out to his vehicle.

* * *

Cain took the elevator from the second basement, which he had turned into an interrogation area, up to his office. The elevator trip took approximately 43 seconds to travel the 320 meters up to his office on the 77th floor. Inside the lift, he paced around frustrated over Nya's escape. He had planned all along to take her as soon as she completed the code she had been working on. He pounded his fist against the wall and yelled in anger, "How could she have possibly gotten away?! How could she have known we were coming?! Nobody knew we were even watching her!"

Back at his desk, he pulled a bottle of Scotch out of the desk drawer and poured a hefty splash into a glass. He took a sip and leant back in his chair.

The phone rang and he grabbed the handset. "What now?"

A voice responded: "We have information that the detective escorting Isaac survived."

Cain's eyes bulged and his face twisted into a red mass. "Then deal with it!" He slammed the phone down.

Chapter 4 – Frank

"Frank, can you hear me?" The soft, female voice sounded in his ears but he had no strength to respond. "My name is Sarah. I'm a paramedic. You're on a trolley. We are wheeling you to the emergency room. Hang in there."

Frank was dazed, cold, and tired. He gazed at the glow of the florescent lights passing quickly above him but couldn't focus. He let his heavy eyelids close and listened to the buzz of voices all around him.

A male voice asked, "What do we have here?"

The female voice – was it Sarah? – replied. "Vehicle accident, gunshot wound. Mountain bikers found him lying in a ravine in a forest near Caboolture. They called emergency services who alerted officers who were tending to a nearby accident scene. A CareFlight helicopter brought him here for emergency treatment. I've stabilized his bleeding. After the vehicle accident he apparently ventured into the forest for some reason and was shot."

"So that's the case of the day so far," the ER physician said. "Does our John Doe have a name?"

"Yes, Doc, according to his I.D. he is 'Detective Senior Sergeant Frank Mercer.'"

"A police officer?"

"It would seem so."

While checking Frank's blood pressure and pulse the doctor said, "Have a nurse start an IV and get him straight to x-ray. We need to see where that bullet ended up."

Frank passed out.

On regaining consciousness Frank heard a woman's voice again. "He's waking up, Doctor."

"Are you with us, Sergeant Mercer?"

Frank managed to open his eyes a little and the doctor gradually came into focus. The doctor was a youngish gentleman in his early 30's wearing the customary white doctor's cloak over a pair of stonewashed jeans and a blue sweatshirt. Frank said, "I think so."

"You are an extraordinarily lucky man, Sergeant. The bullet missed your heart by a hare's whisker. And... Well, the way the slug missed it is rather unusual." He paused for a moment and adjusted his glasses. "It's as if the bullet changed course after entering your body."

Frank cleared a little tickle in his throat with a short deliberate hack. "How bad are my injuries, Doc?"

"Aside from the head wound and bullet hole, the rest of your injuries are superficial. You will be sore for a couple of days. I've prescribed some morphine to help with the pain."

Frank tried to sit up but the nurse, whom Frank only now noticed, quickly interjected and pushed him gently but firmly back down. "You need to rest, Sergeant. You don't want to tear your stitches."

"I *need* to get back to work," Frank said as he massaged the back of his neck.

"It'll have to wait, Sergeant," the doctor stated in a commanding tone. "You are in no condition to get up. I am admitting you for observation. I'll come check on you tomorrow and we will take it from there."

Frank turned to the nurse. "Do you have my mobile phone?"

"Yes, it's just over here." The nurse retrieved it from a nearby table and passed it to Frank. "Can I get you anything?"

"No, I'll be fine," he said. "Thank you."

The doctor added some notes to Frank's chart and then left the room with the nurse.

Frank checked his emails and missed calls. A very enthusiastic salesman wanted to sell him some pricey solar panels for his house on the promise that after a few years he could save several dollars a month. "What a deal," Frank muttered. Then there was the annoying young woman who was still trying to get him to change power companies. "The deals keep on coming," he said, sighing. The last call was from Leigh at head office. He immediately called the Federal Police Headquarters.

A young woman answered. "AFP. How may I help you?"

"Detective Frank Mercer here. Please put me through to Leigh Hammond."

"Yes, sir. He is expecting your call."

As he listened to the on-hold music, Frank thought back to the many cases he and Leigh had worked on together at the Australian Federal Police. Frank trusted Leigh and had a good rapport with him. Fitness wise, Leigh was the better man, which Frank credited to his being a few years younger. But, the real reason was that Leigh spent an hour every other day at the gym toning his muscles and working his cardio. Frank did not. Leigh fancied himself a bit of a ladies' man, and in some ways he was. Frank used Leigh's charismatic ways to great advantage whenever they worked a crime that required the trust of a lady.

A moment later Leigh came on the line and, in a concerned but friendly voice, bellowed, "Frank, what the hell happened?"

"A black SUV jumped us on the highway and some goons started shooting." Frank took a second to catch his breath. "They were good – good enough to off Constable Stevens, take out the car's tires, and run us off the road."

"Damn shame about Stevens."

"Yes, it is."

"Do you know who they were, Frank?"

"I only got a brief look at them before I was shot." He tried to visualize their faces from his foggy memory. "I may be able to identify them from mug shots. Have a bunch of mug shots sent down. White males in their 30s."

"I'll get someone on it right away, Frank."

Frank heard the sounds of keys clicking as Leigh created an email request as he spoke.

"How bad are your injuries?"

"I'm sore and stiff, but I'll be OK. Apparently the bullet missed my vital organs. Guy's a bad shot. He was at point-blank range."

"Good thing," Leigh said.

Frank stared out of the window of his private hospital room at the tops of tall gum trees swaying in the breeze. "Any news on Isaac?"

"No. The detectives on the scene said the initial evidence appeared to suggest the shooters dragged him back to the road and took him away by vehicle. From there, they have no idea where they took him. No eyewitnesses. They found his mobile phone close to the ravine where the mountain bikers found you."

"What about Nya?" Frank asked. He wondered if a storm was brewing, given the restless trees and darkening sky.

"She is missing, and it looks as though she was involved in an incident in New Zealand. Several witnesses report that gunmen chased a woman who escaped with a man in a white BMW. Other witnesses say they saw a white BMW go airborne and crash through a speeding wooden freight car on a rail crossing trying to outrun some black SUVs. It's quite a story, like something you would expect to see in an action movie."

Frank pressed the phone harder against his ear. "Black SUVs, eh? What do you think, Leigh?" Frank had his own ideas but thought he would ask. "Who is behind this?"

"Until we understand the motive it is hard to say. But several black SUVs have been purchased recently in New Zealand and Australia by N.O.D. I certainly wouldn't put something like this past our old pal Cain."

"Yes, that is my gut feeling." Leigh confirmed Frank's own suspicions. "If I can ID someone from the mug shots that should help. I don't think they expected me to live so they didn't try to hide their identity." He stroked the bandage covering the wound on his chest. "Whoever is behind it, their first mistake was not making sure I was dead."

"Do you need protective detail in the hospital, Frank? Will they come after you?"

"It's possible. I don't plan to stick around here for long. Can you send over a fresh set of clothes? I'll be needing them soon. My old ones are a little tattered at this point, with the bullet hole in the shirt and the pants they cut off of me."

Leigh chuckled. "Already done, Frank. They should be in a closet near your bed."

"Thanks, Leigh. I'll talk to you later. Expedite those mug shots." Frank laid the mobile phone beside him on the mattress then closed his eyes. The morphine they had given him for the pain made him drowsy. He dosed off.

* * *

Two men wearing black suits approached the hospital reception desk. The older of the two said, "We're looking for Frank Mercer."

The cheerful young receptionist said, "Just a second." She entered the name into her computer. "Here we go. He is in room 2L. Take the elevator to the second floor and follow the corridor down to the right."

The man smiled. "Thank you."

On entering the room, one of the men shut the door while the other walked quietly over to Frank and covered Frank's mouth with his hand.

* * *

Frank woke from his light sleep to the sight of a silenced 9mm pointed directly at his forehead. The man holding it was vaguely familiar. After an instant Frank recognized him as the colleague of the man who had shot him in the forest. He thought about struggling, but recalling his last encounter decided not to. These people did not mess around.

The assailant was an ordinary looking man in his late 20s, average build, black hair. He waved the 9mm in Frank's face. "Frank, all I want to know is if you have spoken to anyone."

Frank shook his head from side to side.

"Why don't I believe you?" He snatched Frank's mobile phone off the mattress and tossed it to his partner. "Check out the call log. See if he has called anyone."

Frank watched as the man by the door scanned through the recent call list. "He spoke to a 'Leigh Hammond' about five minutes ago."

"When you lie, it's going to hurt." He moved the barrel of the 9mm over Frank's chest and pressed it hard down into the bandages. The stitches underneath the dressing split apart. Blood seeped out and turned the white cloth a deep shade of red. Muffled by the hand over his mouth, Frank cried out in pain.

"Now, let's try this again." He raised the 9mm so it was pointing directly between Frank's eyes. "Who have you spoken to about what happened?"

Frank stared directly into the eyes of his assailant. His detective instincts warned him that they would kill him if he told them the truth. Then they would go after Leigh. They already had too much information from his phone records. He silently cursed himself for increasing the screen lock from 1 minute to 15 minutes recently after becoming annoyed at having to enter his password each time he wanted to make a call.

Once again the man poked his 9mm into the bloodied dressings. Frank winced, holding back screams while enduring the pain. At this point he thought: *Thank God for the morphine.*

Just then there was a knock on the door. The man interrogating Frank holstered his gun while whispering, "Say anything – anything at all – and whoever comes through that door will be killed, and then you."

A nurse entered the room pushing a cart bearing cardiac monitoring equipment. "Oh, you have visitors, Sergeant," she said, smiling at each in turn. "Sorry to interrupt. I just have to take your vitals and fill in the chart. Then I'll be on my way."

Doing his best to stay calm Frank replied, "No problem."

The two men stood in silence and watched the nurse and Frank for any sign of a tip-off. Frank did not recognize the nurse. She had long raven-black hair that flowed down over her shoulders and dazzling emerald-green eyes. There was a strange aura about her. She glanced at Frank and gave him a quick smile. Then she moved behind the observation cart and all at once gave it a mighty push with both hands sending it hurtling towards the man near the door. The cart collected him and sent him careening towards the wall where he hit his head and passed out cold.

As the other man pulled his gun from under his coat, the nurse leapt onto the edge of the bed, took a giant step, then whirled into a spinning back kick that landed her right foot on the side of his left cheek which sent a spray of blood accompanied by several of his teeth flying across the room. His 9mm fell from his hand as a bullet shot out of the barrel and lodged in the far wall as he tumbled to the floor and lost consciousness.

Sophia, urgent, said, "We have to get you out of here, Frank. Can you walk?"

Frank, amazed and startled, replied, "I think so…. But who are you?"

"Sophia."

Chapter 5 - Curiosity

Nya awoke from a deep sleep to the sounds of birds chirping. She squinted and tried to recall what had happened, how she had gotten there. She remembered the man in the BMW who said his name was Elijah Hael. That was it; the rest of her memory was blank.

She pulled herself by her elbows into a sitting position and took in the unfamiliar surroundings. She was still in her own pajamas on a queen-size double ensemble bed under a green silk sheet in a room about five meters square with log cabin-type walls. To the right, an opening led into what appeared to be a living room. Through a slightly-ajar door she could see a frosted-glass shower door: en suite. Against the wall opposite the end of the bed was a window overlooking distant mountains. Beneath the window on a black oak dresser lay a pair of jeans, a white top, and underwear.

Nya swung her legs off the bed and walked over and examined the clothes, wondering whether they were intended for her. *Who else?* she thought. She spun around and spotted on the bedside table a sheet of folded paper with "Nya" scrawled on it. She opened the note and read:

> *I've had to leave to attend to some business. I'll be back later. You'll find some clothes in your size to change into on the dresser. Do not use your Ultrabook. They will be tracking it, but feel free to use the computer in the living area. We can talk when I get back. Elijah.*

Several questions formed in her mind. *Who is this Elijah? Who are "They"?* She shrugged and scratched her head. A hot shower would help her make sense of it all – *maybe*. She entered the en suite and locked the door behind her. The small metal bolt gave her some small sense of security although she knew that any solid blow to the door would snap the lock like a matchstick. She stepped under the steaming water and let the pulsing jets massage her tired muscles and clear her foggy mind. As she slathered the creamy soap over her soft skin she hesitated to explore around her breast and her fingertip went to the small lump on her left breast. It was a ritual of sorts. Each morning she felt for the lump in hopes that it would not be there. She feared the worst and kept shoving the thought to the back of her mind only to be reminded every time she took a shower that the mass was not going away. Her thoughts drifted back to that doctor's appointment she had before taking her assignment in New Zealand.

* * *

"Nya," the gentleman's voice had called out to her across the waiting room.

Nya looked up from the magazine article she was reading on gluten sensitivity and saw Dr. Philip Michaels. "Yes," she said as she rose and followed him back to the examination room.

He closed the door behind and said, "Please take a seat, Nya," in his warm, comforting voice. He gestured toward the chair beside his desk.

Nya sat down and scanned the sparse room – a desk, the patient's chair, the doctor's chair, an examination bench, and a few certificates displaying his credentials on the wall.

"How may I help you, Nya?"

She hesitated at first and avoiding eye contact she replied, "I felt a lump in my left breast and thought I had better have it examined."

"I see," he said, his expression showing a bit of concern. "When did you first discover this lump?"

She had dreaded that question. She looked down at the floor. "A couple of years ago."

He rotated his chair and faced Nya directly. His eyebrows narrowed. "And you waited this long to come and have it checked?"

Nya dragged her fingertips gently across her forehead as if to cover her eyes. "Yes, well, you see, I was going to…." She paused for a moment working on excuses. "But, you know how it is. I got caught up with work, this and that, didn't think it was anything, certainly nothing serious. I hoped it would just go away."

"Like a mild headache?" he said. "Just let it pass."

She nodded.

"OK, let's take a look." The doctor slipped on a pair of latex gloves. "Please remove your blouse and bra and have a seat on the examination bench, please."

Nya did as instructed. She felt exposed but in no way threatened being topless in front of the doctor.

Dr. Michaels approached the table. "Where exactly is this lump?"

"Right here," she said, guiding his hand towards the mass.

He examined the lump and then both breasts and said, "OK, Nya. You can get dressed now."

While Nya dressed the doctor sat down at his desk and began punching the keys on his computer.

"So, what do you think, Doc? Is it anything to worry about?"

"It's difficult to say, Nya." The small laser printer on his desktop spat out a sheet of paper. "But to be on the safe side I'm going to send you for an urgent mammogram. We will know more then."

"Oh," Nya said. "I see. OK."

The doctor continued typing a few additional notes into his computer then gave Nya the printout to take to reception on the way out for billing. "And here's your referral to the breast screening facility. The number's at the top."

Back at home she made the appointment for the scan the very next day. Isaac was away for the week fishing with some friends. Nya felt alone, more alone than usual. In one way she was glad, for she wanted to do this independently. She had never mentioned the lump to Isaac. She just didn't want him to know.

All that evening Nya's mind raced with all sorts of scenarios about what might happen if the mammogram showed that the lump was … *something*. To distract herself, she sat down and put on old episodes of *Seinfeld*. She took comfort in watching Seinfeld even though she could never quite work out why. Maybe it was the droll humor, a show about nothing whose characters rarely took anything seriously. Whatever the reason, the sit-com distracted her from the lump. Several episodes passed before her eyes became heavy and she fell asleep for the night.

Nya awoke to the sound of her mobile phone ringing. She scrambled over to the kitchen counter and picked up. Her employer, ASIO, asked her if she was able to go on an assignment in New Zealand that would begin immediately. She would need to fly out that very morning. She contemplated the request for a moment knowing that she would have to cancel her mammogram appointment. She figured she could have the scan when she got back. She accepted the assignment.

* * *

The hot shower was working its relaxing magic. Several minutes passed as Nya allowed her body to unwind and her muscles to relax. She stepped out of the shower and dried herself with a fluffy white towel before returning to the bedroom. Elijah was right. The jeans fit her perfectly; in fact, they fit better than any she had ever had. So it was with all the garments – the knickers, bra, shirt, and socks. She slipped on the pair of brand new sneakers on the floor beside the dresser. Again, perfect fit.

She walked into the living room and found that the log cabin was anything but rustic. It was quite luxurious, in fact. Not self-indulgent in the way of expensive goods but classy in the way the design complemented the beauty of nature. A gentle blaze in the fireplace on one wall provided pleasant ambient light and a gentle warmth to the room. On the wall opposite, two picture windows afforded a gorgeous view of snow-capped mountains. She figured she was still in New Zealand. The mountains appeared to be the Southern Alps Ranges with Mount Cook in among them. A thick rose-colored woolen rug in front of the fireplace lent a cozy atmosphere.

Her Ultrabook was on a small oak coffee table. In the far corner she spotted a computer system – the model was not familiar to her – on a ledge protruding from the wall. As she approached it she saw an unusual image rotating on the screen. It was a logo consisting of two crossed feathers. She touched the keyboard and sparked the display to life. The logo vanished and the familiar Bing search engine appeared. The first question that came to mind was: *Who is Elijah Hael?* So she typed his name and pressed Enter to begin the search.

The first search hit was a link that read: *Pushbike accident takes life of devoted father...* The name Elijah Hael was mentioned in the search blurb. She clicked the headline and up came an entire news article with a picture of the man she remembered from the BMW who identified himself as Elijah Hael. The article read:

> *A freak accident killed devoted husband and father of two*
> *Elijah Hael when the pushbike he was riding home from work*

*struck a tree. Paramedics treated Elijah Hael at the scene
before transporting him to a local hospital where he died soon
after undergoing emergency surgery for massive internal bleeding
believed to have been caused by a severed artery caused by blunt
force trauma from the handlebars of the bike. The accident
occurred on a drizzly afternoon in the fading light of a gloomy
day. Hael's sister Claricia Hael, a police officer, described him
as a "good Christian family man." She added, "It's such a
tragedy that this could happen to such a nice man." Hael's wife
Juliana is said to have been devastated by the news and frets
over how to explain the loss of their father to the couple's
children, Kaley, aged three, and Reece, aged five. Officer Hael
said, "Kaley is too young to understand, but Reece is aware
Daddy has gone up into the sky. After a few days when Daddy
doesn't come home it will likely become all too real to the poor
boy." Officer Hael stated that police are still investigating the
presumed accident and are as yet unsure exactly what happened.
"He was riding home from work and the roads were wet, but
we don't really know what happened except that obviously he
came off his bike." Police urge anyone who might have witnessed
the accident to phone Crime Stoppers.*

Nya returned to the search results and noticed another link: *"Man
claiming to have been involved in the accident that caused the cycling death of Elijah
Hael surrendered to police…."* She skimmed the news story that told how
a man named Jeremy startled Elijah by shouting at him as he passed by
him in a car, causing Hael to lose control of his bike and collide with
the tree. Jeremy entered a plea of guilty to man slaughter in the second
degree and was given a prison sentence.

Nya pinched her nose up high between her eyes. She shook her head
in wonder. *Must have been a different Elijah Hael,* she thought. *Dead men
don't drive BMWs.* Unless he was some sort of a spy or an endangered

witness who had faked his death as some sort of witness protection ploy. Which would mean that the whole story about the perpetrator "Jeremy" was a ruse. *Hmm.* She clicked the link to the first story and studied the photo of Elijah Hael. *No doubt, it was the man who was driving the BMW….*

Just then a voice spoke behind her. "I guess you could say I am dead."

Startled, she spun around wide-eyed and came face-to-face with Elijah Hael. "You scared me. You're dead? Wh—?"

"Sorry, I didn't mean to startle you."

Elijah's kind eyes were intensely non-threatening, and Nya let go a sigh. "What do you mean, you are *dead?* How could you be standing here talking to me if you're dead … unless I'm dead, too?"

Elijah nodded at Nya and spread his angel wings out to full stretch so they became visible. "I'm an angel." He waved his wings slightly and created a breeze that cooled Nya's cheeks and set her long blond hair swirling about.

"Oh," she said, her bright blue eyes gazing at him in astonishment. Her knees went weak and butterflies danced in her stomach as a rush of endorphins flooded her mind. Her first thought was: *I must be dreaming.*

Chapter 6 - Balancing Choices

Shrouded in darkness with that burlap sack still over his face, Isaac sitting in the back of the vehicle, which he assumed was the black SUV which had run them down on their way to the police station, stretched his jaw to force a yawn to relieve the pressure building in his ears. From the mounting pressure he surmised the vehicle was heading up a mountain. An anxious thought plagued his mind: *Is this my last, best chance to escape before I end up locked away in some compound, probably tortured, killed, or both?* His attempts to devise a plan were constantly interrupted by a strong desire to scratch his face where the sack grated against his skin. The best he could do was shake his head because the black duct tape securing his wrists behind his back prevented him from getting at the blasted itch.

After several minutes of wrestling with his apprehensions and the futile attempts to relieve the itch, Isaac muttered, "I need to pee."

"Can't you hold it?" the man's voice asked from the front of the vehicle.

"No." Isaac shook his head. "I *really* need to go."

"You've already wet your britches once," the man said, with a tone of disgust. "The whole car stinks."

Good, Isaac thought. The vehicle was rich with pungent smell of the stale urine from his earlier accident. "It'll stink worse."

"All right," the man relented. "I'll pull over up ahead, and you can go by a tree."

"Thank you," Isaac said. He felt the vehicle slowing and pulling onto the shoulder of the road. The front passenger door opened, then closed, and a moment later he felt a strong arm pulling him out of the back of the car.

"Don't get any ideas," the man said as he positioned Isaac beside a tree and said. "There you go: Relieve yourself."

"It's going to be kind of hard to do." Isaac raised his bound wrists as high as he could behind his back. "Unless you want to pull my zipper down and grab hold of my—"

"Ah," the man said. "No, no, no." He shouted in the direction of the driver. "Hey, Seth, he says he needs his hands free so he can relieve himself."

Obviously frustrated the driver hollered, "Just give him a hand so he can pee, Jared."

"I ain't touching this guy's junk. There's some things I just will *not* do, not even for Cain."

Isaac could hear the driver, Seth, pound the steering wheel. He shouted, "Just release his freakin' hands then."

The man attending him, whom the driver had called Jared, seemed to be fumbling around in his pocket. Then he cut the black duct tape around Isaac's hands releasing them. "There! Now *go*."

"I can't see," Isaac said, turning towards Jared.

"You don't need to see to take a piss," Jared said, landing a solid punch on Elijah's shoulder.

"I don't think I can go unless I can see."

"What? You pee with your eyes or something?"

"Well, no, but—"

Seth's voice boomed. "He's already seen your face, Jared. Now let him go before we make a night of this!"

Jared ripped off the duct tape and Isaac cringed as the sticky substance tore at the skin on his neck. Tape removed, Jared lifted the sack.

"Thanks," Isaac said, and as soon as the daylight hit his eyes he swung his arm forward and then back as hard as he could, slamming his elbow back and upward. A sudden but expected pain erupted from his elbow. Direct hit. Jared staggered backwards as he grasped his chin.

Isaac ran, faster than he had ever run in his life, straight into the dense bushland. He darted between the trees, leapt over fallen logs, and dodged around the uneven terrain as if he were in a video game. Only this time he knew he had only one life and no retries. Game over meant *game over*.

Behind him, he heard Jared curse and then shout, "He's getting away!" Followed by Seth's booming voice yelling, "Get after him!"

Isaac's heart pounded, his lungs burned, his legs cramped. But slowing down was not an option. He pushed himself way past his fitness level and hoped his body would hold together long enough to get away. Up ahead a small clearing came into view between the trees. He could see nothing on the far side of the clearing and realized that he must be approaching the edge of a cliff. He planted his feet, stopped suddenly, and lost his footing and rolled forward into a slide towards the precipice.

Stop! He cried silently as he clawed at the ground trying to curb his momentum. It didn't work. The momentum from his sprint propelled him over the edge of the ridge. In a last-ditch effort to save himself, he grabbed at the cliff's edge with the tips of his fingers. And to his surprise, it worked. He managed to halt his fall. His feet scrambled for firm ground in the open air beneath him. He cut his eyes down and made out the tops of trees in the ravine far below. He swung his feet out and back in a desperate search for a foothold. After a few attempts, his foot landed on a little ledge in the gap between a few jagged rocks that he could wedge his foot into. He extended his legs so he could reach out with his arms over the top of the cliff edge and try to pull himself the rest of the way up onto firm ground.

Slowly, he hoisted himself back onto firm ground. He lay face down in the dirt for a few seconds and regained his breath. Then he got up and immediately saw Seth and Jared approaching the clearing and blocking his only route of escape. His fitness level was obviously not as high as Seth's and Jared's. He thought he had outpaced them by a good distance, but they had no problem tailing him. Isaac struggled to regain a steady breathing pattern and his head throbbed with each quick beat of his heart.

Seth pointed his 9mm at Isaac. "Why are you making this so hard for me? I'm just doing my job."

Isaac glanced over his right shoulder. The cliff edge was just one short step back. Isaac felt a lump in his throat and whimpered, "I'm not coming with you. I'll jump first."

"Don't be a fool, Isaac." Seth very slowly and deliberately holstered his gun. "If you jump, you die. You're too young to die. Just come with us and everything will be all right."

Jared and Seth slowly but steadily approached him. Isaac took a step backward, loosening some rocks and sending them cascading over the cliff face. The heels on his shoes sat just on the edge.

Isaac considered his options. If he jumped he would surely die. If he went with them he would probably be tortured. If he refused to give them the information they wanted they would kill him. He shuddered at the thought of torture, having his eye cut out or worse, and figured that however they decided to execute him – electrocution, drowning, firing squad, hanging – it wouldn't be pleasant. That left one option. He decided dying right then would be a better and quicker option than the unimaginable agony of torture.

Seth and Jared moved closer still.

Isaac raised his arms at his sides until they were parallel with the ground. Shaped like a cross, he closed his eyes, leant backwards, and let gravity take him over the cliff edge....

* * *

Seth ran to the precipice shouting, "Nooooooooo...," which echoed through the gorge

Jared followed close behind. The two looked down and saw Isaac disappearing into the trees below.

In a sarcastic tone Jared noted, "Cain is *not* going to be happy about this."

Seth swung around and punched Jared in the nose. "You think!?"

Jared pinched his bloody nose and dropped to his knees. He glared at Seth. "What was *that* for?"

"What do you think?" Seth asked.

Chapter 7 - The Genetic Code

Nya struggled to make sense of what she was seeing. Part of her said, *you are dreaming.* Another part was excited at the prospect of being face-to-face with an angel. Nya had believed in angels since she was a little girl listening to stories her mother would tell. As she grew older, though, her belief in angels had gone the way of her belief in Santa Claus and the Easter Bunny.

Later in life, during a heated debate on the validity of Christianity, a colleague challenged her to find one wrong thing in the Bible. At first, Nya was not interested in taking up the challenge. She believed, as many people do, that man made up the Bible to control people. Or worse, that the good book was created as a way to extort money from the desperate and needy. The fact that her friend and colleague who was a very well-educated historian held the Bible in such high esteem piqued her curiosity. *Why did he believe the Bible? How could he believe the Bible?*

Nya took the challenge. Surely she could find one thing wrong in a book she considered a work of fiction written 2,000 years. Should be easy enough. But, the more she read the more wisdom she discovered flowing from the pages. It became increasingly difficult for her to conceive how the biblical writers knew so much about so many different topics back in the days when the Bible was written. Back then there was no Internet for sharing advice. Books were rare and travel prohibitive. For over a year she researched the Bible and studied the texts, and although she did not agree with some things in the writings, she realized that simply opposing a view does not make the view wrong. Later, she came to realize that her disagreements were due more to her own lack of understanding. Over time, the wisdom in the Bible changed her beliefs as she gained fresh knowledge. In reading the New Testament she formed a relationship with a man named Jesus whom she came to understand and truly believe was and is the Son of God. A year later, she accepted Christ Jesus into her heart.

So actually meeting an angel, well that was amazing.

"You are not dreaming, Nya," Elijah said. "I am an angel. I was sent to protect you."

Still not convinced she was awake, Nya pinched herself, twisting her flesh until she winced. "Sent by whom – *God?*"

"Not directly," he said, "but I guess you could say that, yes." Elijah returned his wings to the center of his back where they became transparent to the naked eye. "Come, let's sit down on the rug near your Ultrabook. I need you to show me the software of yours that does the decoding."

"But I thought you said they could trace my Ultrabook if I used it."

"Disable the wireless networking and remove the sim card before turning it on. That may buy us a little time."

Nya slid the switch on the side of the Ultrabook back to turn off the wireless capabilities, removed the sim, and lifted the screen to wake the machine up and resume where it had left off.

They sat down together on the rug around the coffee table, eyes fixed on the screen, as the software continued decompiling the genetic code from the point when Nya made her dramatic escape from her apartment.

"So what is the program doing, Nya?" Elijah asked.

"Well, you know how computer programs are made up of ones and zeroes when they are compiled, and in that state are rather meaningless?"

"Yes," Elijah said, nodding. Having been a programmer in his earthly life Elijah understood exactly what she was talking about. "Meaningless, unless you decompile them using a disassembler that translates them back into something readable."

Nya glanced at Elijah. "Right," she said, smiling. She pressed a few keys to bring up a genetic sequence. "A human gene sequence is made up of the letter's G,T,A,C. So instead of two possibilities for each bit – a one or a zero – you have four in a human gene, a G, T, A, or C."

She pointed to the screen. "Here is an example of assembled code in a computer, made up of ones and zeroes."

10001110101101010100111010101011010101011110010101
10010101011101010101010111110101010110101011110101
00010101010101010101010101010101010101010010101010

"And here is a genetic sequence." Nya pointed to a sample on the display.

ATGTTTTATACAGGTGTAGCCTGTAAGAGATGAAG
TAGAAATTGACTTATTTTATTCTCATATTTACATGTGC
ATATGCCAGAAAAGTTGAATAGTATCAGATTCCAAA

Nya continued. "Scientists have discovered that certain sequences pertain to different things. For example, a person with Cystic Fibrosis will probably carry a particular defective genetic nucleotide sequence made up of G,T,A and C's. The software I have created decompiles the genetic sequences into a readable language – a set of instructions. In cases where disease is present the instructions that would normally appear to maintain correct functionality are damaged and distorted and thus cause issues in the human body."

Elijah's eyebrows raised and his eyes lit up. "So what you are saying is that the human genome is really like a software program that controls the human body. Just like software that runs on the hardware of a computer, the human genetic code is software that runs on the human body?"

"Yes," Nya said, grinning widely. "Exactly!"

"Incredible stuff." Elijah shook his head. "Just conceptualizing the idea would have been quite an achievement, but actually accomplishing it…. Well, that's astonishing."

Nya blushed and shrugged her shoulders.

"You worked out all of this on your own?"

"Yes," she said. "Well, most of it. The actual development took over a decade though!"

Elijah scratched his chin. "So why do you think Cain wants your software badly enough to kill for the code?"

Nya tilted her head and looked Elijah in the eye. "Who is 'Cain'?"

"He is the man whom the henchmen pursuing us work for. He heads an organization called Nanorobotic Organ Development."

"Well, his motive is rather obvious. I mean, my software could help with any sort of genetic research." Nya paused for a moment to collect her thoughts. "I'm sure that knowledge of the decompiled instructions would help the work of the scientists at Nanorobotic Organ Development. That must be his motive."

"I don't think so," Elijah said, shaking his head. "There has to be more to it than that." He rubbed his forehead and narrowed his eyes. "How does the genetic code control the body? With a computer, the software responds to human input – a mouse-click, a text entry. Software typically doesn't do anything without first receiving some form of input."

Nya glanced back at the computer screen. "That's the exciting part. This morning before you told me to escape my apartment the software was working on a part of the genetic code that a lot of people refer to as *'Junk DNA.'* I never believed those parts were 'junk,' so I set my software to work on decompiling them. It's been working on processing them for years. The intriguing part is those parts of the genetic code are external interfaces."

Elijah cocked his head. "Interfaces to ... *what?*"

"To what I believe is the human soul." Nya paused.

"Go on," Elijah said, nodding slowly.

"See, I think the human soul interfaces with the human genome, the genetic code, which controls the body. Think of one of those humongous Mech Machines you see in the movies." She wondered if angels watched movies. "You know, where you have a person sitting in a cockpit of sorts and controlling a giant Mech warrior, which is the body so to speak. He inputs instructions to the software of the Mech by moving a joystick, which then causes the various motors in the Mech to carry out the desired function. The human in the Mech is like the soul in our body. Our soul serves a similar function: It interfaces with the genetic code through the external interfaces that instruct the body to carry out an action."

Nya looked back at Elijah whose face was grim. She said, "You look like you just heard some bad news."

He looked down at the rug beneath them. "A horrible thought crossed my mind about just what Cain may be up to."

"What?"

He shook his head. "Until I know more, I would rather not say at this time. But I know this: Keeping this code away from Cain is extremely important."

Nya looked up at the ceiling. "Hear that? What is that noise, Elijah?"

Elijah locked his head and set his ear toward the ceiling. "A Helicopter. Cain's men have located us. Come! We have to move."

Chapter 8 - Frank & Sophia

Frank pulled the IV needle from the back of his right hand, grabbed his mobile phone, and then eased into a sitting position. Feeling a little dizzy, he took a moment to steady himself before getting out of bed.

"You don't look so good," Sophia said. "Are you OK, Frank? Sure you are up for this?"

"Yes." He gritted his teeth as a sharp pain shot from the open bullet wound on his chest up through his shoulder. "Yes, I'll be OK."

"If you say so," Sophia said. She disarmed the unconscious men while Frank captured photos of them with his mobile phone. Sophia held out one of the men's Glock 9mm pistols to Frank. "Here take this."

Frank took the weapon, checked the magazine clip – it was loaded, then laid the pistol on the mattress. "I'll probably need this," he mumbled.

"Sorry, I know you're not at full bore," Sophia said, "but we must move quickly, Frank. Get dressed." Sophia removed the bullets from the second gun, placed them in her pocket, and tossed the 9mm under the bed.

Frank found a fresh set of clothes in the little closet next to the bed and pulled off the hospital gown. Stripped to nothing but a pair of hospital underwear, he lifted the blood-soaked dressing and inspected the wound. A gaping hole, with broken stitches on either side, wept blood. He reseated the bandage and slipped on a white cotton shirt, a pair of conventional grey suit trousers, a brown leather belt, and the matching suit jacket. Frank picked the 9mm off the bed and tucked it under his jacket between his belt and back. He wondered where his Federal Police assigned Glock 22 and holster were. Either the hospital had taken the weapon to a secure location or the gunmen in the forest had seized it.

"Looking snappy," Sophia said. "Let's go, Frank."

"Snappy, eh?" Frank followed closely behind Sophia as they proceeded down the corridor toward the elevator.

On arriving at the elevator Sophia said, "Call the elevator Frank, I'll keep watch."

Frank nodded and pressed the elevator call button. A moment later the doors opened and he motioned for Sophia to enter first. As they descended, Frank entered a number on his mobile phone. "I'll call Leigh for transport." Leigh's voice mail came on. Frank sighed and left a message: "Leigh, Frank. I need you to come to the hospital right away and pick us up out front. I'll be with a woman. I'll explain later. Come as quick as possible."

They stepped out of the elevator on the ground floor and spotted two men in suits seated on a lounge near the reception desk looking towards Frank. "Quick this way," Sophia said as she turned on her heel and grabbed Frank's arm and turned him about. They walked briskly back towards the elevator trying not to draw attention. Sophia gestured toward the door to the stairwell next to the elevators. "Pick up the pace," she said as they descended the flight of stairs to the basement door.

"Quick," Frank said, as they heard the stairwell door open above them.

The basement was a car park with spaces marked in yellow paint on the tarmac. An exit ramp wound over to their right.

Sophia took Frank's hand and they slouched low as they meandered between the parked cars over to the left side of the basement. They hurried along the basement wall as fast as Frank could move.

The basement door opened and immediately gunshots rang out as the two assailants began firing their 9mm in Frank's direction. Frank and Sophia ducked behind a red sedan where Frank pulled out his 9mm and began returning fire. The two gunmen took cover behind a white Ford Escort near the basement door. Windows smashed on vehicles and car alarms started to sound as gunfire rang out and bullets ricocheted off the concrete walls. The noise became deafening.

"Ah," Frank said as checked his clip: two bullets left. "We have to get out of here, Sophia. Quick!"

"Wait here," she said. Frank watched her move behind the cover of the vehicles towards the side of the Ford Escort the gunmen were using for cover. When the attackers came into view she sprinted towards them.

Fearing that she would be shot, Frank came out of cover and shouted, "Wait!" He squeezed off his final two shots and heard a click: Empty. His distraction worked. The gunmen, unaware of Sophia approaching them, returned fire. One bullet struck Frank in the left shoulder and another pierced the right side of his chest, up high near his collarbone. He sensed no pain but passed out almost immediately, collapsing where he stood.

* * *

Sophia struck the first gunman with a swift kick in the head that knocked him to the ground and then leapt into a spinning double-side kick towards the second aggressor. He looked at his accomplice, wondering what had happened, just before Sophia's feet struck him in the chest and sent him tumbling backwards into the nearby wall. The impact popped the air out of his lungs like a pin-prick in an overfilled balloon. He gasped in an attempt to refill his lungs. His hands trembled as he scanned around for the invisible attacker and fired his 9mm in random directions before Sophia's right hand landed squarely on the side of his head. The gunfire stopped. His eyes rolled as he passed out.

Sophia ran back and knelt beside Frank. She undid the buttons of his jacket and then his shirt to expose the fresh wounds. She placed her hands over the bullet hole on his chest and closed her eyes. A white light of energy formed a sphere around her hands. The ball of dazzling vitality, like gathering clouds swirling in the sky, grew from the size of an apple to the size of a melon and then streamed directly into the open chest wound and came flowing out of the puncture in Frank's shoulder. One spent slug popped out of the hole in his shoulder and another of the hole on the right of his chest. Then both wounds closed and were healed in a matter of seconds.

Sophia then circled her hands over the earlier gunshot wound, relocating the sphere of healing energy. White light danced around the broken stitches and the threads reattached closing the wound. The sphere collapsed in on itself and vanished as Sophia opened her eyes. She stuffed the blood-soaked dressing into her pocket and rebuttoned Frank's shirt. She then placed her hands over Frank's shirt. As she concentrated, the blood rose from his shirt into a red mist as the puncture holes in the fabric closed. Several seconds later, the shirt appeared as new.

Just then Frank's mobile phone rang, but he remained unaware, unconscious. Sophia left hastily as security guards began arriving. She knew they would be followed shortly after by local police and Leigh.

* * *

Frank heard a familiar voice calling out to him. "Frank?" He slowly opened his eyes and saw Leigh down on one knee bent down over him.

"Are you OK, Frank?" Leigh asked.

"I think so," Frank said, realizing that he was lying on cold tarmac in an underground parking lot. "What happened?"

"That's what everybody's asking," he said. "Two gunmen were arrested. They were found near the basement door unconscious, but there's evidence of bullet spray all over the place. Looks as though they were knocked out after receiving blows to the head."

"Blows, as in gunshot blows?" Frank asked.

"No, blows as in a prize-fighter or kung fu master."

"Sophia," Frank said. He closed his eyes and shook his head trying to relieve a little dizziness. "She must have taken them out after I was shot."

"Who's Sophia?" Leigh asked, eyebrows raised. "And where are you shot?"

Frank glanced down at where he believed the bullets had hit him. No blood. He unbuttoned his shirt and pulled it open. No wound. He ran his hand over the right side of his chest searching for the wound. Left shoulder: No wound.

Leigh pulled Frank's hand off his chest. "The wound is on your left side, Frank, where the stitches are."

"But, but," he stuttered, "I, I was shot in my right chest. That's what caused me to pass out." Frank glanced down at the wound near his left breast. The stitches were intact. *But how can that be?* He shook his head.

"Relax," Leigh said. "Maybe you lost more blood than you realize and passed out. We should get you back up into the hospital."

Leigh stood up and extended his hand. Frank took hold of it and slowly gathered himself to his feet and then brushed off his jacket and pants. He took a moment to think, then said, "No, no, let's get out of here. Take me to AFP headquarters. I will be safer there." He scanned himself mentally from head to toe. The pain in his chest wound, which had been so excruciating, was now only a slight throb. Puzzled as to why his pain levels had dropped so dramatically, he thought: *Maybe it's the morphine.* "I feel fine. We need to find Isaac."

"If you're sure," Leigh said. "All right. The local police will take the two guys into custody and transfer them to AFP headquarters for questioning. I'll arrange to get CCTV footage from the hospital to see if that turns up anything."

Frank nodded once.

Leigh located the local cop on the scene, Sergeant Andrews, and gave him instructions in regards to the gunmen and CCTV footage. Then he returned to Frank, said, "Let's go."

Chapter 9 - The Fall

As he fell, weightless, Isaac became filled with a sense of freedom. He gave up his will to live and prepared for the inevitable nothingness he believed would greet him upon impact with the ground. All his fears, all his worries and concerns, vanished – even the fear of death itself, for death became his way of escape. Knowing there was no return from this exit, he pictured Nya and whispered, "I'm sorry."

Then his mind went blank and his body, numb. A few moments passed before a question sparked in his mind: "*Am I dead?*" He opened his eyes slowly and took in the surroundings. White. Everything around him was as white as a newly formed cloud. The ground was white, the sky was white, and the horizon was white. He couldn't tell if he was standing up or lying down. He had no sense of direction or gravity.

An ominous voice, impossibly deep, seemed to come at him from all directions and echoed through the whiteness: "Do you want to be?"

Isaac spun, eyes wide, searching for the source of the voice. "Want to be *what?*"

"Dead?" the ominous voice boomed.

Isaac glanced over his shoulder, left then right. "Not really, no."

Out of the whiteness appeared a middle-aged man dressed in a long trench coat, faded blue jeans, and a 1940s-style fedora. "Good."

"Who are you?" Isaac said, his voice quavering.

"Castiel."

Isaac scratched his head. "Where am I, Mr. Castiel?"

"Castiel works fine. I'm not the 'mister' type." Castiel looked Isaac square in the eyes and in a serious tone said, "Where do you want to be, Isaac?"

Isaac took a moment to think. "Back home, in my lounge room." He shrugged. "Playing Xbox would be quite good."

The whiteness surrounding Isaac began fading, very slowly, revealing more and more detail until at last Isaac was standing in a room that looked exactly like, right down to the tiniest detail, his lounge room. Castiel was seated on the couch with a wireless Xbox controller in his hand. On the screen, Halo was playing.

"Halo is a remarkable game, Isaac," Castiel said without taking his eyes off the screen. "One of my favorites." With swift movements he quickly dodged a few incoming missiles seeking him in the game. "The struggles old Master Chief goes through to save humanity are quite interesting."

Isaac stood there wide-eyed and wide-mouthed, trying to make sense of what was happening. "Uh, uh…," he stuttered. "This can't be real."

"OK, then, which would you prefer, Isaac – this or reality?"

Isaac thought back to his final moments. "I was falling, Castiel, just about to hit the ground, or perhaps I have hit the ground." He paused, eyebrows raised. "Maybe this is the—"

"You're not dead, Isaac," Castiel interrupted. "Well, at least not yet."

Isaac sat down on the couch next to Castiel and whispered, "Not yet?"

"You ask a lot of questions, Isaac," Castiel said, still working the game controller. "So tell me: What do you want out of life?"

Isaac clasped his hands together and pressed his steepled thumbs against the point of his chin. "Um, I don't know." That was a question that Isaac had never given much thought to. "I guess, well, just to be happy, enjoy life, and get the most out of living."

Castiel replied, "Jesus Christ once said, *The gateway to life is very narrow and the road is difficult, and only a few ever find it.*'"

"What's that supposed to mean?" Isaac asked, tapping his thumbs against his chin and narrowing his eyes.

Castiel paused the game, put down the Xbox controller, and focused his attention directly on Isaac. "Before Jesus shared that He said, *'You can enter God's Kingdom only through the narrow gate. The highway to hell is broad, and its gate is wide for the many who choose that way.*'"

"Um, uh, sorry, but I still don't understand, Castiel."

Castiel lowered his eyes. "A simple interpretation might be that the right path in life is not going to be easy."

Isaac struggled to find anything meaningful to say.

Castiel continued. "Life is designed to challenge you, Isaac, to allow you to develop and learn what true faith is. Some people say that God does not give us what we request in our prayers but rather God creates situations to let us experience what we requested. So, if you pray for patience, God will create situations in which you will acquire, or at least require, patience."

"I don't pray, Castiel," Isaac confessed. He shook his head. "I'm not sure I believe in all that God stuff."

"Perhaps that is the lesson God is trying to teach you, Isaac – to pray."

Isaac turned and faced Castiel and considered his explanation. Seconds later everything around him started to dissolve into the whiteness that had originally surrounded him after – or during – the fall. Then it too vanished into blackness. Next came the sensation of wind rushing past his body causing him to open his eyes. Above him, the clear blue sky provided a backdrop for the cliff's edge he had fallen from. Isaac realized he was falling and would very soon strike the ground.

As he closed his eyes his inner voices said, "God, I don't know whether you exist or not, but I guess I believe in you enough to say this: Please help me, help me to find my way, help me to survive this fall. I want to live. I want to see Nya again."

Leaves slapped Isaac's back and legs, followed by branches swiping him all over his body which made loud cracking sounds as he collided with them. Sharp pains racked his body as he descended further into the canopy of the trees. A large limb caught his legs and flipped him over so that he was falling chest first towards the ground. Eyes still closed, Isaac believed he was about to die when his abdomen slammed into a large branch causing his body to fold around it. The force of the impact knocked the wind out of him and snapped the branch off the tree. He continued to fall, wrapped around the branch, until the tree limb snagged among other branches and came to a stop with a loud thud. Isaac slipped off the branch and continued down feet first. His knees buckled under him as he hit the ground. He stretched out his arms in a reflexive attempt to curb the impending impact. He turned his head to the sides to protect his face and braced himself. The collision was hard and he lost consciousness.

Sometime later Isaac let out an agonizing moan as his eyes opened and he saw the bush floor beneath him. He hurt all over but for once considered the pain a good thing. Palms flat on the ground he pushed himself up and rolled slowly over and into a sitting position. He scanned his body mentally to make sure all of his limbs were working. They were. He glanced down and saw that his shirt was ripped open. His chest and stomach had large bruises, reddish-purple contusions, and several gashes where branches had shredded his skin. His legs were no better off. Small patches of blood formed around holes in his jeans where the whip-like branches had torn through the denim and lacerated his skin. Slowly, he rose to his feet and tried to stretch his stiff body. The left side of his jaw felt as though someone had taken a sledgehammer to it. He ran his hand over his swollen face. Then he tried to pivot it from side to side and up and down. Only the slightest movements were possible.

He wondered how long he had been unconscious. Then the thought formed in his mind: *I'm alive.* He struggled to understand how he had managed to survive the fall, which should certainly have been fatal. He tilted his aching head back cautiously and surveyed his descent path. *What are the odds of surviving that?* The trees must have provided just enough cushion to break his fall. His legs wobbled and dizziness blurred his vision. He staggered over and leaned against a tree, hoping he would not lose consciousness and that the wooziness would pass. The rushing sounds of a river nearby and of various wildlife and bellbirds pleasantly chirping filled the air.

He glanced around searching for a reason to travel in a particular direction when he heard a voice – a frustrated, tired voice – in the distance saying, "There is *no way* he could have survived that fall, Seth. No stinkin' way. Why are we even searching for him?"

A stern voice replied, "Shut up, Jared. If I want your stupid opinion I'll ask for it."

The voices made up Isaac's mind as to which way he should go – away from them. With a renewed desire to live Isaac fought through the pain and trudged through the bushland as quietly as he could. He could sense Seth and Jared gaining on him. Although he moved as stealthily as possible he left a trail of crushed undergrowth and droplets of blood on a leaf here and a branch there.

Isaac paused by a tree for a break from the searing pain and crushing exhaustion. He tried to breathe deeply but each breath he drew in felt like a knife stabbing him. He guessed he had broken a rib or two and they were digging into his lungs. The dizziness was overwhelming as he heard Seth's mocking voice say, "Ahhh, there you are."

Seth raised his gun as Isaac's vision swirled into a kaleidoscope of blurry colors. Jared was sarcastic. "You are looking a tad bit pale there, Isaac. I reckon your running days are over."

Isaac struggled to keep his body upright and his eyes open. He opened his mouth to speak when, suddenly, both Jared and Seth clutched their necks as if they had been stung by wasps. Both men jerked their heads wildly as they tried to pull something out their necks. Then their legs buckled under them sending them tumbling to the ground.

Isaac passed out.

Chapter 10 - Nya & Elijah

Nya slapped her palms over her ears as the cabin shook. Elijah shouted over the roar of the descending helicopter. "Quick! We need to go! Step back." Elijah stepped off of the rug the two had been sitting on and, with a wave of his hand, he seemed to be willing the floor covering to slide away. It did, revealing a wooden trapdoor. He hurried over to the trapdoor, lifted the bulky hatch, and said, "You first Nya. I'll be right behind."

With her Ultrabook under her arm, Nya climbed quickly down the three-meter steel ladder. Elijah bolted the trapdoor behind him and then placed his hands and feet on either side of the ladder and slid down to the ground below.

The cabin floor above them dulled the thunderous roar of the helicopter engines. They stood in the small cellar room illuminated by a single small candescent light bulb suspended from a rafter by a short span of cord. A few wooden shelves caked with dust carrying various supplies lined the three front walls. On the far wall an opening led into a dark tunnel.

Elijah fetched a flashlight from one of the shelves. He wiped dust off the lens with the hem of his shirt, pressed the *On* button, and then slapped the side of it to bring the beam to life. "This way, Nya," he said, tossing his head toward the tunnel. "This tunnel leads to the boat house."

Nya followed Elijah who led the way through the dank and musty tunnel carved out of the earth. Every few meters, deteriorating old wooden posts on each side of the shaft supported an overhanging wooden beam.

The narrow passage was just wide enough to accommodate one person. Nya felt the narrow earthen walls closing in on her. Suddenly dizzy, she reached out to steady herself against a wooden post. A sharp stinging pain racked her stomach and she was suddenly nauseated. "Oh," she moaned, placing a hand on her belly.

Elijah stopped and turned to face her. "What's wrong, Nya?"

She closed her eyes and let out a breath and her voice quavered when she said, "I think the events are catching up with me."

* * *

Elijah's eyes narrowed as he placed his hands close to her chest and tried to sense the source of her pain. He detected something but he couldn't determine exactly what. His sensing and healing capabilities were nowhere near as strong as Sophia's. She was the healer of the trio consisting of Sophia, Castiel, and himself. After several attempts, he placed his hands by his side and asked, "Are you able to continue, Nya?"

"I think so," she said. She winced as she drew in a deep breath and held the breath for several seconds before expelling the air from her lungs. The pain and the dizziness subsided just a little.

Elijah wrapped his arm around her waist. "Lean on me, Nya. Let me take your weight." Nya placed her arm over his shoulders and they continued down the passage.

A loud explosion boomed behind them followed by a plume of dust swirling from the source of the blast down the tunnel. They closed their eyes, turned their faces away from the approaching dust cloud, and covered their noses and began moving much more quickly towards the boathouse.

"They blew the trapdoor open, Nya," Elijah said. "They will be coming. Keep your eyes closed. I'll be the eyes for both of us." He opened his eyes just a bit and navigated the pitch-black passageway.

Fifty paces ahead they came to a small rusty metal ladder leading up to a trapdoor that led into the boathouse. Elijah scrambled up the rungs, unbolted the hatch, gave the underside a few shoulder thumps to unstick the hinges, pushed the door open, and climbed into the boathouse. He reached down through the opening. "Take my hand, Nya."

Nya reached up and grabbed his outstretched arm. Several muffled voices carried from down the passage. Elijah lifted Nya through the trapdoor and into the boathouse. She coughed a few times to clear the dust from her lungs and then crawled to a nearby wall and leant against it, breathing deeply, trying to catch her breath.

Elijah shut the hatch and then searched around for something to secure the trapdoor. A nearby cabinet seemed his only option. He dragged the heavy metal tool cabinet over and slammed it down over the door.

The room was sparse. A few fishing rods and several shelves, empty but for a couple old tins, rags, and a dusty plastic tackle box, hung on one wall. Mounted on another wall were two spools of thick rope. The space between two wharves in the center of the boathouse where a boat would float was vacant. Nya said, "Where is the boat, Elijah?"

Elijah turned to her and smiled. "It's on my wish list."

Nya covered her mouth and coughed, a deep lung-clearing cough, and when she pulled her hand away from her mouth they both noticed several droplets of blood. She swatted at the blood spots as if to make them go away.

A loud bang echoed from the trapdoor as the cabinet bounced up, shaking the room. "We have to go now, Nya," Elijah said, as the cabinet leapt up a second time. "We'll get you through this."

Nya shook her head. Her breath was ragged and her voice husky. "I feel terrible, Elijah."

Elijah stood motionless for a few seconds and pondered that new revelation. Nya's being physically ill was not in any of the assignment briefs. He decided to consult EVE. His state-of-the-angelic personal computer. EVE appeared, floating in front of him. Elijah always compared his EVE with the iPad he had before his death. EVE, however, consisted of a paper-thin display screen and was operated by thought alone. Elijah instructed EVE to scan the area for human activity. As expected, two persons were in the passage under the trapdoor, and from the sound of it were trying desperately to get it open. Four other were on land approaching the boathouse from the cabin. He returned his EVE to eSpace. eSpace still puzzled Elijah. He always forgot to research what the invisible storage zone actually was. He understood the space to be some sort of holding area between the Earth and Spiritual Realm, a dimension of infinite space where things could be stored and recalled with the blink of a thought.

Elijah sat down next to Nya, took her hands in his, and stared deep into her eyes. "You are going to have to trust me, Nya. They will be here in minutes to take you."

She shook her head. "No."

"But considering the circumstances," he said, squeezing her hand, "it is probably better to let them. Nobody will be able to see me. I'm invisible to most people *unless* I grant them the ability to see me. I am 'out of visible phase,' to be precise."

Nya was shivering and her eyes screamed panic. "Will they hurt me?"

Elijah squeezed Nya's hands gently. "No. They need you, Nya. They need you and your software. I suspect the first thing they will do once they realize you are sick is get you medical help. Cain, the man behind this, while not a gentle man is a sensible one."

A small explosion rattled the fishing rods on the wall and then the far door of the cabin burst open. Four men rushed in, their assault rifles pointing in all directions, and searched the room. One of the men spotted Nya and said, "Well, look who's here. Who else is with you?"

"Nobody," Nya responded while gazing into Elijah's eyes. "It's just me."

Two of the men kept their assault rifles trained on Nya while the other two continued to search around until one yelled out: "All clear!"

The man who had first spotted her knelt down and looked her over. He cocked his head and squinted, obviously realizing that she was in distress, and pulled out his mobile phone and punched in a number. "Williams here. We have the subject Nya in custody, but … she looks unwell."

He pulled the phone away several inches away from his ear as if the person on the other line was shouting. "No, of course we didn't hurt her." He paused, "OK, will do."

Williams snatched Nya's Ultrabook from her lap and said, "Nya, we are going to take you back to Australia on our private jet. On landing, we will take you to the compound. Can you walk?"

"It's OK, Nya," Elijah said, keeping his eyes locked on hers. He spoke not through words but through thoughts, which Nya heard echo in her head. "I am going to go ahead of you. I have a plan."

Nya nodded towards Elijah, hesitated a moment, then responded to Williams: "Possibly, but I feel really weak. Otherwise I would have run."

In a stern commanding voice Williams ordered two of his men, "Peters, Anderson. Help her up and assist her back to the chopper."

Peters and Anderson, one on either side, helped Nya to her feet. Nya gazed towards Elijah as a tear flowed down her left cheek. The fear was full on her face as Peters and Anderson walked her out of the boathouse towards the Blackhawk helicopter standing by.

After the other two men left, Elijah left the boathouse, spread his wings, and took to the air heading for Auckland Airport.

Chapter 11 - Jump

Nya sat between Peters and Anderson in the back of the Blackhawk helicopter. Williams sat in the row directly across from them, flanked by two other men, with their backs to the cockpit. She watched Williams operating her Ultrabook and figured he was transferring her software and files directly to Cain. *If only I had protected the computer with a secure login and encrypted the hard drive*, she thought.

Out the window in the distance she saw the hangars and runways of Auckland Airport. Out of the corner of her eye she caught a glimpse of Elijah flying parallel with the helicopter. He soared through the air as graceful as an eagle. Nya's eyes gleamed and a gentle smile made her lip quiver as she watched him. The nausea and dizziness faded and she was feeling a little better and her energy was coming back.

"Something amusing?" Peters asked. "What are you smiling about?"

"Knowing that this is not the end," she said, still watching Elijah gliding so freely through the air.

"What's that supposed to mean?"

"Just that life is beautiful."

Peters shook his head and let it go.

Nya lost sight of Elijah several minutes before the helicopter touched down on the helipad at Auckland airport. Peters and Anderson escorted Nya out of the Blackhawk and into a private jet waiting nearby. Williams followed close behind with her Ultrabook securely in hand.

"Ladies first," Anderson said, gesturing for Nya to mount the short stairway leading into the plane first. Though they worked for Cain, to some extent the men were thoughtful and considerate. They were just men doing a job, she knew. Nya herself had at times done jobs contrary to her conscience, such as the time ASIO asked her to break into computer systems to hijack data. It presented Nya with a dilemma. On the one hand, she knew that gaining illegal access to the computer systems was wrong, but on the other she could understand why ASIO needed the intelligence gained to prevent possible terrorist attacks – even if doing so meant violating people's rights. The imaginary line between right and wrong was constantly shifting in Nya's world and it did bother her at times. Nya wondered if any of the five men doing Cain's bidding faced similar conscience battles as they carried out their assignments. She considered the possibility that they did not even know who they were working for.

Nya climbed the narrow flight of stairs into the Lear 45. The jet's cabin had eight leather seats, four down each side of the plane, and Anderson prompted Nya to sit in the third seat from the front on the right. Anderson sat in the seat opposite her. Peters and Williams boarded the jet and took their seats and Williams, still, carrying her Ultrabook, sat at the front near the door on her left while Peters took one of the seats at the rear of the cabin.

A few minutes later the door to the jet was closed from the outside and then the jet engines hummed to life. After a short taxiway, the aircraft lined up on the main runaway and then rolled down the tarmac and took off. Nya leaned back into her seat. She had flown often enough to be comfortable with the odd sensations and noises of the aircraft. In many ways, she found the sensation of the plane gliding through the heavens quite peaceful.

Nya gazed out the window at the passing clouds and whispered, "Where are you, Elijah?" A voice entered her head: *I'm right behind you.* She glanced over her shoulder and, sure enough, Elijah was sitting in the seat just behind her. Nya smiled, filled with a warm sense of comfort, and turned back around to avoid attracting attention. She had heaps of questions for him but did not know how to ask them without speaking.

Elijah's words continued in her thoughts. *I have a plan, Nya. Though I must warn you that I'm not sure you're going to be overly enthusiastic about it…. But, I need you to follow my instructions without hesitation once I start giving them.*

Nya nodded.

For now just sit back and enjoy the flight. We will make our move to get out of here on the descent into Brisbane at around 20,000 feet.

Although puzzled at the prospect of *getting out of here … at 20,000 feet,* Nya nodded.

While trying her best to relax as time passed on the flight from New Zealand to Australia, anxious thoughts flooded her mind: *What caused my bout of fatigue, the coughing, and the blood?* After several minutes of wrestling with her inner voice and arguing within, she managed to subdue the questions by saying a quick prayer and trusting God with her life. Her mind was at ease.

As the plane's engines whirled down to begin the descent into Brisbane, Nya heard Elijah's voice: "*Nya, I'm going to turn off the oxygen supply in the cabin. The reduced oxygen will cause you and the men in the cabin to pass out. Don't be afraid. You will not feel any pain, just slightly dizzy until you lose consciousness.*" Nya's eyes narrowed as she bit the inside of her cheek, closed her eyes, and nodded.

* * *

Elijah left his seat and walked to the cockpit door. Over the past year, Elijah had been working hard on manipulating physics in the Earth

Realm with his thoughts. His training had been going well. At times, he found the process quite challenging and his obvious concern over not making the distance required sometimes bothered him. He didn't want to end up stuck halfway through a wall. The present operation would be a real test to see how his practice paid off. Elijah concentrated on the atoms making up the door as he walked through. The metal plate melted like warm liquid around him. On the other side, Elijah located the cabin pressure switch on a panel towards the rear of the cockpit. When the pilot and co-pilot were busy he flicked the switch to the off position. Then he reduced his own breathing to the minimum required and waited.

* * *

Several minutes later dizziness began to overpower Nya. The sensation wasn't awful. It started with light-headedness, which she had experienced from time to time after standing up quickly from a sitting position. Then the wooziness overcame her and everything faded to black as she passed out.

* * *

Elijah kept the pilots engaged by implanting thoughts in their minds to distract them from realizing that the faintness they were experiencing was due to a drop in cabin pressure. By the time the pilots had checked out the other possible issues Elijah suggested, they had lost consciousness. Elijah placed the jet into an autopilot holding pattern at 12,000 feet. He felt proud of himself for knowing how to do that. All those years he had spent playing flight simulators actually accounted for something. Though he had a pilot's license and flew light aircraft, he never had the chance to fly a jet except in simulators.

He left the cockpit and walked back to the exit hatch of the plane. He waited until the plane leveled out at 12,000 feet before unlatching and pushing the door open. The door alarm echoed from the cockpit as air streamed out of the cabin, decompressing with the air inside. The suction was negligible as the cabin pressure had begun to synchronize with the air outside when he disabled the cabin pressurization earlier. Elijah knelt beside Nya and gently shook her back into consciousness. Though the air was thin at 12,000 feet there was enough oxygen to allow her to breathe somewhat normally.

Within a few seconds, her eyes flickered opened. "What's happening?" she mumbled as her mind gradually regained focus.

Elijah smiled. "We're about to leave the plane."

Nya glanced towards the opened exit door. "Oh, and how are we—?"

"Jump!" Elijah replied.

Elijah stood up and moved to Anderson seated opposite Nya and removed the belt from around his waist. "Come, Nya," Elijah said as he walked towards the open door. Nya's reluctance gave way to trust and she followed. Elijah wrapped Anderson's belt around Nya's waist, looped it through his own belt, and cinched the strip of leather tight to bring Nya's back into contact with his abdomen. "Get your Ultrabook from Williams, Nya."

Nya held the Ultrabook firmly as Elijah proceeded to wrap his arms around Nya's chest and moved towards the door. He yelled, "Here we go!" as he pushed powerfully against Nya's hesitation. They began to fall, tumbling at first, but Elijah turned the flip-flop into an elegant dive with the help of his wings, then he brought them into a graceful glide.

* * *

"This is amazing," Nya said, wide-eyed and grinning. "I love it!"

Elijah replied, "It's not your first time."

"Oh," she said. "And when was the first, Elijah?"

"When I took to you to the cabin after our original escape in New Zealand."

"Ah," she said. "That explains why I woke up in bed with no memory of how I got there. How come I have no memory of that?"

Elijah replied, "Well, let's just say that I put you into a gentle sleep."

She contemplated whether she should ask more questions but she had come to trust Elijah and decided to just let it go and enjoy the ride. It wasn't everyday a girl got to fly!

Elijah slowed their descent over a quiet location near Clear Mountain. "Don't want anybody to see you," he said, "so I'm going to land out of view of any observers." He explained that although people would not be able to see him, they *would* be able to see Nya floating in the sky and that might be odd enough to attract unwanted attention.

After slaloming through several trees they landed with a soft touchdown in a small clearing. Elijah undid the belt and released Nya.

"What now, Elijah?" she asked.

"Now we get you to the hospital," he said in a concerned voice, "where they can check you over."

"I feel fine."

Elijah took Nya by the shoulders and looked her square in her eyes and said, softly, "You're not 'fine,' Nya. You need medical attention."

Nya knew he was right. She knew she was in denial because she simply did not want to admit the possibility that…. A tear formed in her eye as she whispered, "I'm scared, Elijah."

Elijah pulled her close and hugged her tight. "It's going to be OK. Have faith."

Nya's legs went limp and her eyes closed as she leaned into his hug.

* * *

Elijah knew she was about to lose consciousness as her adrenalin settled from the jump. He scooped her up into his arms and carried her to a nearby house. He made himself visible and knocked on the door. An elderly man with gray hair and deep wrinkles opened the door. Elijah's voice was urgent. "My friend and I were nearby and she collapsed. I need to call an ambulance. May I use your phone?" The elderly gentleman showed Elijah, with Nya in his arms, to the phone in his lounge room.

Elijah set Nya down gently on the sofa and dialed emergency services. He told them his friend was in need of immediate medical attention, rattled off a few of the symptoms, and suggested they take her to the Holy Spirit Hospital in North Brisbane. The emergency services operator assured him that an ambulance was en route.

The elderly gentleman asked, "Is there anything I can do?"

Elijah, noticing a crucifix on a nearby wall, replied, "Just pray." Elijah sat on the edge of the sofa next to Nya and said a silent prayer of his own as he gently stroked her hand.

Several minutes later he heard the wail of a siren approaching. Paramedics came rushing through the door armed with a stretcher and various medical gear. After a quick check, they lifted Nya onto the stretcher and whisked her into the back of the waiting ambulance. One of the paramedics asked Elijah for Nya's name and identification. He hesitated a moment considering the possibility that Cain could trace the hospital admission and track her down. *Cain has the software and will likely presume Nya is dead after the plane incident.* He gave them Nya's identification.

"Would you like to accompany her, sir?" the paramedic asked.

"No, it's OK," he said. "I'll follow later." Elijah watched as the paramedic hopped into the ambulance and closed the doors. Then the ambulance sped away, siren squealing.

"Will she be OK?" the elderly gentleman asked.

"I'm not sure," Elijah said, with one eyebrow raised and a slight frown on his face. After a moment of silence Elijah extended his hand and introduced himself. "Sorry, I should have introduced myself earlier. My name is Elijah. Thank you so much for your kind assistance."

The elderly man shook his hand. "Sam, that's me. Call me that."

Elijah said his goodbyes and then walked back off into the nearby trees. The time had come for Elijah to report in with Araton. He opened a portal to Elysium and passed through the white oval-shaped gateway.

* * *

Williams regained consciousness and, noticing the door opened, scrambled to his feet and pulled the hatch shut. He scanned the plane while yelling, "Wake up! What's going on?!"

Anderson and Peters stirred, and Anderson said, "Where is Nya?"

Williams shouted, "Check the toilet!"

Anderson scrambled to the back of the plane, opened the toilet, and scanned inside. "Not here!"

The pilot and co-pilot, awakened by the yelling and commotion in the cabin, regained control of the aircraft from the auto-pilot. Williams entered the cockpit. "What happened?"

The pilot said, "I think we lost cabin pressure and passed out. After that we are not sure. We should know more after we land and review the flight computers."

"Lost cabin pressure," Williams said. "But how?"

The pilot shook his head. "Like I said, I'm not sure. Please return to your seat and prepare for landing."

"One last question. Do you have parachutes on board?"

"No. We don't carry any."

Williams returned to his seat and instructed Peterson and Anderson to do the same. Williams mumbled to himself, "She must have jumped. How I am going to explain this?"

Chapter 12 - Courage

As Nya's eyes opened very slowly she heard a female voice saying, "She is waking up, Doctor." Nya glanced around the bright white room trying to figure out where she was. The first thing she noticed was a large cross hung on the wall near a window with drawn blinds.

Above her a TV, black and silent, was set on a metal bracket hung from the ceiling. She looked down at herself: She was in a hospital gown and underwear under a thin white cotton sheet in what was unmistakably an infirmary bed. An IV was fixed to a vein on the back of her right hand and a steady drip pumped fluids into her bloodstream. A hospital bracelet with her name on it in blue biro was on her left wrist.

"Hello, Nya," an elderly man in a white coat said. "I'm Dr. Evans. How are you feeling?"

"A little groggy," she replied in a somewhat monotone robotronic voice, "but I'm not feeling too bad. What happened? Why am I here?"

"Our initial tests indicate that you apparently passed out from exhaustion and dehydration. Your blood work did turn up a few other markers that suggest that your immune system is battling."

Battling what? she thought.

"The IV is getting you some much-needed fluids to help with your dehydration." He held up the clipboard and scrawled some notes on her chart as he spoke. "We'll try to get you to eat something a little later."

Nya took comfort in Dr. Evans' bedside manner. He was a handsome bloke with kind green eyes and an especially fit looking body, and his thin grey receding hair suggested he was in his late 50s.

Dr. Evans stood an arm's length from Nya. "We called your doctor to request your medical records be sent over. He informed us that you had been scheduled to have a mammogram for a lump on your breast, but cancelled the appointment."

Nya could feel her cheeks burn as she blushed. "Yes," she said, "I was getting to that. I had important business I needed to attend to." She swept a few strands of blond hair away from her face. "But I was going to have the scan as soon as I got back."

Dr. Evans cocked his head and nodded. "Well, since you're already here we're going to go one better, Nya." He scribbled something on her chart. "We will be sending you off for a full body MRI, just to be on the safe side." He handed the clipboard to the nurse who then penned some of her own notes on the chart.

Nya wondered what she was writing.

Dr. Evans proceeded to check Nya's blood pressure and her heart rate: "Blood pressure: one-fifteen over seventy-five. Heart rate: seventy-four. All looks good, Nya," he said as he removed the cuff from her arm. "They will take you down to the MRI room in a half hour or so. In the meantime, try to get some rest. I'll come by later today after we have had a chance to look at your scans."

"Thanks, Doc." Nya said.

The nurse passed Dr. Evans the chart after recording the blood pressure and heart rate readings. He glanced over the notes then hung the clipboard on the end of the bed. Before leaving the nurse said, "If you need anything, just use the buzzer on the side of your bed."

Nya thanked her and then closed her eyes. Her mind raced. *Where is Elijah? Is Isaac OK? Is that lump anything to be concerned about? What is my immune system battling?* She thought back to the blood on her hand after she coughed and wondered whether she should have told the doctor about it. *Was that important? Maybe the red droplets were nothing….*

After thirty minutes of such wrangling with her anxious inner voice, a nurse and an orderly whose name tag identified him as Andrew entered the room. The nurse introduced herself as Amanda and removed the drip attached to the IV.

Andrew moved around the bed, raising the sides and unlocking the wheels. "Here we go, Miss," he said as he took his place behind the head of the bed out of Nya's view. "The radiography department is a short trip."

He wheeled her down to the MRI suite on the first floor. A young radiologist who looked to be in her late 20s and was very pregnant introduced herself as Samantha. "This procedure will take approximately sixty minutes, and you may feel a little claustrophobic inside the tunnel. That is completely normal, and you'll be just fine. I will be talking to you throughout the scan through a microphone. If you need anything just talk to me. I will be able to hear you."

Samantha's comforting voice and kind manner put Nya at ease.

She pressed a few buttons to adjust the bench height and switch on some lights. "The main thing is to lie as still as possible and keep your breathing steady."

Nya smiled. "I'll do my best."

Samantha left and went to control room behind a glass window on Nya's right. Nya began sliding into the tunnel headfirst until the plastic tube surrounded her body from head to toe. It was tight. There was barely a hand's width between her and the sides and ceiling of the tunnel. Samantha's voice spoke: "OK, I'm going to start the machine now. Just breathe normally." A whirring noise began.

Nya closed her eyes, drew in a slow deep breath whispering "Inner Awareness," and then released the air whispering "Outer Awareness." She had learnt how to control her breath long ago from a friend she met in a dark place and it always helped her manage anxiety whenever she was in tight spots.

The air was cold, probably to help keep the MRI machine cool. The thin hospital gown did not provide much cover from the chill. As she continued her breathing exercises Nya's mind wandered to thoughts of the past. She pictured herself back home on the farm where she had grown up in Nanango, Northwest of Brisbane. She had many happy memories of her childhood on the farm.

She saw herself as a 9-year-old running through a grassy paddock towards the old well. Nya wondered to herself, *am I dreaming? Did I fall asleep?* And then the scene in her mind took over entirely.

The small A-frame roof over the well had seen better days and its wood shingles were well-weathered and grayish. The structure cast a late afternoon shadow across the grassy knoll. Under the roof a wooden water bucket suspended from a frayed rope swayed to and fro in the breeze. The circular walls of the well house were fashioned of bricks and stones of various sizes cemented together.

Nine-year-old Nya leant over the well wall on her tip-toes and peered into the darkness below trying to see how deep the shaft was. She gave the swaying water bucket a gentle push to the side so she could get a better view. And when she did, all of the sudden a cracking sound rang out as the brick well wall gave way. The wall collapsed inward and Nya lost her footing and stumbled down towards the deep hole. She flailed her hands out for the closest thing she could get a hold of – the bucket fastened to the winding spool – and took it with her as she fell into the well, slowly, slowly, as if in slow motion, gazing ever upward at the forever-shrinking light at the top of the well.

The rope spun off the spool at the top of the well as she and the bucket went down until she was literally at the end of her rope and came to an abrupt stop that sent a jolt through her arms. The sudden jarring stop alarmed her, but she clung to the bucket for dear life. Then, her weight and the sudden stop, caused the old rope to snap. Still clutching the bucket in both arms, she resumed falling, fast now. An instant later her feet hit something solid, but whatever it was it gave way to her weight. She descended into the cold dark water below. It did not take long for her feet to hit bottom. Her knees buckled and she lost her grip on the bucket. The air in her lungs was forced out of her nose and mouth sending large bubbles floating to the surface.

Nya straightened her legs, pushing away from the ground with all her might while focusing on the dim light above. She raised her arms and swam upwards. Her head broke the water's surface and she treaded water gasping for air. The icy liquid caused her lungs to burn. She stretched out her arms and began pawing frantically at the rough walls of the well shaft for something – anything – to hang onto. After a short search, she found a few protrusions she could get a purchase on.

Nya shouted, "Help! Somebody help me! I'm down here!" She heard her voice reverberate with a muted echo and, though she knew nobody would hear her, her natural instincts overrode her intellect. Nobody came to the old well, which was a good two-mile walk from her home. She was the only one who came to explore that area of the farm. Nya yelled again with the faint hope that someone would hear her cries. Her heart rate and breathing increased as fear began creeping into her mind.

Then suddenly she grew scared, dreadfully scared. Panic started to overwhelm her. Her arms began to tremble with fatigue. Her fingers clutching the rocky wall screamed with pain from fingertip to knuckle. She realized that she would not be able to cling to the well's wall much longer. The cold water sapped her strength and took her breath away. She felt along the surface of the cold dark water with her left hand thinking: *It must be here somewhere.* She located the bucket and dumped the water out. She took her hands off the well wall and cradled the bucket, which was her wooden life-preserver, in her arms. It served as a crude, but effective, floatation device that allowed her to hover on the water's surface.

Her panic started to subside just a little and her breathing steadied and heart rate dropped. Minutes passed, long and dark, each seeming more like an hour. She glanced occasionally up at the light at the top of the well in the hope that someone would be looking back down at her. Her heart skipped a beat as something rubbed against her leg. Her mind raced with worrying thoughts: *There is something in the water! A rat, a snake, what was that?!*

She floated motionless, scanning the surface of the water in the darkness, waiting to see if *it* would touch her again. Moments later *it* did. This time she freaked and jerked her leg away from it. Whatever *it* was wrapped around her leg. She let go of the bucket and splashed around punching the water trying to free herself from whatever had her. Her attempts to free herself failed. She could not shake it loose. Terrified, she struggled harder and lost the bucket. Unable to stay afloat her head went under. She thrashed, kicking her legs frantically, trying to free herself. Her lungs began to burn from lack of oxygen. She was sure she was going to die. This was the end. She was going to drown, caught by something in the water.

In a final desperate effort to free herself she reached down with one arm to grab whatever was clinging to her leg. On doing so, she realized *it* was the rope from the bucket. She untangled her leg with both hands, swam back to the surface, dumped out the now water-logged bucket and resumed her floating position. Somewhat relieved, but still fearful, she hovered on the water's surface, cradling the bucket.

Her troubled inner voice complained. *I'm going to die. I'm going to freeze. There is no way out.* Night will soon fall. Panic, once again fueled by terrifying thoughts, started to take hold of her. Her heart rate and breathing increased. She paddled around and explored the inner wall of the well in search of larger indents to aid in climbing up. No luck. The well shaft was smooth and slippery. She began yelling again: "Help! I'm down here!" Then she lost hope and gave in.

She gazed towards the dimming circle of light at the top of the well. The sun was setting, and soon all light from above would be gone. Nya held out hope for a clear night with the moon lighting the sky to provide some comfort.

Two hours had passed and, with each passing second, Nya found it more difficult to keep her eyes open. The cold water continued sapping her strength. She shivered and her teeth chattered and she met two new friends or enemies, depending on how she thought about them: Mr. Fatigue and Mr. Hyperthermia.

A male voice echoed in the depths of the well: "Nya? Hello, Nya!"

She peered up into the darkness. "Who's there?" she asked.

"I'm here to help, Nya. I'll keep you awake and teach you how to breathe to fight off your fears."

"Who are you?" Nya questioned.

"So many questions, Nya," the voice said. "You are a curious little girl."

"What do you want?"

"Just to teach you, Nya. Now listen very carefully: With each breath you breathe in think *Inner Awareness*. With each breath you exhale think *Outer Awareness*. Do this each time you breathe and focus on the words and just breathe."

Nya figured she did not have anything to lose so she gave the method a go. Several breaths later, she did find it comforting and her fear subsided. Focusing on the words and breathing kept her mind from obsessing about negative outcomes.

The voice spoke again. "Very good, Nya. You're a fast learner."

Nya continued to concentrate on her breathing and acquired a steady rhythm. Hours passed. High above the well, echoing down the shaft, she heard distance voices yelling her name, "Nya, are you out here? Nya! Nya?!"

Nya yelled, "I'm down here! Help! Help!" No words left her mouth, only silent gestures. Her throat was dry, her vocal cords rigid. She tried again. "Help, I'm down here!" This time her voice did radiate up the well and was heard.

A soft female voice met her eardrum. "Nya." She opened her eyes and saw Samantha standing over her. "We're all done, Nya. The scans are complete. Looks like you fell asleep."

After taking a moment to regain her bearing, Nya replied, "Yes. I think I did. I dreamed a memory of the past."

"Well, you're not the first one to fall asleep during an MRI. For some people that is a blessing. Being stuck in the tunnel for a length of time can be quite disturbing."

"Or down a well," Nya added.

"A well?" Samantha asked, eyebrow raised. "What do you mean?"

"Oh, doesn't matter," Nya said. "Just memories."

Samantha smiled and nodded.

Andrew and a second orderly entered and placed Nya back onto her hospital bed and wheeled her to her room.

During the short trip, Nya thought about how they had rescued her from the well. The rescue did not take long. They sent down a harness that she looped around her waist and then they pulled her up. She remembered the ride in the ambulance to the hospital where they treated her for hyperthermia and a few scrapes. She even made the local newspaper, something that she was somewhat proud of. Many people from around the town had joined the search after she had not come home that evening. Her parents alerted the local police, who quickly organized a search party from members of the community. They saved her life. She never did understand where the voice that taught her the breathing trick had come from. At the time Nya had mentioned the mysterious voice to her mother, who told her she was probably hallucinating from the hyperthermia. Her mum stayed with her throughout the night in the hospital, lying beside her.

Thoughts of her mum stung her heart and tears welled in her eyes. She missed her mum, and the father she barely had a chance to know.

Chapter 13 - Elysium Megiddo Building

In the past year since he had become an angel Elysium had become Elijah's home. The vast city spanned miles and miles and consisted of futuristic buildings intertwined with lush vegetation that created a perfect balance of technology and nature working together. Flying cars, which resembled modern luxury buses without wheels, called Ancars – short for Angel cars – zipped around the city. No teleporting, portals, or angel flying was allowed in Elysium. This policy kept the Ancars busy along with the many Transport Points, which port an angel from one place in the city to another in a matter of seconds.

Standing at an Ancar station, Elijah raised his hand to the sign bearing the Ancar logo. The logo glowed and slightly pulsed bright white indicating that his transportation request had been received. Moments later an Ancar arrived hovering in front of Elijah. Its doors opened upwards and a pleasant female voice from within the vehicle said, "Please take a seat." Elijah hopped in and took a seat in one of the several empty seats. Elijah said, "Megiddo Building," and the Ancar replied, "Destination set to Megiddo Building, expected travel time is twelve sectants." Elijah quickly calculated how long 12 sectants would be in Earth time – around four minutes. Thanks to inertial stabilizers the Ancar twisted and turned and changed elevations without even a hint of movement, other than the visual stimulus through the windows.

Elijah expected to meet up with Castiel, Sophia, and Araton at the Megiddo Building. Araton's job was managing the angels' assignments and working out which team to send. Araton reminded Elijah of Major General George Hammond who managed the SG1 teams in the television series *Stargate*, not in appearance but in job role and personality. Elijah got on well with Araton. Even though the two did not always agree on things, they understood where each other was coming from. Not everything is black-and-white, and Elijah realized his tendency to view things from his own personal perspective while Araton took a much broader view of situations.

As the Ancar slowed to a hover and the doors opened the female voice said, "Megiddo Building." Elijah exited the Ancar and made the short walk to the Megiddo Building, a grand multi-story structure with a stately entryway framed with two polished marble pillars that supported a little alcove above the entrance. The building was sided in sandstone-type brickwork but with a futuristic gleam.

Elijah entered the Megiddo Building and proceeded into the assignment briefing room. Araton, standing behind a round table with a holographic image of the earth floating above it, greeted Elijah with a warm smile. "Ahh, Elijah. Welcome back."

"Thank you." Elijah gave Araton a brief handshake then placed his hands loosely behind his back. "Good to be here. However, I think my stay will be short."

"From what I'm seeing, I would agree with you, Elijah." The glassy tabletop displayed a wealth of information. "Castiel and Sophia should be here any minute." He paused and took a good look at Elijah. "If I didn't know you any better, Elijah, I'd say that those furled eyebrows and rather phony smile meant you are unsettled."

Elijah nodded.

"Level with me, Elijah. What is bothering you?"

"Nya. She has a physical illness," Elijah said, narrowing his eyes. "I couldn't quite detect what it is. What is wrong with her?"

"She has cancer, Elijah." Araton's own smile turned bitter. "It's in a late stage, I'm afraid."

Elijah stared at the ceiling, shuffled his feet. After a moment he said, "Can we send Sophia to heal her?"

Araton cocked his head. "We are not allowed to heal diseases or trauma without a directive from above, Elijah. You know that."

"Yes." In a sincere though somewhat defeated voice Elijah said, "But shouldn't she be an exception?"

Araton raised his voice. "The only exception is when trauma or disease occurs as a direct result of angelic involvement."

Elijah crossed his arms and raised his voice a little louder than Araton's. "I don't see the issue. Why not?"

Sophia and Castiel entered the room as the debate between Araton and Elijah continued. Elijah nodded to each of them as they arrived. Castiel nodded back and Sophia raised her right hand and waved. It wasn't the first time Elijah had gone toe-to-toe with Araton over an issue he felt passionate about.

Araton greeted Sophia and Castiel with a quick nod and continued his conversation with Elijah. "Let me tell you a little story, Elijah. Back in 1897, on Earth, a little eight-year-old boy sang in the church choir. He even considered becoming a priest. His guardian angel became particularly fond of him. Three years later the little boy contracted a case of the measles, and his guardian angel became concerned over the way the boy struggled with the condition. So the angel went rogue and decided to cure him while he slept. The angel was well aware that healing him was against policy but did not consider the action would be an issue. After all, curing measles is *no big deal*, right?"

Elijah weighed the question but decided to withhold his first impulse, which was so say, "Right. It was no big deal." He wondered where the catch was. He just nodded.

Araton paused for a moment as if knowing that he had Elijah right where he wanted him – right at the place where he could get the point across. He continued, "The younger brother had contracted measles around the same time and, unfortunately, passed away. His guardian angel did not break the rules. The older brother was deeply affected by his brother's death. The little boy's name was—"

Elijah took a step back, almost stumbling, as Araton said the boy's name: "Adolf Hitler."

After a moment of silence, Elijah clenched his teeth and lowered his eyes. "So are you saying that the Holocaust was a result of an angel healing Hitler?"

In a lower, softer, gentler voice, Araton responded. "No, not at all. It is quite likely that Adolf would have healed naturally from the measles and that his brother would still have died. The problem was this: The angel who healed Adolf took it to heart when the destructive reign of Hitler began."

"Wh-who, who," Elijah stuttered, "was the angel?"

Sophia turned to Elijah with wet eyes and said with deep sadness in her voice, "The angel was *me*, Elijah."

Elijah did not know how to respond. His stomach sank. He felt sorry for Sophia, but at the same time he couldn't help but wonder whether Sophia may have been responsible for the millions and millions of people who died at Hitler's hands. Within a few seconds, though, he dismissed the thought knowing Araton was right and the events probably would have played out the same way if Sophia had not intervened. He could also understand how Sophia had carried the burden. He stepped over and placed his hand on Sophia's shoulder and looked her in the eye. "I'm so sorry, Sophia. I didn't know."

"It's OK, Elijah," she said. "I've learned to live with the pain."

Araton said, "Healing someone isn't simple. We angels do not know what a person will continue to do in the future. To protect us, we are not given the option to freely heal whomever we believe we should. If healing someone comes as a directive, we don't bear any responsibility if the person turns out to be bad."

At a loss for words Elijah stood there motionless and absorbed the issues. On the one hand, he wanted Nya healed, but on the other he realized the policy regarding healing was in place for a reason. "How can we get a directive for Nya to be healed, Araton?"

Araton replied, "A request has already been made, but we are yet to hear a response. These things sometimes need to play out for reasons we do not understand until we witness the result. Even then, they can be hard to comprehend."

Elijah nodded. He knew that sometimes the picture made no sense *as it was being painted*. He remembered back to when Castiel explained the concept like a jigsaw puzzle. When you have only a few pieces in place it is hard to visualize the complete picture. With life, we don't even have all the pieces of the puzzle – only God does.

In a more optimistic voice Araton said, "OK, well let's get on with your next assignments. Castiel, how is your progress with Isaac?"

"He is safe for now with the Joondaburri."

Araton faced Sophia. "What is the status with Frank?"

"Safe as well."

Araton looked at Elijah and stated, "I've been watching your progress with Nya. The Holy Spirit Hospital is a good place for her, Elijah. They will treat her well. The escape you pulled off over Brisbane, Elijah, jumping from a plane, was quite compelling and very well-executed."

Castiel and Sophia both faced Elijah and said in tandem, "Jumping from a *what?*"

Elijah shrugged and Castiel muttered, "Typical Elijah, always the show pony."

"All right, then, your next assignment." Araton moved his hand over the table's surface causing some of the screens to change. "All three of you are to investigate Cain's compound. Our sensors are being blocked from the area, and we cannot monitor inside the buildings." An overview shot, similar to a satellite image, displayed the compound on the table's surface. "I want you three to go inside and explore. To our knowledge, you should be invisible to everyone. So getting in should not be much of a problem. However, several security systems and armed guards are in place so you will need to be careful. Although invisible, you will still trigger alarms and can be shot."

Araton paused for a moment as the various displays on the table's surface changed to show further instructions. He looked back at the Trio. "You all have been granted X1 status, which permits you to use whatever force is necessary in the human realm. If you deem it necessary, you may also disclose your true nature to believers. Nya, to whom Elijah has already revealed himself, and Detective Sergeant Frank Mercer both believe. Isaac, however, does not, so do not reveal your true nature to him. Cain believes but has pledged his allegiance to the Underworld. He knows about the Shadows and us. Information from various sources report that he has some sort of alliance with the Shadows. We are not sure how much his employees know or do not know, so you will have to use your best judgment to determine their awareness."

Castiel, Sophia, and Elijah glanced at each other briefly before Castiel said, "We will succeed."

"I hope so, Castiel," Araton replied. "The stakes are very, *very* high. It is possible that the very survival of humanity is at stake. Things are changing rapidly in the human realm. Something just isn't right."

Araton took a moment to shut down the holographic display on the table. Then, with a concerned expression on his face and an unsure tone, said, "Just between us: Things are changing. This is the first time in a thousand earth years that X1 status has been assigned to angels. For X1 approval to come from above, something is happening … something *big*."

For a long moment no one said a word before Araton closed the meeting with a warning: "Remember, guys, no heroics. Fatal wounds in the Earth Realm will lead to your spiritual death, which is a result none of us wants. Elysium needs you all. Do not put yourself in immediate danger." Araton pointed towards the exit. "Now go visit Nemamiah and grab some armaments. You will likely need them when investigating the compound."

Castiel, Sophia, and Elijah thanked Araton then headed off to see Nemamiah.

Chapter 14 - Preparation

A quick Ancar ride followed by a short journey via a Transport Point led the trio of Castiel, Sophia, and Elijah to Nemamiah's training area. Nemamiah was the angel in charge of training the angels for combat and distributing armaments for their assignments.

Elijah peered through the entranceway that led into the place where Nemamiah conducted his training. Seeing the room empty Elijah said, "Castiel, you first."

"Why thank you, Elijah." Immediately upon entering the training area Castiel clutched the back of his head and let out a painful yelp as though he had been struck with a cricket bat. His eyes were watery and clouded over as he lost balance and fell face-first onto the ground.

A moment later Castiel regained his composure, swiveled around and rose to his feet, and found Nemamiah standing in a horse stance holding a long staff at arms' length in front of him. Elijah and Sophia, both grinning, stood on either side of Nemamiah.

Nemamiah said, "I see you have learnt from your past experience in entering my training field, Elijah."

Castiel cut his eyes to Elijah. "I get it. You set me up. Well, you just wait, Elijah," Castiel said, smiling. "Two can play at that game."

Elijah, a little anxious about the possible retaliation, cleared his throat. "It's all in good fun."

Nemamiah walked towards the wall opposite the entrance. The training room consisted of a single entrance. No furniture and no windows, only muted white walls. He placed his hand flat against the wall at shoulder-height and began to push. The portion of the wall he touched dissolved revealing a doorway into the next section. "Right this way. This will be something new for you, Elijah. You get to experience our testing and equipment readiness area."

Elijah's eyes widened, his eyebrows raised. "Cool."

"Follow me," Nemamiah said.

Elijah's eyes were drawn to an angel standing at the end of an exceedingly long corridor. The angel spread his white feathery wings like an eagle preparing to take flight. On each wing, close to the angel's body, was a shiny metallic cylindrical device resembling a mini torpedo, only hollow, sparkling under the yellow-tinted ceiling lights. Ten-inch-thick floor-to-ceiling glass walls formed the sides of the corridor, which was about a football field in length. On the far side the glass joined a smooth stone wall painted sky blue. At the end of the corridor, opposite the angel, stood a human crash dummy.

"Ahh, Elijah," Nemamiah said, "curious, are you? Those are our Angel Light Ares. Stand back a little and watch the test."

The angel lifted into the air as he flapped his wings and began flying forward just above the ground towards the crash dummy. Two beams of white light streamed out of both Ares and simultaneously struck the crash dummy at the far end of the corridor. The crash dummy disintegrated, amid a cloud of dust, into thousands of tiny fragments. Then a large bright-white flash erupted from the rear of each Ares which thrust the angel forward at an incredible speed. The angel sped like a missile and, as he approached the wall, maneuvered each of his wings into a full vertical position, using them as speed breaks, and then came to a soft landing less than a meter from the wall.

Nemamiah said, "The Ares serve two purposes." He held up his hand and raised his index finger. "Firstly, they shoot Angel Light beams that can disintegrate Shadows and material other than human flesh and bones." He raised his second finger. "Secondly, they can give a sudden boost of forward thrust to the angel wearing them, similar to afterburners on a jet."

"Awesome," Elijah said as rush of adrenalin energized him and his eyes gleamed. "I have to get myself a set of those."

"You'll have to wait a while, Elijah," Nemamiah replied. "They are still in the testing phase. We have a few bugs to iron out."

"Oh, well," Elijah sighed with a shrug.

Castiel patted him on the back. "Just think how much safer the walls will feel without you having a pair."

Elijah smiled. "You have a point."

As they followed Nemamiah to the armaments room the Trio glanced around at the extraordinary equipment being produced and tested. Elijah shook his head. "There is some pretty cool stuff going on here."

"My guess is we are going to need every last one of them in the future," Sophia said as she whipped her long black hair over her shoulder with a tilt of her neck. "The Shadows are getting better armed all the time."

Elijah reminisced about Shadows. He had not confronted one in some time. They appeared much like human shadows, dark and without features, just outlines of a body except for glowing and typically red eyes. Elijah knew of four types of Shadows. The first type of Shadow was generally unarmed and fed off of Red Energy that humans produce with negative emotions. The second type were Shadow Knights that were, of course, shaped like Knights. Armed with swords and shields they were worthy opponents. The third type were Shumans that resulted from Shadows' possessing a human being and taking full control of him or her. The human host's eyes would turn black as night to any angel viewing them. Under control of the Shadow, the human host would do almost anything – and typically negative things – to create more Red Energy for the Shadows to feed on. Shumans were the type that most bothered Elijah. Fortunately, they were rare because a Shadow could only possess a human if the human allowed it to do so – in other words by selling his soul to the Underworld, or as some would say, *"Sell their soul to the devil."* Lastly, were the Shadow Scavengers that scurried around on the floors and walls of environments feeding off any Red Energy they could find. Scavengers were not much bigger than the average human hand and resembled spiders in their movements and furry outlines.

"Right, Sophia," Nemamiah said standing by a blank white wall, "we have something of an arms race with them. Time to get your weapons."

"Uh, hmm," Elijah said raising an eyebrow. "There is nothing here."

"Right you are, Eli. Well not yet anyway." Nemamiah placed his hand on the white wall and this time the wall vanished around his hand revealing a large narrow closet space which spanned further than the eye could see. The endless walls were lined with neatly arranged armaments. Elijah realized that the armory was another one of those spaces in Elysium like Gethsemane that was larger on the inside than on the outside and opens into a different dimension.

A pleasant female voice radiated from inside the armory. "Your weapon code, please." Elijah wondered why all the virtual voices sounded female.

Nemamiah said, "6AP312A." A white floating sphere with a silver ring around it scurried to the back of the armory. When it hovered at a specific spot, a ray of blue-light beamed towards the wall, spanning out into a large oval shape around a pair of 9mm Uzis. The sphere glided backwards, pulling the weapons from the wall, and then rotated and headed to Nemamiah. As the sphere pulled to a halt near Nemamiah, it emitted several beeps of different pitches. The sounds reminded Elijah of R2D2 from *Star Wars*.

Nemamiah took the pistols and handed them to Castiel. "Your Judgement Twins, Castiel. I know how much you like them."

"I sure do," Castiel replied. He placed them around his waist under his trench coat.

"They are loaded with Angel Light Mk2 bullets," Nemamiah said. "They act the same as Angel Light bullets. They will damage all physical matter and Shadows without damaging human flesh and bone. The difference with Mk2 bullets is that, on contact with human flesh, they will send out an electric shock that stuns the human, rather like a stun gun without the need for probes attached to a battery."

Nemamiah spoke another code and the sphere brought him two Katana swords glowing with a white haze, along with their sheaths. "For you, Sophia, I have your Sisters of Light," Nemamiah said as he handed them to her. Sophia thanked Nemamiah and then attached them to her back where they crisscrossed. After another command, the floating ball delivered a necklace with a large cross on the end to Nemamiah who handed it to Sophia. She hung the cross around her neck.

A voice echoed from up high on the wall of the armor, in amongst the armaments. "Leaving me till last. You *always* leave me till last. Do you think I have nothing better to do than just sit up here?"

Elijah smiled on hearing the familiar moaning of Gunthor. Nemamiah commanded the sphere and accepted Gunthor from the hovering ball on its return. "You know what this is, Elijah, no doubt," Nemamiah said, holding the sword by the sheath and offering the hilt to Elijah.

Light sparkled off the pure gold hilt and glistened from the three different colored gems embedded in the handle. Elijah took Gunthor from Nemamiah and pulled it from its sheath revealing the sterling silver blade glowing with a white aura. He slashed the sword through the air a few times admiring how balanced Gunthor felt.

The cheeky, moaning voice spoke again: "Hey, Hey, slow up! You're making me dizzy here!"

Castiel said, "Do it faster, Elijah."

"You're cruel, Castiel," Elijah said, laughing as he sheathed Gunthor and attached the sheath to his belt.

Elijah sheathed his sword, and Nemamiah returned from the armory with a bow. "And of course we have your Bow of Sentencing."

"Of course," Elijah said. He took the bow from Nemamiah. As always Elijah admired the craftsmanship of the bow, which was emblazoned with many inscriptions in a language unknown to Elijah and glowed with a faint white light. He fastened it to his back under his right wing.

Nemamiah said, "As always, the bow shoots Angel Light arrows, Elijah. We have upgraded them to Angel Light Mk2 arrows just as we upgraded the Angel Light bullets. The arrows will automatically appear when you drawback the bow. If for some reason you want to use regular Angel Light arrows, you can do so by holding the bow horizontally instead of vertically before drawing back the string."

Elijah nodded thinking, *that's pretty neat*. Elijah turned to leave thinking that he had received all his usual armaments

"Not so fast," Nemamiah said. "We have something new for you Elijah." Elijah spun around and watched as Nemamiah directed the hovering sphere to retrieve an armlet from the armory. "This armlet Elijah is the Shield of Faith."

"But, uh, Nemamiah," Elijah said, pursing his lips and lowering his eyebrows, "it doesn't look like this little piece of jewelry will be much of a shield to me."

Nemamiah passed the armlet to Elijah. "Put it on." Elijah slipped the armlet over his hand and up his left arm until the breadth of his forearm brought the decorated metal circle to a stop. Elijah examined the silver armlet that was wreathed in a soft white aurora and noticed that it bore inscriptions similar in style to those on the bow. They glowed with a faint golden hue.

"All right, Elijah, now simply raise your left forearm to about chest height and push it slightly out from your body as if you're trying to push someone away."

Elijah raised his forearm parallel to his chest then pushed his forearm outward. A large shield suddenly beamed out of the armlet in front of him. The magnificent shield glowed translucent white and had the form of a Medieval Kite Shield with a sky blue cross adorning its center. It was weightless. "Magnificent," Elijah said.

Nemamiah nodded. "The shield will stop just about anything, Elijah. However, it will not stop any inertia an object that hits the shield carries with it, so I wouldn't try to stop a bus with it." Nemamiah winked at Castiel and Sophia and, in a sarcastic tone, added: "After your last adventure – you know, the one in which you decided to use your body as a shield to stop some bullets – we figured you would be better off with a real shield."

"Huh," Elijah said, blushing. "You know about that?"

"Only what Castiel and Sophia told me," Nemamiah said. "You were lucky you were not killed."

Castiel cut his eyes over at Sophia and she glared back, perhaps thinking the same thing he was thinking: *If they only knew what really happened....*

Elijah shrugged it off. "How do I retract the shield, Nemamiah?"

"Simply touch the back of the armlet with your other hand, Elijah."

Elijah touched the back of the armlet and the shield vanished instantly. "This could come in handy, Nemamiah. Thank you."

"You're most welcome, Elijah." He clapped his hands together. "Well, that about wraps this meeting up." He addressed the Trio: "All the best with your assignments, and don't forget to return all of your illustrious weapons in one piece."

Sophia and Castiel thanked Nemamiah while Elijah continued admiring his new armlet.

Castiel said, "Right. Let's go. We have work to do."

They headed out the way they had come and headed for the nearest portal point where they could port to a location near Cain's compound on Earth.

Chapter 15 - Investigate Compound

Elijah, Castiel, and Sophia stepped out of the Portal in the midst of a copse of trees behind the 10-foot-high razor-wire perimeter fence of Cain's compound.

Elijah retrieved his EVE from eSpace and brought up a scan of the compound. He studied the layout. "Hey, Castiel, check out this scan. What is this red outline around the outer walls of the compound?"

Castiel squinted and took a close look at the image on Elijah's EVE. "It means the walls are impenetrable by manipulating their physical properties. In other words, we can't pass through them."

"How is Cain pulling that off, Castiel?"

Castiel shrugged and scratched the back of his head. "Probably by some sort of energy field generator. Remember what Araton said: 'Cain believes but has pledged his allegiance to the Underworld. He knows about the Shadows and us.'"

"Right," Elijah said. "He's prepared."

"Indeed," Castiel said. "The problem for us is that although we can manipulate and morph matter, energy fields are a bit trickier – especially if they consist of Red Energy."

"I see," Elijah said, nodding. He continued to analyze the layout of the Compound on his EVE. Elijah pointed to the front door to the compound on his EVE. "It looks as though this door is the only access point available to us. It's the only place in the whole compound where the energy field isn't present."

"Yes," Castiel said. "But it shouldn't be too difficult to pull off. Let's stake out those guards."

Elijah joined him in studying the position and movement of the guards. Some armed with sniper rifles were manning watch towers about four stories high positioned at the two corners of the front perimeter fence. Others were on patrol marching end-to-end along the perimeter fence and stationed at the main gate. All were armed with a heavy assault weapons.

Castiel looked at Elijah and said, "Looking at the guards, I don't believe any of them will be able to see us while we remain out of phase." Castiel rubbed his chin. "What do you think, Sophia?"

"I think you're right," Sophia replied, analyzing the guard's movements. "But we should move one at a time, covering for each other, in case we're wrong and they can see us."

Elijah moved closer to the galvanized chain link fence and began preparing to pass through by manipulating the physics when Castiel grabbed him by the shoulder. "Wait a second, Elijah." Castiel picked up a fallen tree limb from the ground and poked it through a loop in the fence. He proceeded to move the twig sideways through the wire. As the wood touched the wire, a stream of smoke rose and the stick was split in two as if by a laser.

Elijah shook his head. "Hmm, if I had tried to pass through that would have been a rather unpleasant experience."

"Rather, indeed," Castiel agreed.

"Shall we fly up and over?" Elijah asked.

"No, I think dear old Gunthor should be able to sever the wire and make a hole for us to pass through."

Elijah drew Gunthor from the sheath around his waist. In a whiny voice Gunthor said, "Wait a second. If this doesn't work *I* will be severed. Easy now. Give me a moment to think about it."

Without hesitation Elijah pushed Gunthor towards the wire.

"Wait, wait! I don't like this. I don't want to." Elijah swiped the wire fence with the blade. Gunthor screamed, "Ahhhhhhh, no, help!" The wire cut and Gunthor stayed in one piece. "Oh, that wasn't so difficult. See, I told you I could do it," brave Gunthor said.

Castiel faced Gunthor and lowered his voice. "You're just lucky no guards heard you scream like a little girl, Gunthor, otherwise you would really have had something to squeal about."

After a few more swipes Elijah had carved a hole in the fence large enough for them to step through.

"Why the extended protection, Castiel?" Elijah asked, sheathing Gunthor. "Do you suppose Cain is aware of possible angel intrusion?"

"I'm not sure, Elijah. It does seem strange." Castiel kicked aside some of the chain-link fence on the ground in front of the hole Elijah had created. "He obviously has quite a bit to hide and some high-value loot. These security measures would work as well against humans."

"OK," Elijah said, "here goes nothing." He dashed to the side wall of the compound as Castiel observed the guards on the right and Sophia observed those on the left for any sign that they had noticed Elijah's move. Castiel went next, followed by Sophia. They walked together as close to the wall as possible until they arrived at the corner. Around the corner were two guards standing directly in front of the compound entrance.

"Time to test whether we are invisible to the guards," Sophia whispered.

"I'll go first," Elijah said. "If they start shooting I can use my shield."

"Sounds good to me," Castiel said.

Elijah strode around the corner and headed towards the front door, making a wide arc around the guard closest to him, and then approached the door directly between the two guards. He remembered that *the closer he was to a human, the more likely it was that they would sense his presence.* Using his ability to manipulate matter, he ventured through the solid metal doors as if they were liquid. On the other side, he waited for Castiel and Sophia.

Castiel passed through the doorway next. The guard on the left tightened his grip on his assault weapon and raised it slightly. He cut his eyes around at the guard on his right and then at the door, said, "Did you just feel something?" The other guard said, "Feel *what?*" The guard shrugged and gazed around aimlessly.

Sophia waited until the guard had settled back into his normal, relaxed stance and then passed through the door, a little more cautiously than Castiel.

Just inside the front door was a succession of security gateways to pass before entering the main hallway – a metal detector portal followed by a laser body scanner and then an x-ray machine. A glass-walled room on the second floor overlooked the corridor. Behind the glass Elijah spotted an unshaven security guard wearing a blue long-sleeve shirt a size too small with mustard and ketchup stains down the front from the hot dog he was eating as he sat there monitoring several screens.

A female technician entered the x-ray scanning station. As she did, the security guard fixed his vision on a display monitor. Elijah saw a grin on the man's face as he leant in toward the monitor for a closer look, enjoying his job just a little more than he should: the screen displayed a full-color high-resolution image of the technician's nude body. Elijah had to hand it to old Cain; his technology was certainly better than that of the airports and was not hindered by any concern for people's privacy, much less modesty. The lady glanced up at the window and gritted her teeth before shaking her head and continuing on.

Telepathy is part of angel communication when silence is required. Although invisible and inaudible, they can be heard. Elijah, via telepathy, queried, "Castiel, can we walk straight through these security check points?"

"We'll be OK passing through the laser scanner," Castiel responded, "but the metal detector will sound due to our equipment, and that x-ray scanner will display our physical bodies."

Elijah, recalling that all the walls were reinforced with the energy barrier, took a moment to think before replying, "I have an idea. Follow closely." Elijah walked into the metal detector causing several loud beeps to sound. The guard shot his head around and glanced at the metal detector. Elijah took a step toward the entrance of the x-ray scanner and gestured for Castiel to come through the metal detector. Again the metal detector sounded its alerting beeps. This time the security guard stood up, shoved the last bite of the hot dog into his mouth, and peered towards the metal detector. Elijah gestured for Sophia to come through. She did. Once again the metal detector beeped. The security guard disappeared from sight for an instant before appearing at the end of the corridor. The guard headed towards the Trio. Through telepathy Elijah instructed Castiel and Sophia to move as close to the walls as possible to allow the guard past. Once the guard passed, Elijah instructed them to move through the x-ray machine and proceed to the end of the main hallway.

Castiel whispered along the way, "Good plan, Elijah. Seems old Cain thought of everything except providing a back-up for that lone hotdog loving ladies' man of a security guard. Looks like he'll be there for a while trying to figure out what triggered the metal detector."

Near the end of the main hallway, they came across several rooms that appeared to be some kind of holding cells. Each contained only a chair, a small table, and a spotlight suspended from a metal wall-mount. Further along Elijah came to a doorway signed "Breeding Area." His mind raced: *Breeding what?*

"This doesn't sound good," Sophia said, shaking her head.

They passed through the door. Elijah gasped at the sight before him. The large warehouse contained male and female bodies floating in some sort of stasis pods suspended from pulley systems that were connected to a myriad of conveyors attached to the ceiling. It was an eerie sight. The bodies in the pods were entirely devoid of hair, their eyes were closed, and each had a semi-transparent tube containing reddish liquid extending from their navel into the rear of the pod. Elijah's rough count was several hundred pods with bodies in them.

Castiel and Sophia were clearly as disturbed as Elijah.

Speechless, they continued further into the warehouse. They tracked the body-pods out of the main Breeding Area room and down a long hallway. The pulley-driven conveyor system was carrying a single line of pods into a room at the end of the hallway marked "Assembly." The Trio entered the room and saw scientists placing lifeless babies, no more than six months old, into the pods. Once the baby was in the pod the scientists attached tubes to the belly button, closed the capsule, and hitched it to the pulley system.

Elijah moved about the room and discovered a substantial glass-walled chamber. He could see many lifeless babies at various stages of development, from embryos to around six months old. The babies moved along a slow conveyor system that led from a large chamber. Elijah heard one of the scientists explaining the process to a trainee. They were taking human embryos and cloning them to produce the fetus. Then they used a sophisticated aging process to accelerate their development. When the babies reached the equivalent of six months old, the scientists placed them in the pods where their development continued at an advanced rate for several months until they reached 25 years old, at which time they put them into stasis inside the pods. The bodies were lifeless, merely flesh and organs in the form of a human. The process made Elijah's stomach churn.

Sophia grimaced in disgust and Castiel shook his head in disbelief at what they were seeing. They traded thoughts and various theories on what Cain was doing with these bodies. Sophia said, "Are they using them to harvest organs?"

Castiel replied, "Might be. What a horrible, creepy thought. What do you think, Elijah?"

"I have no idea," Elijah replied. "Let's keep looking around and we will find out."

They all agreed. After entering a room marked "Testing Area" they immediately spotted Cain himself talking to a scientist. "Will it work this time?"

"We believe we have made progress, sir," the scientist said, pacing back and forth between workstations, "and are hoping that the Shadow will be able to bring life to the body."

Cain crossed his arms over his chest and frowned. "I don't understand why you are finding this so difficult. A Shadow can possess a human, so why can't it simply possess the bodies we have created?"

The scientist pointed to a display screen showing an outline of a human body, a gassy substance, and line after line of scrolling code as he responded to Cain. "Technically, the Shadow doesn't control the body. It influences the soul inside the body to do its bidding. Since the cloned bodies we have produced don't have a soul, we have to provide a direct interface for the Shadow to control the body."

Cain glanced through a window at a hairless naked male body suspended by ropes from the rafters. Its head was tilted forward. Cain approached the window and slammed both hands down onto the surface of a large bench beneath the window. "Just run the experiment!"

Elijah, Sophia, and Castiel stepped quickly out of direct sight as a Shadow entered the room on the other side of the glass where the body was hanging. The Shadow would be able to see them. They watched as the dark black Shadow in the shape of a man looked over the hanging body before entering into the interior of the cadaver through the flesh. A couple of minutes passed, and nothing happened.

Cain grew restless. "What's taking so long, or is this just another *failed* experiment?!"

Just then, in a slow menacing way, the body lifted his head, opened his eyes, and started to convulse as though in the throes of electrocution. The wild quaking continued for several minutes before his eyes closed and his head dropped down. Emerging from the rear of the body the Shadow came back into view. The Shadow looked around, seemed somewhat disappointed, and then vanished. Castiel, Sophia, and Elijah moved into the room so they could hear every word of Cain and the scientist's conversation.

"We have made some progress, sir," the scientist said, as he scanned the latest information scrolling down a monitor display. "The Genetic Code decoding software you have provided is helping, Cain."

Cain thumped the table. "You call that *progress?* I have several hundred bodies waiting for Shadows and this is all you have come up with?"

"I'm sorry, sir, "the scientist replied. His hands were trembling as he stepped back away from Cain. "We will work harder."

Cain cocked his head in the direction of the hanging body and muttered, "See that you do … or you'll find yourself hanging from these ropes."

Elijah sent a thought to both Castiel and Sophia: "So this is why Cain needed Nya's software. He is trying to give life to lifeless, soulless bodies by using Shadows as their 'souls.' If he accomplishes that, the Shadows will be able to do anything they want without having to battle a human's will. Cain is trying to play God and give life to the lifeless."

"Well, not quite giving life," Castiel replied, placing his hands in his trench coat pockets. "Cain is creating undead bodies that appear human to serve as vehicles for Shadows without a human soul's conscience and moral law getting in the way."

Sophia added, "That is one of the more disturbing ploys of the enemy I have ever seen. Can you imagine how much destruction the Shadows could wreak if they have a physical form in the Human Realm? Cain is creating his own Shadow army."

"So did you enjoy the show?!" Cain shouted.

Is he talking to us? Elijah wondered.

Cain moved over to a console and pressed a button. Glass walls suddenly shot up from the floor to ceiling around the Trio, confining them in a cell-like enclosure. Cain turned and faced them. He winked. "This bionic eye implant isn't for show. It allows me to see things that normal humans cannot. I have been waiting a long time to catch myself an angel." Cain smirked. "To catch three, well maybe I'm *blessed*."

Elijah, Castiel, and Sophia stood motionless, stunned.

"Ahhh," Cain said, as he approached the glass encasement. "If it isn't Elijah Hael, and let me guess…." Cain pointed to each in turn. "Castiel and Sophia. Am I right?"

Elijah nodded. "How do you know?"

"You don't work with Shadows without hearing the latest gossip from the Underworld." Cain placed his hands on the glass and leant in towards them. His breath created fog on the glass surface with each word. "You three caused quite a flood in the Underworld with your little stunt to shut down that rift. That sort of thing gets you noticed, you know?"

"Well that's all well and good, and it's been a pleasure indeed," Castiel said, "but we must be going. Elijah, open a portal and get us out of here."

Elijah opened a portal. It opened then closed and disappeared just as quickly.

Cain laughed. "You don't think I'm *that* stupid, do you?" He strode back to the console and punched a few buttons. Small holes no bigger than the head of a pin and spaced about an inch apart opened up beneath Castiel, Elijah, and Sophia's feet. Then a hissing sound filled the enclosure.

"It's gas!" Castiel shouted, retrieving his Judgement Twins from under his cloak. "Stand back!" He fired into the glass. The Angel Light bullets sprayed the glass creating tiny fractures. Castiel kept firing but to no avail, the glass was apparently bulletproof, even Angel Light bulletproof. Castiel holstered his Judgement Twins. Sophia collapsed to the floor. "Sophia!" Castiel shouted. She was the first to succumb to the gas.

Elijah tried his best to cover the holes and prevent the gas from coming into their glass tomb. There were too many holes to plug – thousands upon thousands. Seconds later, he felt himself fade to black and lost consciousness.

* * *

Cain laughed hysterically at the amusing scene. Castiel pawed at the glass aimlessly in a desperate attempt to escape. Then his hands slid slowly down the glass as he, too, dropped to his knees and then folded over onto his face.

Chapter 16 - Reality Bites

Nya lay in the hospital bed watching an episode of *Dr. Phil* to distract her from the negative, anxious thoughts that threatened to send her into a full-blow panic attack as she waited for Dr. Evans to return with her scan results.

Try as she might to stay focused on Dr. Phil's pop psychology advice, she found her mind wandering back to an episode that occurred eight years earlier when she was 25 five years old.

* * *

In her newly purchased blue Holden Vectra, Nya navigated peak-hour afternoon traffic on the way to her mum's house. She had relied mainly on taxis and public transport to get around before she purchased the hatchback. Her new job working for ASIO came with a substantial income that made getting a loan for the vehicle quite easy. Getting the car was a truly thrilling occasion. On this day, however, she sensed that something was not quite right. Something in her mum Lisa's voice when she called an hour earlier and said she wanted to talk to Nya in person just left her uneasy. Lisa, who lived an hour and a half's drive from Nya, had only asked to talk to Nya, her daughter, in person once before. They generally communicated about everything by phone and email. Though Lisa did not share her daughter's enthusiasm for email, she did use it to stay in touch with her daughter.

The only other time her mother had wanted to talk to her in person was when Nya was 11 years old. That day was forever burnt in her memory. It was the time her mum told her about the plane crash that had taken her father's life and broke the news that he would not be coming home – ever again.

Nya pulled the little Vectra into her mother's driveway and parked in front of the garage. The three-bedroom brick veneer home was relatively modest. With the life insurance payout from her husband's death she could afford something more extravagant. But Lisa decided to live modestly, avoiding the spoils of wealth, and to donate her disposable income to sponsor children in Christian ministries that served abused and neglected children. Seeing a child's life transformed meant more to Lisa than all the flashy furniture, latest electrical gadgetry, and large houses in the world. The return on her investment? Well, that was the sweet smile of each child she helped, which reminded her of all the positive memories she had shared with her husband. The sponsorships were something good and positive that had come out of his untimely passing.

Lisa greeted Nya at the front door and led her to the kitchen table where they sat across from each other. Nya admired her mum's beauty. She had a stunning smile that radiated enough warmth to melt the coldest heart. Lisa had never dated after losing her husband. She chose instead to devote all of her time, energy, and resources into her relationship with Nya and her work with a call center set up to help children talk to someone about troubles they were facing in life. Lisa considered her volunteer work with the call center her "calling in her life." Her strong Christian faith fuelled a desire to help others. Sponsoring children was as a result of working in the center for she had witnessed firsthand just how much the sponsorships helped.

Lisa took Nya's left hand and cradled it in both of hers. "Nya, I have some unfortunate news."

"What mum?" Nya asked, the blood draining from her face, the joy from heart. "You're scaring me?"

"I've been —." Lisa swallowed before continuing. "Diagnosed with Breast Cancer."

Her voice ragged, Nya replied, "It's treatable, isn't it, and you'll beat it?"

Lisa cast her eyes down at the table for a moment and when she looked back at her daughter her eyes were wet with tears. "It's spread, Nya. The cancer has spread throughout my body."

"It's OK, Mum," Nya said, placing her right hand over her mum's hands. "You'll beat it. You are a fighter. We can fight this together."

Lisa tried to manage a smile. "The doctor gave me two options, Nya. The first is to have radiotherapy and chemo."

"OK," Nya said, nodding, "and the second was—"

"To make the most of the time I have left. He said if I chose option one there was only a slim chance that the treatment would work. And I would be quite ill due to the ravaging side-effects."

Inside she felt herself dying, but Nya willed herself not to show it but to be brave. She took her mum's hands in hers, squeezed them tightly, and gazed directly into her teary eyes. "You have to fight it, Mum."

Lisa pulled a tissue out of her pocket and blotted her eyes. "I'm not going to, Nya. My life feels complete. I miss your father. You are all grown up now and have your own life. This is not the end for me, Nya, but only the beginning."

Although Nya's Christian faith was strong and she believed in the afterlife, it was not as strong as her mother's. Tears snaked down her cheeks as she pleaded. "Don't talk like that, Mum. I want you around. I need you in my life. Please, please let's fight this together."

"Oh, my dear Nya," she said, smiling through her tears. "I've spent some time thinking about my choice. I have made arrangements for my funeral and secured the plot next to your father's grave."

"Oh, Mum." Then Nya lost it and began sobbing. "I'm so so sad. My heart is breaking."

"It's going to be OK, Nya."

Nya stayed with her mother that afternoon. The next day she gathered her belongings and moved back home to be with her mother for the time she had left, which Nya believed would be several months. It turned out to be only two weeks. A nurse came by daily and assisted with pain management and Nya tendered to her other needs. In the end, the cancer triggered an aneurysm that claimed her mother in her sleep.

Her mother had arranged for the song "This Is Not The End" by Gungor to be played during her funeral service. The short verses played over and again in Nya's mind:

> *This is not the end*
> *This is not the end of this*
> *We will open our eyes wide, wider*
>
> *This is not our last*
> *This is not our last breath*
> *We will open our mouths wide, wider*
>
> *And you know you'll be alright*
> *Oh and you know you'll be alright*
>
> *This is not the end*
> *This is not the end of us*
> *We will shine like stars bright, brighter*

Nya listened to the beautiful song quite often and reminisced about her mother. It reminded her of all the good times they had spent together and would spend together again.

* * *

Dr. Evans walked into the room and jolted Nya from her reminiscing. The dreaded moment had come. Knowing that breast cancer tended to run in families, Nya had feared she, too, would have it ever since her mother's death. When she had first felt the lump in her breast mortal fear had wracked her. She somehow found it easier to deny the possibility, as if she could just hope the lump away, than to face the alternative – the reality that her mother went through. She wondered now if choosing the dangerous refuge of denial had cost her more than she was willing to spend. Nya was well aware that early detection gave the best chance for a positive outcome. *Oh, Nya, why, why, why?* she thought, knowing that putting off seeing a doctor for two years would prove to be the great mistake of her life.

Nya searched Dr. Evans' face for a clue as to what he might say. *Will it be good news, or will it be bad? He looks a bit sad.… Does that mean it's grim news? Or maybe that is just his serious, professional look.…*

Nurse Amanda entered the room and stood beside the bed very close to her. Nya became increasingly nervous. *Why is the nurse here? The news must be bad.*

Dr. Evans spoke. "Do you have any family other than Isaac, Nya, whom we can contact and let them know you are with us? We have been trying to contact Isaac, who is listed in your records as your primary contact. Thus far we have not been able to reach him, but we will keep trying, of course."

Nya thought it likely that Isaac was on one of his fishing trips. She recalled him mentioning something about going away the day before she last spoke with him on the phone. Isaac quite often went to Stradbroke Island to camp near the beach and fish for a few days, sometimes with friends and sometimes alone. She had never minded, especially when she was away working on assignments.

"No," she said. "Isaac would be the only one. I have a few friends, but I would rather catch up with them when I'm out of here."

"I see," Dr. Evans said. He hugged her chart against his chest with both arms and sighed. "We have your scan results, Nya, and unfortunately," he said, frowning, "I'm terribly sorry to tell you that the diagnosis was not what we had hoped."

A wave of nausea hit her full-force and every muscle in her body stiffened. Amanda took hold of her hand and squeezed softly.

Dr. Evans continued in a very compassionate tone. "It's cancer, Nya, and it has spread from your breast throughout your body. The scans show it in your liver, stomach, and some areas of your brain." He paused as though he dreaded sharing the information as much as she dreaded hearing it. "Unfortunately, due to the number of masses, they are inoperable. But a few options are available to us, such as——."

Such as whether I'm cremated or interred. The morbid thought came from nowhere. Nya interrupted. "How long do I have, Doctor?"

He hesitated for a moment before saying, "From our experience people diagnosed with cancer at this stage rarely survive more than a few months, often much less without treatment."

Nya knew it was true from her mum's experience: two weeks. Her stomach flip-flopped, the nausea took hold. Thoughts of her mum came rushing back. She was living her mother's diagnosis. Nya retched, and Amanda fetched a silver bowl and placed the container on the bed. Nya vomited.

Amanda poured a glass of water for her and a moment later she vomited again. Her mind was reeling. Several minutes passed before she regained her composure with the help of the nurse.

Dr. Evans whispered, "I'm so sorry," and then said: "Nya, you can undergo radiotherapy followed by an intense regimen of chemotherapy. Some patients respond well, and treatments have a positive impact on their cancer. I know that it is a tough road to take for someone in your situation given how far the cancer has already spread. This approach increases your chances of survival – but not by much. It typically does slow the growth of the cancer, however, and extends the time you have left. The treatment requires regular visits to the hospital, and there are usually side effects, some rather unpleasant."

Loss of hair, nausea, fatigue…. Nya knew all that. Her mother had explained them all to her the day she told her she had cancer. As she considered her options, a nagging thought played in her mind: *Deep down I really wish Mum had just tried the treatment.* But she also understood why her mother had made the decision not to.

Dr. Evans said, "Nya, I know that the decision won't be easy, but if you wish to start treatment, the sooner the better."

"Yes," she replied. "Let's start straight away."

Dr. Evans looked somewhat surprised. "I must advise you, Nya, that for someone in your condition the chance of the treatment working – as in a complete recovery – is less than one in ten thousand." He paused. "Having said that, however, I support you and admire your will to fight. The treatment at the very least will likely prolong the time you have left."

"I know, Doctor," Nya said, smiling through her fear. "My mother was given the same options."

He nodded. "OK, Nya. Well if you have any questions, please have one of the nurses contact me. I'll make the necessary arrangements to begin your treatment as soon as possible."

Nya prepared for the fight for her life.

Chapter 17 - Joondaburri

A pair of soft hands rubbing cool lotion on his chest roused Isaac from his unconscious state. Rich, luscious aromas filled his nostrils as his eyes fluttered open and he gathered his bearings. He tracked those soft gentle hands to a young aboriginal lady sitting to his right clad in a matching top and dress fashioned from sea grass and interwoven palm leaves. He was lying atop a blanket in a cave neither large nor small with sandstone walls embellished with hand-drawn indigenous scenes. Sunlight entered the cave from a distant triangular gap formed by the junction of two rocks. Additional light glowed from a small fire in the corner flickering yellow and red. A breeze from further back in the dark cavern carried the smoke out of the cave. The woman picked up a mortar and pestle and worked the salve she was applying to his various wounds.

In a croaky voice Isaac said, "Where am I?"

"With the Joondaburri," she replied in a comforting tone. You're in a cave deep in the bush." After wiping her hands on a piece of whitish cotton cloth, she picked up a small wooden bowl of orange liquid and held it out to him. "Drink this," she said. "It will help."

Isaac held the bowl under his nose and took in a whiff of the refreshing scent of citrus fruit. He was not keen on consuming mystery drinks from strangers, but if his aboriginal *captors* had wanted to hurt him they would have done so by now. His throat was parched and it was risk worth taking. He took a sip and swished it around in his mouth before swallowing to analyze the taste of the warm liquid. It tasted sweet at first and then turned a little sour and had a distinctive citrus tang.

He looked at the young woman. "Thank you."

She nodded.

"How did I get here?"

"An ancestral spirit called our people to your aid," she said as she added some powder to her mortar. "The spirit said you were in trouble and needed our help." She ground the ingredients together with her pestle. "Our hunters went to investigate and found two men with guns hunting you. They shot the two men with blow darts to put them into a deep sleep. You collapsed from your wounds. So they brought *you* here and left the two assailants behind."

Isaac's eyes narrowed to a mere squint. "What spirit?"

"A great and wise one that our people call 'Castiel.'"

Isaac nodded. "Castiel," he whispered, thinking: *Wasn't that the name of the man in the dream I had when I was falling? That would be quite a coincidence. Was that the name?* In his foggy mental state he couldn't be sure, and it nagged him. His suspicion turned to curiosity. *Why would some spirit magically come to his aid?*

He looked at the girl. "What does this spirit look like?"

"Our people have never seen the spirit," she replied. "Here," she said, lifting his arm so she could apply more of the ointment to a purplish contusion on his side. "We only hear the spirit."

A cool soothing sensation numbed the pain in his side as the concoction did its work. "What is that stuff you're massaging into me?"

"For your open wounds I've created a blend of Ageratum, Dendrobium affine, Eleocharis dulcis, Melaleuca, and Planchonia careya."

His eyes widened and his mouth drew open. "Ah," he said, having no idea what any of it meant and sorry he had asked, but she wasn't finished.

"On your bruises," she continued, "I am using a combination of Acacia auriculiformis, Canavilla rosea, Eremophila freelingii, and Calophyllum inophullum. The treatment will help you heal."

Isaac said "Thank you" and then lay quietly as she continued applying her salve to his body. He realized then that he was wearing only underwear. He felt a bit exposed but knew that given the extent of his wounds they had no choice but to undress him.

Since they were so intimate, the least he could do was introduce himself. "My name is Isaac."

"I'm Loorea," she said. "It means 'The Moon.' It's nice to meet you, Isaac."

Isaac smiled. "It's nice to meet you, too, Loorea." Loorea, who was in her mid-20s, had a pretty face, a warm comforting smile, a slender but curvy figure, and rich chocolate-brown eyes that perfectly complemented her flawless auburn skin.

"Tonight you can join us in Joonbas."

"What's that?" Isaac asked, eyebrow raised.

"It's a dance we use to express our lives and beliefs." She gently worked a dollop of the salve into a laceration on his arm. "Joonbas is also a time of thanksgiving to the creators for creating the world we live in."

Isaac's jaw dropped. "You believe in God?"

"You mean Altjira, God of Dreamtime? Yes, we believe he created the Earth then retired to the sky." Her eyes sparkled as she talked about the creator. "During Dreamtime all things were made. Men and women were created and our laws and our culture were given to us."

Isaac sighed, thinking: *The poor people had obviously not attended enough science classes to realize the truth about the origin of life and had probably never even heard of the Big Bang.*

She studied his face. "So you *don't* believe in God?"

Not wanting to offend her, he replied, "I find it difficult to believe anything until I have either seen it with my own eyes or it has been proven by science."

Loorea just smiled and continued her work. When she was finished, she unfolded a black-and-white striped blanket and placed the warm woolen cover over him. "Sleep now, Isaac. I will wake you for the Joonbas."

"Thank you," he said. Isaac closed his eyes, suspecting that the warm drink may have contained some sort of relaxant as a wave of fatigue washed over him. Oddly, even though he was a stranger in a strange land he felt unusually safe and comfortable and sleep came easy.

After a few hours of deep, dreamless sleep, Isaac woke to Loorea running her hand through his hair and whispering, "Isaac, Isaac: Wake up now. Time for the Joonbas."

Loorea passed Isaac some clothes to wear and, to his surprise, they were *normal* clothes, well, normal to him — a pair of blue jeans and a white cotton shirt. He slipped on the jeans very cautiously, expecting the soreness from his injuries to wrack his body, and then worked the shirt over his head. He winced, but only slightly, from a stinging pain in his shoulder as he wormed his arm into the sleeve. Those multi-ingredient healing potions Loorea was treating him with were working quite well.

Once he was finished dressing, Loorea stood up and extended her hand and helped him to his feet. His legs were a little stiff and he had an ache here and a pain there, but for a man who had hurtled headlong off a cliff he was doing just fine. Loorea took him by the hand and led him out of the cave.

An enormous raging bonfire illuminated a large grassy area between a dense forest and the cliff wall that housed the cave. Over the sounds of burning wood crackling through the night air Isaac could hear the whirr of falling water, suggesting that he had plunged over a cliff near a waterfall. A potpourri of flowers and smoldering incense mounted on spears stabbed into the ground around the clearing filled the air with a heady fragrance.

Loorea gently squeezed Isaac's hand. "The fire is beautiful."

Isaac turned and saw the blazing flames reflected in Loorea's big brown eyes and the glow on her smiling face. He smiled and said, "Indeed." Loorea led him to a spot in the clearing where they could enjoy the warmth of the bonfire without overheating. He sat down cross-legged facing the bonfire and Loorea sat next to him.

The rhythmic click-clack of sticks clapping filled the air. Isaac trained his eyes on the source of the sound as an aboriginal man materialized from the dark wearing a reddish loincloth strung with decorative wooden bangles. His face and body were covered with white hand-painted symbols. The carved sticks he was playing had various inscriptions burned into them and, although small, they cracked each time he clapped them together. With each stick-clap, the man moved, systematically simulating some type of animal action. Isaac found the dance mesmerizing. The man continued moving towards the bonfire until he found a vacant place. Before sitting he crouched down with his legs crossed in front of him and continued playing a breathtakingly intricate beat with the sticks.

Then the deep bellowing sound of a didgeridoo met Isaac's ears. He glanced around but could not locate the source. He squinted into the dark spaces between the trees until a second aboriginal man appeared as though stepping from the dark air itself. Wearing garb similar to the first man, he moved slowly towards the bonfire playing the didgeridoo. Isaac had heard the instrument on TV but never in person. The incredible sound penetrated his ears, echoed down his back, and rattled inside his ribcage. Isaac sat spellbound with a shiver down his spine as he listened to the didgeridoo accompanied by the cracking rhythm of the sticks. The didgeridoo player sat down next to the man playing the sticks with his legs crossed and the didgeridoo out in front of him.

Isaac marveled at didgeridoo player's lung power because the constant playing made it seem as though he never took a breath.

From different directions several other aboriginals – some male, some female – emerged from the darkness. The females wore skirts fashioned from weaved grasses and straw and tops made of leaves that covered their bosoms. A few of the women wore no tops but had hand-painted symbols that featured their breasts as part of the art. They all moved in unison with smooth animal-like movements and danced around the bonfire, singing. Although he didn't understand a single word they sang, the way they sang the lyrics was both beautiful and hauntingly spectacular and filled Isaac with a deep sense of comfort and happiness.

Loorea passed Isaac a wooden bowl containing orange liquid. Thirsty, Isaac drank without hesitation. The dancing continued for quite some time, and Isaac found the experience both incredibly enjoyable and quite relaxing. Feeling a little drowsy, likely from his injuries and the drink, he closed his eyes and listened to the music.

Memories from his childhood came seeping in. The bonfire reminded him of a moment he had shared with his father back when he was 12 years old.

* * *

Isaac sat in the cool white sand gripping his fishing rod with both hands waiting for a fish to bite. On the other side of the crackling campfire his father sat in a low beach chair holding his own fishing rod. Moonlight cast a white aurora across the calm surface of the ocean that reflected countless twinkling stars filling the night sky. Isaac gazed up at the stars and said, "Hey, Dad, do you believe in God?"

"Why do you ask, Isaac?" his father replied.

"Some kids at school were arguing over whether God exists or not. One believed in God, and one said he was an atheist. They almost got into a punch up before a teacher broke them up."

His father picked up his soft drink can and took a sip. "What do you believe, Isaac? Do you think something created this world?"

Isaac pulled up on his fishing rod and touched the line to discern if anything was nibbling at the bait before answering his father's question. "I've never given creation much thought. You?"

"Well, Son, I guess from an engineer's perspective I don't find it plausible that the world came into existence by random chance. Even if by some long shot Earth did come into existence by itself, it seems highly unlikely to me that the world would continue to exist for any length of time. See, if Earth occurred by chance, then random variables would be the only thing keeping everything stable, so that at any moment everything could cease to exist. So if scientists are correct and the Earth has been around for billions of years...." His father paused, rubbed his chin, and narrowed his eyes before adding, "I can't see how the universe stays in balance if its governed by chance —unless ultimately something created some boundaries for the variables to stay within. So creating is not the only thing; there's also maintaining everything."

Isaac's rod bowed down. He had a bite! "I've got a fish on, Dad," he said, excited. He tightened his grip and began winding the reel determined to wheel in the fish. He wound the line as fast as his wrist would go bearing in mind what his father had taught him earlier in the night about using the correct drag to avoid snapping the line. He stood up and walked towards the water's edge. His father collected a net and ran over and stood by his son as together they waited for the fish to emerge from the salty water. The fish broke the surface, and Isaac's heart fluttered with excitement as he watched the fish toss and turn trying to get free. "It's a bream, Dad, and not a bad size by the looks of it."

"Let's see what you've got there," his father said as he walked over and scooped the fish into the net. After removing the hook from the bream's mouth, he placed the fish in a nearby ice chest where a few other catches lay. "Well done, Son! That's a good-size bream."

Seeing the smile on his son's face, he couldn't resist the pun: "You're *breaming* with pride!"

"Good one, Dad," Isaac said, and they both snickered. As he re-baited his hook, cast his line, and sat back down, Isaac thought back to what his dad said just before the fish took his line. "So, Dad, does that mean you *do* believe in God?"

"I suppose it does, Son."

Isaac wound the reel a few times to take up the slack in his line. "But, Dad, what about natural selection? Doesn't *that* explain our existence?"

"Do you remember our old black-and-white TV set, Isaac?"

"Yeah, how could I forget?" Isaac replied, rolling his eyes and grinning. "All my friends had those nice color TV's and we had that old black-and-white clunker."

"Do you think that black-and-white TV could somehow randomly evolve into a color one?"

Isaac thought about the question for a moment. "No, not really. Somebody would have to invent the color TV and build it."

"The world is infinitely more complex than a television, right? Yet, some people believe monkeys could have randomly evolved into significantly more complex and distinctively different humans."

Isaac picked up a stick and poked the fire several times and watched as yellow and orange embers rose into the sky.

Lost in that moment when all the world was right, Isaac felt as content just then as he ever had. "I love you, Dad," he said from his heart.

His father smiled and replied softly, "I love you, too, Son."

* * *

Loorea's words roused Isaac from his dream. "Time to wake up, Isaac." As his eyes slowly opened and adjusted to the light, he saw Loorea's fine face come into focus. "What happened?" he asked, noticing that everyone had left and the music had stopped. "Where did everyone go?"

Loorea said, "You fell asleep and slumped over onto your side, so I placed a pillow under your head and let you sleep. Nearly four hours have passed."

"Four hours?" Isaac said, pulling himself into a sitting position. "But it only feels like only a few minutes."

Loorea rose. "The potion that helps with the pain can make you drowsy. Come, let's return to the cave."

She helped him onto his feet and Isaac followed Loorea into the cave.

"Can you help me get back to Brisbane?"

"The spirit has asked us to keep you here for seven sunrises."

Isaac presumed that meant seven days. He considered the alternative – being hunted down by Seth and Jared. He nodded. "OK." Still curious about the mysterious spirit, he thought: *If this spirit existed … why would he be looking out for me?*

Loorea had prepared some food while he was sleeping at the bonfire. She prepared a plate and handed it to him. "Eat," she said. "You need your strength back."

"Thank you," he said, as he began eating the delicious meal of fresh fish along with some tiny potatoes, beetroot, beans, and onion, with some pleasing herbs scattered among them. They ate together.

"Loorea, how come you're looking after me?"

"The elders assigned me the duty of caring for you during your stay here. I was happy to do so. In your culture, I would be like a nurse."

"How do you know so much about my culture?"

"I live in both. I have an apartment in Brisbane and work as a schoolteacher. I come back here on weekends and holidays."

"Why come back here?" he said, screwing up his nose. "I mean there is nothing here. No offense. I didn't mean anything by—"

"None taken," she said, smiling. "That's the reason I come – because there is nothing here, nothing but my people and nature." She took a sip of water. "We are connected to nature, and being close to nature allows us to feel complete."

Isaac thought about the fishing trips he took to a sandy beach on Stradbroke Island or to a peaceful lake. He just loved the experience of being close to nature. He had never thought about having a connection with nature but simply enjoyed it. "You're right," he said. "I can see why you would want to come here. I do something similar, though not as often. Maybe I don't spend as much time with nature as I should."

Loorea smiled. They sat for some time chit-chatting until Loorea told him to get some sleep, said goodnight, and left.

As much as he was enjoying the company of Loorea Isaac was quite concerned about Nya. *Where was she? Was she looking for him?* He remembered telling her two days earlier that he would be off fishing for a few days, the one place he didn't have mobile phone reception. She should not start to worry for at least three days. Before falling asleep he made a mental note to ask in the morning if there was some way he could get a message to her.

Chapter 18 - Games

Awakening from his stupor, Elijah shook his head trying to cast off the lingering effects of the gas. He was lying naked on a cold dirt floor. The air was cold and moist. He gazed around the room but everything was a blur. He rubbed his eyes and looked again. The room gradually came into focus. It was about four meters square with walls made of rough-hewn stone that were covered in places with moss. A wooden door in the wall to his left appeared to be the only exit. The steady drip of water from a crack in the stone ceiling formed a damp puddle on the hardpan floor. The only source of light was a flickering incandescent bulb mounted in the center of the ceiling. A little glass panel high up on one wall provided cover for a camera. On a small black monitor screen next to the camera displayed white text: "E:1-1 C:1-1 S:1-1." Elijah played the code over and over in his head, trying to decipher its meaning. He figured the panel housing the camera was made of the same type of glass which had formed the gas chamber that trapped him and his colleagues.

He got to his feet, shaky, and staggered over and leaned against the cold stone wall until the gas sickness wore off enough for him to stand without wobbling. He padded over to the lone piece of furniture in the cell, a small wooden table against the wall opposite the door, and found his clothes. They had confiscated his weapons, including his armlet. As he dressed he tried to retrieve his EVE from eSpace but nothing happened. *Sly one, that Cain*, he thought and sighed.

Just then he heard three knocks on the door. "Come on in," he said.

He glanced toward the door and watched as a yellow envelope slid across the floor and stopped at his feet. He picked up the sealed envelope with a color logo – a red circle inside a blue triangle – stamped on the front. He read the note inside:

WELCOME TO GOLGOTHA
THREE PLAY
ONE SURVIVES

Not interested in playing Cain's game, Elijah wadded up the note and tossed it and the envelope onto the floor. As he paced around the cell he got the sensation that he was on the set of some sort of reality TV show. He closed his eyes and concentrated hard and tried to contact Castiel and Sophia through telepathy. No avail. Either Cain had figured a way to block their telepathic skills or they were too far away from each other.

Elijah mumbled, "OK, so let's start with getting out of this cell." He considered using his power to manipulate physics so he could just walk through the door. But of course Cain would have added an energy field to provide another layer of security.

Plan B: He turned his attention to the door. Starting with the obvious, he tried to open it. He pulled, then pushed, then pulled again. The door did not budge. The old-fashion warded lock securing the door had a large keyhole complete with a shank in a metal casing. Elijah peered through the keyhole and saw that it was blocked. *Aha!* He picked up the crumpled note, smoothed it out, and slid it under the door, in line with the lock, leaving just an inch protruding on his side of the door. Then he grabbed the envelope, rolled it into a tight cylinder like a giant cigarette rolling paper, and used it as a rod to poke through the keyhole *... and it worked.* It forced an old-style skeleton key out the other side. The key fell to the floor with a clanging sound and came to rest on the paper. Elijah bent down and slowly pulled the piece of paper with the key on top under the door. He slipped the key in the lock and turned it: *Success.* With a little clunk the door unlocked. 'Right, well that was easy enough. What next?"

The door opened to a corridor running left and right, illuminated by incandescent bulbs strung from the ceiling every several feet. At the far end of the corridor to his left, high up near the ceiling, Elijah noticed another camera with a small display screen beside it, just like the one in the cell. He decided to head right and follow the corridor away from the camera. At least that way Cain would only be able to see his back.

Thirty paces down, Elijah turned and walked down another hall that opened to the right. He stopped at the entrance to a room about half the size of a basketball court. This room was no cell. The floor was mosaic tiles in various shades of grey and the walls were constructed of ash-colored stone bricks of various sizes. On the back wall, a series of vertical rusty metal bars screened the entrance to a small alcove with an old chest inside. In front of the bars, on either side of the alcove, stood a stone statue of a menacing open-mouthed gargoyle. There was a plaque beneath each statue. The one beneath the gargoyle on the left read:

I ALWAYS TELL THE TRUTH AND I NEVER LIE

The one beneath the gargoyle on the right read:

I ALWAYS LIE AND NEVER TELL THE TRUTH

On the floor between the two gargoyles was a small clear glass ball atop a yellow envelope. Elijah picked up the ball and the envelope. The note inside read:

REWARD AWAITS IF YOU FEED THE TRUTHFUL
GARGOYLE
LIFE WILL BE LOST IF YOU FEED THE LYING GARGOYLE
ONE GARGOYLE ALWAYS TELLS THE TRUTH AND ONE
GARGOYLE ALWAYS LIES
A GARGOYLE CANNOT TELL THE TRUTH STRAIGHT
AFTER LYING

Elijah thought: *If I get the puzzle wrong life will be lost? Whose life – mine or —?*

He took a few steps back so he could gaze at the gargoyles as he pondered the puzzle. Just then a beam of light shot out of each Gargoyles open mouth. Startled, Elijah flinched as he spun around and focused on the far wall on which the beams were projecting an image of a large golden spike attached to a solid marble block suspended from a marble ceiling. The image panned slowly from side to side as it zoomed out to reveal more of the room. The room had exquisite marble walls with intricate patterns hand-drawn in gold flake. When the entire room was in view what Elijah saw made his jaw drop and his eyes bulge.

It was Sophia, strapped down on a long marble altar with her panicked eyes fixed directly on the point of the golden spike just a foot above her. If the spike dropped it would certainly impale her directly through the heart. She struggled to free herself from the bindings securing her wrists and ankles to the altar. The image cut to a close-up of her eyes, eyes frantic and desperate.

Elijah realized then whose life would be lost if he got the puzzle wrong. A riot of thoughts assaulted his mind. *What if I do not play but rather do nothing? Is there any way I could stall? I cannot – **cannot** – afford to get this wrong!* As the image cut to an overview of the room the answer to his thoughts came quickly. The golden spike had begun descending. That explained the sheer desperation in Sophia's eyes.

He took the glass sphere and popped it into the mouth of the gargoyle on the left. The projection ceased. Seconds later, a low rumbling noise erupted from the walls. Dust fell from the ceiling. The sound of metal grinding echoed from above the bars as they started to rise. He had gotten the answer right and could only assume that the spike had stopped descending.

Elijah fell to his knees overwhelmed at having Sophia's life hang in the balance of his choice. He exhaled. Relief. He closed his eyes and gritted his teeth and cradled his face in his hands.

It was possible that both statutes could have been telling the truth, but even if they were, the truthful gargoyle would always be the one that *always* told the truth. If the plaque on the right was true then questioning the gargoyle on the right would always result in a lie. The riddle's clue was a red herring that was meaningless for solving it.

After rising to his feet, Elijah paused for a moment to collect himself before carefully stepping forward into the alcove to analyze the chest. The black oak chest had an angled lid with raised flanges on either side and short milled legs. There appeared to be no locking mechanism. Elijah raised the lid and heard a familiar voice whining: "About time you got me out of this dark box. What took you so long?"

"You're welcome," he said as he retrieved Gunthor and his sheath from the chest. Not wanting to spend any more time than he had to in the alcove, Elijah quickly backed out and fastened Gunthor's sheath around his waist. "Gunthor, can you make a quick scan of this room? We need to find an exit."

Elijah noticed that the display beside the camera had changed. The text now read: "E:1-1 C:1-1 S:3-1."

Gunthor said, "Elijah, I'm noticing the stone brick in the wall to our right – three from the left and two from the floor – seems to have different properties from the others in this room."

Elijah paced over to the wall and located the brick. He analyzed the stone closely and discovered that the ash color was paler than the other bricks. He tapped it and discovered that it was slightly loose to his touch. He gave it a gentle push and the stone brick receded into the wall. The ground rumbled, dust fell from the ceiling, and the room started to shake. Elijah glanced around and watched a square area, like a trapdoor, the width of a doorway, descend in the middle of the room. The section of floor, once partially descended slid sideways under the floor revealing a stairway leading down into darkness.

Covering his mouth Elijah let out a small cough as he shook the dust from his hair. He muttered, "Cain needs to get some maid service down here. This dust is ridiculous." He glanced up over his shoulder and shouted into the camera, "Did you hear that Cain?!"

Elijah approached and peered down the staircase into darkness. "Gunthor, light, please." With Gunthor's brilliant white glow lighting his way, Elijah descended the stairs gradually, step by step, wondering what would come next.

After moving off the last step Elijah passed through a small archway that opened into a larger room. Gunthor's light was not strong enough to illuminate the whole room, so the far side was dark. Huge granite tiles covered the floor and the stone walls were just like the previous room's. A torch on the left side of the archway burned brightly. A small ledge extended from the base of the lit torch to an unlit torch, which in turn was connected to another unlit torch, and so on around the wall as far as Elijah could see. The torches along the wall were spaced about five feet apart. The ledge appeared to connect all the torches to each other.

Elijah walked over to the ledge for a closer look. Some sort of dark liquid filled a groove carved into the ledge. Elijah dipped his finger into the liquid and ran it under his nose: Oil. He removed the burning torch from the wall and touched its flame to the oil. Instantly the flame flared up and ran along the ledge and lit the next torch, then the next, and so until all the torches were lit, the last being the one at the right hand side of the archway. The full extent of the room, which was about the size of an Olympic swimming pool, was now visible. On the far wall a large archway led into darkness beyond. Elijah noticed the familiar cameras in the room – one on each wall. Old Cain apparently was keen to observe the events in his game from every angle.

"You can turn off your light, Gunthor," he said. "This room is bright enough." Gunthor stopped glowing.

Elijah paced ahead until he heard the sound of metal crashing behind him. He spun around. Vertical bars had dropped from the top of the archway blocking the passage he had come through. Footsteps echoed from the other end of the room. Elijah turned toward them.

A Shadow figure about the height of Elijah and wielding a staff emerged from the darkness of the distant archway.

Elijah said, "This isn't like any Shadow I've seen before, Gunthor. What can you tell me about it?"

"It's dangerous," Gunthor replied in a rather cheeky voice.

Elijah sighed. "Care to expand on that, Gunthor?"

"It likely wants to kill you."

"All right, Gunthor," Elijah said with urgency rising in his voice, "this is serious. I need info, and I need it fast."

"OK, OK," Gunthor said. "Sheesh. I just don't like being treated as a talking Wiki."

"Gunthor...."

"It's a Shadow Mystic. They are quite rare and have not been seen in the Earth Realm for many thousands of years. They operate under the legion of Belial and are part of the Sons of Darkness. They were banished to the Underworld during the great angel war in the time of Enoch."

The Shadow Mystic emerged fully from the darkness, and Elijah got a good look at the unknown entity. It wore a golden crown with 12 small pointed spires equally spaced around the top. It had a face, dark as night, with a nose and mouth. Its eyes were long flat ovals that glowed pale white and had no pupils. Its physique was no more impressive than an average human. After it passed through the archway, vertical bars clanked down behind it, sealing the exit.

Gunthor continued. "Shadow Mystics use spells as their method of attack. Their spells manipulate the physics of the Earth Realm to create elements such as fire and ice. The staff they carry enhances their mystical powers and can also be used to smack you upside the noggin."

"Keep it technical," Elijah said, shaking his head. "Sounds just great."

The Shadow Mystic raised its left hand with the palm facing upwards. A ball of fire about the size of a baseball appeared and levitated just above the dark shadowy hand. Several smaller fireballs the size of golf balls emerged from the ball of fire and streamed out towards Elijah. Elijah weaved to the left. Like heat-seeking missiles, the fireballs changed direction mid-flight and honed in on Elijah, but they failed to turn as quickly as Elijah moved out of their line of flight. The fireballs singed the hairs on his arm as they passed by and then slammed, one after another, into the wall behind him and exploding, leaving dark scorch marks on the stone bricks.

"Close call," Elijah whispered. He pondered his next move while watching the Shadow Mystic raise its staff, a black wooden stick with a shrunken monkey's skull on top, slightly upwards, towards him. A blinding white flash erupted from the top of the staff, followed by a stream of ice that flowed from the skull and hit the ceiling above Elijah. "Hah, you missed!" Elijah shouted.

Gunthor exclaimed, "Look Up!"

Elijah threw his head back and saw a number of sharp stalactites forming as several other established stalactites broke away from the ceiling and began falling. Elijah dived to his left into a roll as the first of many stalactites impaled the ground like razor-sharp knives skewering an apple.

Elijah sprung out of the roll onto his feet. He glanced back at the stalactites. "Woo, close."

"Looks like you could use a good shave," Gunthor said. "Next time, just stand—"

"Get serious, Gunthor!" He returned his focus to the Shadow Mystic. He sprinted towards the enemy with Gunthor raised above his head. As Elijah closed within seven feet, the Shadow Mystic raised his hand palm out as if to make a stopping gesture. At first, a few sparks danced around the shadowy palm before they erupted into lightning bolts aimed directly at Elijah. One bolt connected with the tip of Gunthor and proceeded down the blade and into Elijah's arm, which jolted in spasms. He lost his grip on Gunthor who dropped to the floor with a loud *clang*. A second bolt of lightning drove through Elijah's chest sending him shuddering to the ground convulsing. The Shadow Mystic aimed its staff towards Elijah while closing the distance between them. Still shuddering from the jolt, Elijah started to levitate.

The Shadow Mystic smiled a wicked smile, its eyes burning bright white, as it flicked its staff to the right sending Elijah hurtling through the air. He slammed into the wall and crumpled to the ground. "That hurt," he mumbled, writhing on the floor, "just a little."

Elijah realized he could not take much more of that. He tried to think of a way to stop the Shadow Mystic. In his mind he heard the distant voice of Nemamiah whisper, "Use the force, Elijah." He remembered how Nemamiah used that quote when he was teaching Elijah how to control material objects in the Earth Realm. Nemamiah drew parallels between his own teaching style and that of Yoda in educating Luke from the *Star Wars* series. Elijah had been quite fond of *Star Wars*, and the correlations helped Elijah realize his own potential.

He clambered to his feet and studied the Shadow Mystic, trying to predict its next move. Wielding his staff with both hands the Shadow Mystic started twirling it in a frenzied fan-like motion. Elijah's hair fluttered in the wind it whipped up, which grew stronger by second until the force was strong enough to drive Elijah backwards. He leaned forward at the waist, clenched his fists, and stiffened his whole body to prevent it from sweeping him away. No good. His feet skidded backwards as though he were on ice until his heels hit the wall. The relentless wind stood his body bolt upright and pinned him against the wall.

The room echoed with a great howling sound as the Shadow Mystic continued spinning the staff with his right hand to keep it at gale-force strength. He held his left palm out in front of him and Elijah saw knife-like ice crystals beginning to form. Elijah screwed his eyes shut and concentrated hard. Gunthor started to lift slightly off the ground, see sawing a bit at first, before rising up and rotating in midair. Gunthor rotated until he was pointing directly at the Shadow Mystic. An instant later he shot like a dart toward the Shadow Mystic. The Shadow Mystic placed its left hand full of ice crystals in front of the staff and let the wind pick them up and send them careering towards Elijah. Gunthor crashed into the Shadow Mystic's staff and knocked it from its grip. The ice crystals dropped to the floor, the rushing wind stopped, and the room fell silent. Free from the wind's crushing embrace, Elijah charged towards the Shadow Mystic holding out the palm of his right hand.

The Shadow Mystic appeared confused and a little stunned at losing the staff and just stared as Elijah rushed him. Gunthor rotated and was darting hilt first towards the Shadow Mystic. When the hilt was but a foot away from the Shadow Mystic Elijah grabbed Gunthor and entered into a spin that brought Gunthor's blade full circle towards the Shadow Mystic's neck. Leaving a streak of white light in his wake, Gunthor sliced cleanly through the Shadow Mystic's neck sending the Underworld creature's head tumbling onto the floor: *thump-thud-thump*. A second later, the headless Mystic collapsed. Black smoke erupted from the corpse followed by a small explosion of blackness leaving behind no trace of the remains.

Clanking sounds echoed from both archways as the bars raised. Elijah stood up and straightened his clothes. "Right," he said, smiling. "Who's next?" He noticed that the display had changed: "E:1-1 C:3-1 S:4-1"

Striding solemnly towards the open archway that the Shadow Mystic had come through, he wondered with some concern how Sophia and Castiel were doing.

Chapter 19 - Finding Isaac

"How are you coming along with the mug shots, Frank?" Leigh asked.

"No good." Frank shook his head and rubbed his eyes, strained and bloodshot from staring at page after page of mug shots.

"Take a break, Frank," Leigh said, shaking his head. "You look like a train wreck."

"Feel like one, too," he said, rolling his eyes at Leigh, "but I can't. These mug shots are our best – and at the moment *only* – shot at finding out who tried to kill me and where that fellow Isaac is. Not to mention Nya." Frank was anxious to interrogate the men they apprehended at the hospital, but the doctors were yet to declare them fit for interrogation. Since both suspects had suffered head injuries the approval was taking longer than expected. Frank was well aware of the old trick whereby suspects in custody prolonged or feigned illness to buy time for their lawyers to work the system and get them released.

Frank's computer chimed, alerting him to incoming email. He clicked a few keys and opened the message with the subject "Nya."

> FROM: Missing Persons
> TO: Frank Mercer
> SUBJECT: Nya
>
> Frank, some information came in suggesting Nya is currently at the Holy Spirit Hospital undergoing cancer treatment. We called the hospital, and they confirmed Nya is admitted.
>
> Regards
> Lesley Summers

Somewhat relieved, although concerned for Nya, Frank looked up above his screen at Leigh seated opposite him. Their desks were set back to back. "Nya has been located. Now we just have to find Isaac – *alive*, let's hope."

Leigh nodded and resumed working his own computer.

A little stumped on how Nya had ended up in hospital – for cancer treatments, no less – Frank made a mental note to check on her after he had more information on Isaac's whereabouts.

A muffled *splat!* made him flinch. A parcel slid across the desk in front of him. "Parcel for you, Detective." He looked up at the police officer. "Thanks." A white label in the top left corner of the yellow parcel read "CSI Video Lab". "About time," he mumbled as he tore the package open and placed the DVD in the drive on his computer and waited for the software to open. "Now we'll get to see Sophia in action, Leigh. Come and watch the CCTV footage." Leigh rose from his seat and walked around and stood next to Frank.

Frank fast-forwarded the footage to the point when the two men entered his room. Some footage after they entered – the section that would have shown Sophia walking into his room – appeared to be missing. Frank rewound the DVD to ensure he had not missed the scenes. No sign of Sophia. He concluded that, according to the tape, she never showed.

He played footage later in the tape in slow motion and watched himself walk out of the hospital room. He skipped backwards and forwards, replaying the segment over and over. Frank shook his head. *Where is Sophia? She left before me, and I followed. How could this be possible?* The CCTV recording showed Frank walking down the corridor to the elevator and pressing the button to call the lift.

Leigh said, "I thought you said Sophia was with you in the elevator?"

Frank ignored Leigh and continued watching the playback. Next, the footage showed Frank exiting the elevator on the ground floor of the hospital. Frank strode up the corridor – alone – and then back down towards the stairwell exit – alone. Later, the video showed Frank descending the stairs. The last of the footage showed Frank about to exit into the basement.

Frank threw his hands up in the air and mumbled. "Where is the basement footage?" He picked up the parcel and dumped it contents on his desk – and found a note:

> Video Footage from Holy Spirit CCTV Camera
> Scenes recorded to DVD as requested from available cameras. The camera in the basement provided only static. On checking with security at the hospital, they reported that the camera was out of service.

He placed the letter on his desk, turned to Leigh, and said, "Well that hasn't helped us much."

"What about the woman – Sophia?" Leigh asked, scratching the back of his neck. "How come she isn't in the footage?"

Frank lifted his hand and pinched his chin between his fingers and thumb. "Maybe the pain medication had me seeing stuff…. I really don't know."

Leigh raised an eyebrow. "Are you OK, Frank? Do you need a psych eval?"

"Hell no," Frank said, shooting him a look. "Don't suggest that. They'll have me on a shrink's couch for months."

Frank was not sure what to believe. He questioned his own recollection of events. *Sophia was real; she was right there and I had seen her with my own eyes. Hadn't I? Surely I could not have imagined the whole scene. Could I? If I did, how did the assailants end up unconscious in the car park? I could not have taken them both out all by myself. Maybe I did.* Frank, feeling ever more confused, shifted his thoughts back to searching for Isaac.

Leigh returned to his desk and resumed working on his computer. A few seconds later he said, "Hey, Frank, this might be interesting. I just got a pop-up news alert on a police report. Police found a black four-wheel drive vehicle abandoned in the mountains. Some locals reported it. Since the plates and VIN were untraceable the police had it towed and impounded."

"Why is that interesting?" Frank replied, tapping his fingers on the desk. "We get reports of abandoned vehicles all the time."

"Well, this is the interesting part." Leigh grinned. "Since the vehicle was untraceable they had CSI run some tests on the vehicle to try to identify the owners."

"And...," Frank said, impatient. He tapped his foot on the floor.

"And ... they found traces of urine in the back seat from which they were able to extract some DNA. The DNA was a 96% match to DNA on file for Isaac. Missing persons requested Isaac's DNA be collected after we lost him. CSI took it off a hairbrush collected from his house."

"Ah," Frank said, his eyes wide. "Why didn't you start with that?"

Leigh's grinned wider and winked. "I like to keep my audience in suspense."

"Load up the mapping software with the location of the vehicle and the direction it was heading." Frank ran his hand over his face. "Then do a 300-kilometer scan to all destinations in that vicinity that are affiliated with Cain or his aliases or that belong to any of his known corporations."

Frank hears Leigh tapping keys on his computer. A moment later Leigh said, "Two hits, Frank. One is an average three-bedroom old Queenslander style family home owned by one of Cain's trust funds. It's a rental property. Let me look up the tenants." Several key-clicks later he said, "Nothing on file for the tenants except an old petty theft charge." Several more clicks. "Now this is the interesting one, Frank. The other hit is a compound, listed as a research facility owned by N.O.D., one of Cain's corporations."

"What sort of research?" Frank asked.

"Let me check.... It's listed as 'restricted military,' and get this, they have clearance for armed guards on site."

Frank checked his wristwatch. "Print out the location of the vehicle and the compound. Let's go pay them a visit. There are still enough hours in the day."

Leigh pressed a few keys on his computer and then the laser printer beside his desk whirled up and spat out a sheet of paper. He snatched the print out, stood up, and said, "Right then, let's go."

Frank turned off his computer, grabbed his car keys, and tossed them to Leigh. "You drive."

Chapter 20 - Risk

Flaming torches lit up the passage Elijah ended up following. The passage opened into an area the size of a large bedroom. On entering, his attention was drawn to a waist-high golden pedestal in the center of the room with his armlet on top. The wall opposite the entrance, behind the pedestal, was glass. Through the glass he could see another room that was almost a reflection of the room he was in but without a pedestal in the center. The other three walls were smooth, dark-grey slate. Elijah looked down and saw a yellow envelope on the floor at the base of the pedestal. He picked it up and read the note inside:

IT WILL TAKE FAITH OR STUPIDITY TO SOLVE THE
PROBLEM

"Gunthor," Elijah said, shoving the note into his pocket, "what can you tell me about this room?"

Gunthor replied, "Scanning."

Elijah strode over to the glass wall and tapped the smooth surface with his fingers.

Gunthor said, "The walls have an energy barrier inside them, including the glass, which will prevent the manipulation of physics to penetrate them. The glass analysis results indicate that is the same as the glass in the gas chamber that Cain used to entrap you, Castiel, and Sophia."

Elijah tapped harder on the glass. "Gunthor, can you cut through this?"

"No, I cannot. Technically, however, you should be able to pass through the glass with your physics ability. Though the energy field would slice you into pieces."

"Hmm, that's comforting."

Castiel appeared from the archway leading into the room behind the glass. Elijah shouted, "Hey, Castiel!" Castiel approached the other side of the glass wall, put his hand on his forehead as if to shield his eyes from the light, and stared into the glass at various angles. Elijah shouted for a second time while banging on the glass. "Castiel!" No response. Castiel knocked on the glass, testing the surface, seemingly oblivious to the Elijah's shouting. "He can't see me," Elijah whispered. "Must be one-way glass and sound proof."

A noise seemed to catch Castiel's attention and he turned to the archway. After a moment's hesitation, he began rushing to each wall, frantically, sweat running down his forehead, as if searching the slate walls for hidden secrets. Every several seconds he glanced back towards the archway while continuing his agitated search.

Why is he in such a hurry? Why is he constantly checking the archway? What is he searching for? "Gunthor, can you scan the room on the other side of this glass?"

"Negative," Gunthor replied. "My sensors cannot penetrate the energy field."

The floor quaked as heavy iron bars slammed down in the archway in Castiel's room, sealing the only exit. Castiel ran over and grabbed the rusty bars and began pulling at them desperately. He placed his hands beneath one of the cross bars and strained as he tried to lift them with all his might. To no avail. The bars were locked in place. He then resumed his frantic search for a way out. Skin tore from his knuckles as he punched various places on the wall to find some hidden latch that would reveal an exit. He alternated between frenzied bouts of punching and kicking.

It was hard to watch. Elijah winced with each blow Castiel landed. He considered the armlet on the pedestal. "What do you think, Gunthor, should I take the armlet? Do you think it's a trap?"

"Maybe it's simply a reward for defeating the Shadow Mystic."

Elijah pulled that note out his pocket: *It will take Faith or Stupidity to solve the problem. What does that even mean? What problem? Castiel's problem? My problem? What?!*

He moved to the pedestal. "Well here goes nothing." He moved his hand slowly towards the armlet. He gave the armlet a nudge with his finger and waited to see if anything would happen. Nothing. He nudged it a little harder and waited again. Nothing. Quick as a flash he snatched it off the pedestal and, anticipating that something would occur, leapt back a few steps. Nothing. While scanning the room, he slid the armlet up his forearm and into place. "Well, that was a bit of a non-event."

A vibration began in Elijah's feet and escalated into a shuddering that shook his whole body. He checked on Castiel who was standing with his back to the glass wall, motionless, watching the archway. Castiel was preparing for something … but *what?* The floor quaked, the walls trembled, and dust rained down from the ceiling creating a brownish haze. Elijah glanced at the camera in the room. The display had changed to read "E:1-1 C:9-1 S:4-1."

All of the sudden water came rushing through the bars of the archway in Castiel's room. Castiel scrambled about the room through the water like a gazelle crossing a shallow creek with a lion in pursuit searching for any possible way of escape. Elijah now understood Castiel's anxious behavior.

Elijah returned to the pedestal, removed the armlet, and set it back on top hoping, somehow, that Castiel would be released or the water would stop rising.

The water continued to rise and Castiel, waist-deep in water, waded towards the center of the room. A moment later his feet were unable to touch the ground, so he began treading water. When the water lifted him to within arms' reach of the ceiling he extended his arm upwards and began searching the stone ceiling for a possible means of escape. Seconds later, the water was lapping at his chin. He tilted his head back and took a deep breath before the water swallowed the remaining air. His face turned white, and the tendons on his neck bulged. Spiritual death was knocking at his door, and the expression on his face showed that he realized his time may have come.

Elijah banged desperately on the glass. That failing, Elijah gripped Gunthor by the hilt with both hands over his shoulder and stepped back from the glass. With all his might, he swung Gunthor into the glass. Gunthor bounced off the smooth surface, sending shuddering vibrations down Elijah's arm.

A few air bubbles trailed from Castiel's mouth.

"Cain!" Elijah yelled, pounding on the glass, with a pained expression and emotion-choked voice. "Don't do this!"

With his eyes drawn together and his teeth clenched Elijah tapped his forehead on the glass and watched Castiel let out his final breath. Castiel's eyes closed. His body shuddered. Seconds later, he went limp and sank to the floor of the room that had become a deadly tank.

It will take Faith or Stupidity to solve the problem. Elijah set Gunthor down and hurried to the far wall. In a mad rage, he charged the glass yelling "Arghhhhh!" As he hit the glass, he used his ability to manipulate physics. The glass melted around him and he passed through. Floating in the water, he tensed, expecting his body to be severed into many pieces. After realizing he was still in one piece, Elijah swam fervently to Castiel, grabbed him beneath the arms, and swam back the way he had come. With a swift kick of his legs and thrust of his right arm, he made a final swimming stroke towards the glass wall. His momentum carried them both through the glass. On the other side, in the open air, they fell a short way down to the ground.

Elijah tilted Castiel's head back and cleared his airway. He placed his lips around Castiel's and drew in a breath through his nose and then blew the air into Castiel's mouth filling his lungs. "Don't you die on me, Castiel!" he said, between cycles. A few breaths later he sat up, placed both his hands onto Castiel's chest, and pushed downwards in an effort to pump blood through Castiel's heart. After repeating the compressions several times, he placed his hands on Castiel's shoulders.

"Come on, Castiel!" Elijah's hands glowed white as White Energy passed from his hands into Castiel's body. He knew his healing powers were weak, but he was determined to do everything he possibly could, both physically and supernaturally, to bring Castiel back.

Elijah repositioned back to Castiel's mouth and gave him another breath of life.

A tear started to form in Elijah's eye. "Castiel, please? I need you." With each passing second, a little more hope drained from his heart. A moment later, when hope was all but gone, Castiel coughed. A plume of water shot out of his mouth. He coughed again, expelling more water from his lungs, and again. Elijah quickly wiped his teary eyes on his sleeve and smiled. "Welcome back."

Castiel opened his eyes and let them adjust to the sight of Elijah hovering over him. "You weren't kissing me, were you?"

Elijah laughed and helped Castiel onto his feet. He hugged him tightly. "You had me worried there for a minute."

"I wasn't worried one bit," Castiel said, patting Elijah on the back.

"Sure you weren't," Elijah said, laughing a little more.

Castiel gazed into the flooded room through the glass wall. "How did you get into the room? Aren't those walls energized?"

Elijah clenched his fists. "Yes, but I figured it would be off." He sneered and his nose crinkled as he said in a strained voice, "It took faith and a bit of stupidity."

"You sound annoyed, Elijah?"

"Yeah, well, I'm getting tired of Cain's games."

Elijah and Castiel, both dripping wet, did their best to wring the water from their clothes. Elijah picked up Gunthor and his armlet. As he put his armlet on he said, "Right, well I'm not sure where to go next. This is pretty much a dead end."

Before Castiel could respond, the slate wall to the left of the archway began to shake. A section of the slate wall in the shape of a door started to emerge from the center. Once the slab receded about 10 inches it slid to the left revealing a passage.

Castiel cocked his head. "Well, I guess that is the way we are going, Elijah."

Chapter 21 - Reunions

In the place the police had found the black AWD SUV Leigh pulled the unmarked silver Holden Commodore he was driving off the road. Frank and Leigh exited the vehicle and began searching the site where the now late afternoon sun cast long shadows through a stand of tall gum trees.

Before long, Leigh shouted, "Over here, Frank! Got something of interest." Leigh was crouched over clawing at some leaves and broken twigs on the ground.

Frank crouched down beside him. "Hmm." Frank knew that a few bent sticks, some disturbed ground, and crushed undergrowth appeared to Leigh like pathways through the scrubland. Leigh had been trained by a man of aboriginal descent named Inkata, who was one of the best trackers, and had exceptional knowledge on how to track people through bushland by the clues they leave behind.

Leigh pointed into the bush and said, "Multiple people ran into the bush this way."

Stroking the newly-formed stubble on his chin, Frank peered in the direction Leigh indicated. All he saw was bush. "Right, after you, Leigh," he said. "Let's find where they went."

* * *

Relaxing on a grassy bank, Isaac tossed a gum tree leaf into the creek. The dead, dried out brown leaf flowed downstream carried by the current from the waterfall. Though the waterfall was not overly large, Isaac still enjoyed hearing the sound of the water falling and the feel of the fresh water mist cool on his skin.

"Isaac!" He turned in the direction of the voice and spotted Loorea jogging towards him. She continued, "I've been looking all over for you."

"Sorry," he said. "I came over here to relax for a while."

She crouched forward with her hands on her knees and, between ragged breaths, said, "Two men appear to be tracking you."

Isaac said, "Cain's goons again – Jared and Seth? The ones who were after me before?"

Loorea shook her head. "No." She sat down next to him with her legs crossed and her hands in her lap. "Our scouts believe them to be Federal Police officers."

"What did they look like?"

"One is slightly taller than you, with a heavier build. Late 40s, balding."

"Sounds like Detective Mercer." Isaacs's eyebrows raised. "I thought he was dead."

"Would you like to go to them, Isaac?" She turned away from him and looked down at the ground. "I can show you the way."

Isaac looked at her and had the strange feeling that she was not sure he should leave. *Was it because she was concerned about him as a nurse, or was it something else, something more intimate?*

Isaac shook his head as if to cast away the thought and contemplated the choice. He was missing Nya and had healed enough to survive on his own, but at the same time he had an overwhelming concern that Jared and Seth may come after him. "The two men who were chasing me when your tribesmen rescued me … do you know what happened to them?"

"After they woke up," Loorea replied, running her fingers through the long grass beside her, "they searched around for you for a while. When they could find no sign of you, they left, making their way back to the road." She faced Isaac. "The scouts did not follow them after that."

"What about the spirit?" Isaac asked as he picked up a small stone and flung it into the creek. "Didn't it say I should stay here for seven days?"

"Yes, Isaac, that is what the spirit said," she said, looking down again. "But spirits ultimately let us decide what we do. They only advise."

Isaac gazed towards the waterfall while continuing to mull over the decision.

Loorea grabbed Isaac's hand. "Come, let me take you to where you can see them. Then you can make up your mind."

Isaac followed Loorea through the bush. Her way of moving was swift and elegant as she weaved in and out of the trees and over the rocks. Isaac struggled to keep up and wondered how she managed to move without even disturbing the ground. He felt like an elephant following a deer.

Standing on the edge of a large stone outcrop overhanging the hillside, Loorea pointed downwards into the distance. "Over there. There they are."

Isaac squinted in the direction she was pointing. "That appears to be Frank, all right."

"If you decide to go with them, Isaac, you must not tell them about us. We like to keep hidden."

"Of course," he replied, shaking his head. "I have no intention of saying anything." In the few days he had lived amongst them, Isaac had developed a new understanding of the aboriginal people. They belonged to the land, and every aspect of their lives connected to Earth.

"So," she said, her voice low, "are you are going?"

"Yes, I have to return sooner or later. Since Frank is alive, he might have already apprehended our pursuers or at least know more about them."

Loorea faced Isaac and her eyelids fluttered when she said, "I will miss you, Isaac."

He placed his hand on her shoulder. "I'm going to miss you, too." He leant forward and gave her a gentle kiss on the side of her cheek. "Thank you for everything."

She smiled.

Isaac blundered through the bush, down the hillside, towards Frank. When he glanced back towards Loorea, she was gone. The sense of loss he felt disturbed him. "Goodbye, Loorea," he whispered.

* * *

A voice shouting "Sergeant Mercer! Detective!" interrupted Frank and Leigh's exploration of the area where the Joondaburri people had found Isaac. The men turned in the direction of the voice.

Is that Isaac? Frank cupped his hands over his eyes and took a second look. "Isaac, you're here!"

Frank and Leigh approached Isaac who continued jogging towards them.

Once within speaking distance Isaac said, "I managed to get away and have been hiding out up here in the wild ever since." He huffed a little, catching his breath. "What about you? You were shot! I thought you were—"

"Dead? No," Frank replied. "Yes, it was a lucky miss, I guess." He wondered how a city boy like Isaac had managed to stay alive in the wilderness and was about to ask but figured for all he knew Isaac was an experienced outdoorsmen and avid camper. "Do you know who took you, Isaac?"

"Their names are Jared and Seth, Detective. I remember their faces fairly well."

"Right," Frank said. "And, listen, call me Frank, so I don't feel I have to live up to my titles." He pulled his notebook from his shirt pocket. "Well we will get you with a sketch artist as soon as possible." He jotted down the two names. "Between your memory and mine we might be able to identify my shooter at least." He slipped the notebook back into his pocket and gestured towards Leigh. "This is my colleague, Leigh. He's got more titles than a library, too, but he'll answer to Leigh."

Isaac nodded at Leigh. "Pleased," he said. He turned his attention back to Frank and asked, "Any news on Nya?"

Frank stared at the ground. He shuffled his feet a little while trying to work out the best way to say what he had to say. Isaac noticed Frank's discomfort. "She is all right, isn't she?"

After a short pause, Frank looked into Isaac 's worried eyes. "She is in hospital, Isaac, being treated for—"

"For what," Isaac said, looking as though he had taken a shot to the gut.

"Cancer," Frank said. "We will take you there."

Frank saw the blood drain from the young man's face as he winced and swallowed hard. The news hit him hard.

"She has cancer? But that can't be. She's so healthy.... When? How?"

"She is being well cared for." Frank said, patting Isaac on the back. "Come on, Isaac, let's go."

Frank figured it unlikely Cain would make a second attempt to abduct Isaac. Nya was in hospital, and even if Cain knew where she was he would realize that she was not any good to him if she was sick. But just to be on the safe side as they were on the way to the Holy Spirit Hospital, Frank called into the Federal Police headquarters and gave orders for a protective detail to be assigned to both Isaac and Nya.

After arriving at the hospital, Leigh dropped Frank and Isaac at the front entrance and then left to park the car in the nearby parking garage.

* * *

Isaac and Frank followed the directions reception gave and made their way quickly up to Nya's room. On arriving at Nya's room, Isaac, not wanting to startle her awake, tiptoed over to her bed, picked up her soft hand, and whispered softly, "Nya."

Nya's eyes fluttered open briefly before her eyelids dropped like lead weights. A moment later she rolled her head towards Isaac and forced her eyes open as if it took all her strength. In a slow, quiet voice, she said, "Isaac, you're here."

"Of course I am," he said, trying to smile and squeezing her hand gently.

Frank moved into Nya's field of vision. "Hi, Nya."

"Frank," she said, as her eyes closed for a moment and took a breath, "how nice to see you." She paused briefly, wincing, and said, "I would prefer it to be under better circumstances."

"Well," he said. "I'm going to leave you two alone and make my way back to headquarters."

"OK." Nya smiled. "Thank you, Frank."

Before leaving, Frank gestured for Isaac to join him by the door. "I'll be right back," Isaac said. "Promise."

Frank took a business card from his wallet and handed it to Isaac. "If you have any troubles, at all, call me directly anytime. My mobile number is on the card. I have organized for a couple of officers to follow you around for the next few days as a precaution in case another attempt is made on you. But I doubt that is likely to occur." Frank glanced at his wristwatch. "They should be here soon. Wait until they arrive so they can also transport you back to your home or wherever you want to go. An officer will also stay at the hospital to keep an eye on Nya."

"Thank you, Frank. Appreciate it," he said. Isaac pondered the notion of Seth and Jared coming after him again. His eyebrows drew together and his eyes dimmed. He pushed the thought to the back of his mind, knowing that he needed to focus on Nya.

Frank extended his hand and Isaac gripped it tightly. "Take care, kid."

As Isaac turned to make his way back over to Nya, he heard, "One last thing, Isaac." Isaac turned and faced Frank. "When you're up to it, have the officers bring you to AFP headquarters, and we'll get a sketch artist capture what you remember of Jared and Seth."

"No worries," Isaac replied, nodding.

Isaac leant against the side of Nya's bed and took her coldish hand. "Frank said you have cancer?"

"Yes," she said, "it's true." Her damp blue eyes were distant. "Stage four. Prognosis isn't good."

Isaac swallowed hard, but the lump was still there. He drew in a long, deliberate slow breath. "It's OK. We are going to work through this together, Nya." He blinked rapidly to hide his tears. "We can beat this."

"That's the same thing I said to my mum."

A lonesome tear coursed down the side of her pale cheek and her lips began quivering. "You don't need to stay with me, Isaac." She began crying. "I'll understand if you want to end our relationship."

"No," he said, shaking his head. He squeezed her hand tightly. Then he was crying, too, and it was no use trying to hide them behind blinks. In a fractured voice he assured her, "I'm not going anywhere, Nya."

"They are letting me go home tomorrow, after the next round of treatment." Nya dabbed at her eyes with the back of her hand. "Then I only need to come in for follow-up treatments."

"It's settled," he said, placing his left hand on top of their holding hands. He forced a smile. "You're going to come home to my place, and I'll care for you."

Nya squeezed his hand gently. "I do not want to be alone."

"You will not be alone." He ran his fingers gently through her long blond hair and traced the top of her ear. "We will do this together."

They held hands in silence, content with being together, for some time until Nya broke the quiet moment and asked, "How was your fishing trip?"

Isaac let out a small sigh. "Eventful."

Chapter 22 - Three

Through a small rectangular glass window embedded in the top half of a solid iron door, Elijah observed Sophia strapped down on the marble altar, that menacing golden spike suspended just inches above her chest. She appeared either unconscious or sleeping. He faced Castiel with eyes narrowed and said, "That gold spike is a lot lower than the last time I saw it."

Castiel looked towards the ground, sheepish. "Well, I had a little trouble solving a puzzle."

"Uh huh," Elijah replied, nodding slowing, in a sarcastic voice. "I'm sure your puzzle was much more difficult than mine."

Elijah pushed on the heavy iron door and, expecting it to be locked, was surprised when it swung open.

Castiel swung his arm out in front of Elijah's, blocking his path through the door. "Wait!" he said, pointing at the floor with his other hand. "It appears to be pressure sensitive."

After surveying the floor and noticing each floor panel seemed slightly elevated, Elijah replied, "I think you're right, Castiel."

Great, Elijah thought. After assessing the distance between himself and the altar Elijah considered leaping onto the altar. But there would not be enough room on the altar itself for both of them unless he literally stood on Sophia. Elijah focused on Sophia's cross necklace as he pinched his chin. "I have an idea, Castiel." His eyes narrowed as he concentrated. The cross began rising from Sophia's chest. As the cross gained a little height, it dragged the chain up over Sophia's head. Then it hit a snag and the cross hovered, caught under Sophia's head by its chain, trying to break free.

Noticing the problem Castiel shouted, "Sophia!" No response. He shouted again, "SOPHIA!" Her eyes opened. Lying completely still she said, "When I struggle the gold spike lowers."

"We need you to raise your head *ever so slightly*," Castiel replied.

She cut her eyes around side to side and caught a glimpse of the chain. "I see," she said. She took a deep breath and then raised her head slightly. The golden spike responded by lowering an inch. But the chain slid free. She let her head fall back onto the altar and slowly released the air from her lungs. This time, the spike did not move.

After guiding the cross to his hand, Elijah slid his fingernail into the small indentation on the side of it and the hollow cross pendant flipped open. He shook out four silver metal crosses within it. He concentrated on the bindings that lashed Sophia to the altar and threw the four crosses. Two crosses glowing with white aurora spun like throwing stars and flew towards the bindings on her wrists while the other two split off towards the two straps on her legs. After slicing through the bindings with ease, they turned like boomerangs and jetted back into Elijah's hand.

Staying low Sophia rolled to her side off the altar onto the floor. The golden spike instantly reacted to her weight on the floor, impaling the altar with such force that the thick marble altar itself was split in two. After leaping onto her feet, Sophia shoved Elijah and Castiel, one with each arm. "About time you guys got here."

"Hey," Elijah said, staggering backwards from the shove, "it's not our fault you're always the one getting tied up."

She sighed. "True enough."

Castiel motioned down the torch-lit rather dusty and slightly damp corridor. "Onwards we go."

Elijah noticed that the numbers on the display next to the camera in the passage had changed. "What do you think those numbers mean, Castiel?"

"Hmm." Castiel glanced up at the display. "No idea," he muttered, shaking his head. "But I reckon the initials stand for Elijah, Castiel, and Sophia."

Shortly, they came to the entrance of a cavern the size of a football field illuminated by a moat of fire framing the walls with flames as tall as they were. Once inside, they assessed the area. In the center stood three white stone pedestals, waist-high, each one holding a square glass container. The first container contained Castiel's Judgement Twins, the second, Sophia's Sisters of Light. Lastly, the third container contained Elijah's Bow of Sentencing.

Behind them, the moat of fire closed the room and sealed the entrance they had come through. The flames leapt higher until they extended from floor to ceiling, creating great walls of fire.

Sophia flipped her hair back over her shoulders. "Delightful."

On guard, they advanced together towards the pedestals. Each pedestal consisted of a single column supporting a square marble slab with the container on top. Elijah analyzed each one in turn. "What do you think, Castiel?"

"A trap, most likely."

"I agree," Sophia said.

The members of the Trio stood in front of the pedestal containing their respective weapons and placed their hands cautiously on the sides of the glass containers. Elijah said, "On three, we lift. Ready; one …

two … *three.*" Simultaneously they raised the glass containers off their armaments.

Castiel lifted his glass container up high above the pedestal and said, "Nothing happened."

Elijah placed his container on the ground beside the pedestal. Castiel and Sophia followed his lead and did the same.

"What do you think, guys," Elijah said, unsheathing Gunthor, "should we grab em?" Elijah gave the Bow of Sentencing a bit of a poke with Gunthor's blade.

Castiel circled his pedestal and inspected his Judgement Twins from every angle. "We could do that."

Sophia curiously felt along the sides of her pedestal and examined the floor. "The pedestal is made of some type of stone, quite cold to the touch."

"Gunthor, what do you think?" Elijah said.

Gunthor sighed, mumbled something about his sleep schedule being disturbed.

"Gunthor!"

"Oh, OK," Gunthor groaned. "It's most likely an order thing. Take them up in the right order and all should be well. Take them up in the wrong order and all—"

"He has a point, Elijah," Castiel interrupted. "Because it—"

"Of course I have a *point*," Gunthor interrupted with a wise crack. "What point would there be to a *point*less sword?"

Elijah shook his head and sighed. "Oh, Gunthor, you and your *pointed* sense of humor."

"Keep at it," Gunthor said, "humor takes practice."

Sophia glanced at all three pedestals, gnawing on her lip. "What order?"

"I have a better idea." Elijah held Gunthor out to his side at waist height. He moved to the end of the pedestals, then ran beside them slicing through each pedestal causing the top of each one to topple to the floor, spilling the weapon it carried. Feeling taller, bigger, and stronger Elijah said, "Sir, madam: Grab your weapons."

Elijah picked up his Bow of Sentencing, Sophia her Sisters Of Light, and Castiel his Judgement Twins. "See simple!" Elijah boasted.

The ground began to rumble and quake. Sophia shuffled backwards away from the pedestals. "Well, maybe not *that* simple." One by one what was left of the pedestals crashed down onto the floor.

A thunderous roar bellowed from the far end of the room. The Trio directed their attention to the source. Through the wall of flames, a giant Shadow stepped forth, four times the height and four times the width of an average human.

Mesmerized by the sheer size of the Shadow, Elijah raised his sword and followed Sophia's lead in stepping back a few steps. "Gunthor, what is this?"

No nonsense, Gunthor responded, "They are referred to as Shadow Lords. Well-armed and well-armored."

The Shadow Lord reminded Elijah of giant all-black ogre. On its head was a large helmet-like the contraption Ned Kelly, the notorious Australian outlaw, wore that concealed its head and revealed only white glowing eyes that peered through small slits in the front. In its left hand, it wielded a pole with an attached chain. At the end of the chain, spinning faster and faster, about the size of a basketball, was a silver spiked ball. In its right hand it wielded a broad black sword glowing red. The Shadow was outfitted with knee-high boots and stiff black chain-mail armor that protected its torso and waist.

With each step, the floor shook as the Shadow Lord advanced towards them. The spiked ball was swirling so fast that it appeared as a solid ring. Then, without warning, the chain slackened and the spiked ball hurtled towards Sophia at incredible speed. A split second before impact, she leapt to the side. A single spike grazed the sleeve of her dress as the ball passed by, slicing the fabric to ribbons. After reaching the limit of the chain's reach, the spiked ball recoiled.

Castiel let loose with his Judgement Twins. Angel Light bullets flew through the air leaving small white trails in their wake. His jaw dropped as the bullets bounced off the Shadow Lord's armor. Elijah, following Castiel's lead and began shooting Angel Light arrows at the Shadow Lord but they, too, bounced off its armor.

"Ummm, guys," Elijah said, retreating backwards, staying out of range of the Shadow Lord's glowing red sword, "any ideas?"

Sophia sprinted towards the Shadow Lord. In response, the creature swung its sword toward her, missing her by only a hair's width as she slid between its tree-trunk-like legs. Twisting back and forth at its waist, the hulky monster tried to locate Sophia as she clambered up its back. She wrapped one arm around its thick neck while jamming her other arm beneath the edges of its helmet trying to bare its head. Back and forth, the Shadow Lord reeled, attempting to throw Sophia off. After a mighty roar, the Shadow Lord raised its sword then swiped towards itself trying to pry her loose. Sophia dodged the sword causing the blade to slice the beast's own shoulder. A flume of black smoke poured from the fresh wound. The Shadow Lord let out a bellowing scream and shook violently to free itself from Sophia's embrace.

Sophia gave up trying to pull the helmet off. She unsheathed one of her Sisters of Light then stabbed the thin sharp blade deep into the gap between the helmet and the beast's neck. Black mist streamed from the wound as the Shadow Lord swung its sword around for another swipe at Sophia. Sophia leapt sideways to avoid the well-aimed strike coming her way then jumped off the Shadow Lord. She landed awkwardly and went tumbling across the floor. She quickly balanced herself as the Shadow Lord spun around and swung its sword directly towards her. She lunged to her left and found herself in the path of the spiked ball, which she had not seen swinging in her direction. She let out a great gasp and her eyes bulged as the spiked ball burrowed deep into her stomach. The momentum of the ball drove her backwards. As the Shadow Lord recoiled the spiked ball, she was pulled with it momentarily before the spikes that had impaled her pulled free of her flesh. She fell to the floor writhing in pain. The Shadow Lord raised its sword, aimed it at Sophia, and then brought the glowing red blade down full force for the kill.

Sophia heard Castiel let loose a loud desperate cry, "Sophia!"

Elijah looked on in horror. Sophia seemed unable to move and just closed her eyes as the Shadow Lord's sword descended.

Chapter 23 - Intent

Seth raised his hand to shield his eyes from the afternoon sun glaring through the windscreen as he drove the little red Ford down the gravel driveway leading to Cain's compound. He pulled to a halt in front of the closed gate and waited for the burly guard dressed in army greens and armed with an assault rifle to make his way to the driver side window.

"Identification," the guard barked, keeping his eyes locked on Seth.

With a dismissive nod, Seth held up his ID. "I'm here to see Cain."

The guard snatched the card, checked over the details, and then flicked the small business like card back to Seth through the open car window. Seth scrambled to catch it but the card fell down between the driver's seat and the center console. Clenching his teeth, Seth dug down and found the card and a moment later the gate opened.

Jared, sitting in the passenger seat, muttered, "That guard has some attitude."

"Nice guy," Seth said as he pulled the car into the compound and parked close to the entrance.

After rapping on the door to Cain's office, Seth entered followed by Jared. Seth felt like a schoolboy having to front up to the principal. Bleak and dimly-lit, the office reminded Seth of an interrogation room. The only interesting thing in the office was a window veiled by closed curtains that spanned the wall behind Cain's desk. Cain sat in a high-back executive chair behind the large cherry wood desk. Cain greeted the duo with a few choice curse words and then demanded: "Right then, where is Isaac?"

Jared's face turned white. He avoided eye contact with Cain. Beads of sweat broke out on his forehead. From experience, Jared knew that disappointing Cain could result in serious injury or death.

"H-uh-he managed to escape," Seth said, pulling at his right ear. "But after he ran away from us, we believe he fell off a cliff and died."

Cain fiddled with the sleeves of his starched white shirt and glared at Seth as he shouted, "Is that right?!" He slammed his fist on the desk. "Tell me, then, how it is possible that he recently visited Nya in the hospital?"

Jared gasped and took a few steps backward. His mind was awash with the vivid, disturbing memory of Cain stabbing the sharp point of his letter opener into the side of his business partner's neck. They were only partners for a short period. His partner was the one in command and thus faced the full-force of Cain's wrath for failing to deliver on one of his requests. Nightmares had haunted Jared for months after the incident, causing him to wake up in the throes of a full-blown panic attack. In the end, the only way he could get a decent night's sleep was with the help of sleeping pills.

Jared watched Seth standing there still and silent, knowing full well there was no correct answer.

Cain rose from his seat and turned his back to Seth and Jared. In a cold, hardened voice he said, "The only reason the both of you are still standing is that my plan no longer requires either Isaac or Nya." He stomped over towards the curtain-covered window. "We got what we needed." He pressed a little recessed silver button in the corner of the window frame. The curtains opened exposing a large room beyond. "And we got ourselves a little bonus."

Seth moved closer to the window. Inside the room, two male and one female bodies lay on narrow beds. Their eyelids were sealed shut with little pieces of tape. Each body had a small implant in the right temple connected by wire to a central spherical device suspended from the ceiling. All the bodies appeared to be asleep or unconscious.

Raising his eyebrows, Seth asked, "Who are *they?*"

"They are angels," Cain replied, gazing at the bodies with a diabolical grin on his face. "Under ordinary circumstances you would not be able to see them. They have an ability to remain out of our normal visual spectrum." He clenched his jaw and narrowed his eyes. "They're like cockroaches, always around, hiding, then scurrying about."

"What are you going to do with them?"

Cain let out an evil laugh and said, "Watch them die."

Back at his desk, Cain pressed a few keys on the computer. "They're in one of my custom-coded virtual environments." The monitor displayed the two male angels battling a giant black shadowy figure. "We can observe them from various camera angles that exist in the virtual environment. The camera feeds are shared amongst my New World Order colleagues." Cain spun around on his chair and faced Seth. "We are placing bets on whom we think will be the last to survive. The whole setup –taking reality TV to a whole new level – is quite entertaining. Who knew that angels would turn out to be good for something after all?"

"If they die in the virtual environment," Seth said, folding his arms across his chest, "won't they just wake up?"

"Not in this one." Cain's eyes widened and a sinister smile furled his lips. "If they die in the virtual environment their mind becomes inherently confused and they fall into a coma. Shortly after that occurs, the heart stops beating."

"Hmm." Seth touched his chin and stared in at the three angels lying on their deathbeds.

Cain spun around on his chair and picked up a wad of papers from his desk drawer. "Now I've got to get back to the Q1 building." He tapped the stack of papers against his desk to straighten them. "We are about to unleash our latest creation on the world. I want you there for the unveiling, Seth."

Still watching the angels, Seth nodded.

Before leaving the office Cain glared at Jared, shook his head, and said, "Seth, do something about Jared. Dispose of him if you have to."

Jared collapsed into a chair in the corner of the office, put his knees to his chest, and rocked back and forth trying to quell his anxieties.

* * *

Seth turned his attention to the computer monitor. The display showed one of the angels distracting the hulking black shadowy figure while the other attempted to drag the female angel away from the action. Their actions made it clear to Seth that they had no idea they were in a virtual environment. Seth glanced at the pathetic form of Jared rocking like a lunatic and shook his head. He left the office and entered the room with the angels. He rubbed his arms and shivered. He could see his breath. The temperature in the room was near freezing, no doubt to keep the computers controlling the virtual environment running at maximum efficiency. He pulled a small wooden cross from his pocket. After gazing at the cross while rotating it between his thumb and forefinger, he placed it into the palm of the female angel's left hand and closed her fingers around it. He placed his hand over hers and closed his eyes. A ball of white light the size of a baseball glowed and pulsated around both of their hands for a brief moment. Seth opened his eyes and then quickly returned to Cain's office.

The curtains over the window had closed. Seth presumed they must be set to close on an auto-timer. He knelt on one knee in front of Jared. "Snap out of it, Jared!" he said as he slapped him across the side of his face.

Jared merely stared at him with lifeless hollow eyes. Seth stood up and grabbed both of his shoulders and shook him. "Come on Jared, snap out of it." No response.

"Dammit," Seth muttered. He placed his hands on either side of Jared's head, cupping his ears. Seth closed his eyes. White light began to glow around his hands. Jared's body began to shake as if he were having a seizure. Seth held Jared's head tightly between his hands. Jared convulsed violently for several seconds before his body went limp. Seth opened his eyes, placed his hands on Jared's shoulders, and shouted, "Jared!"

"Seth," Jared said, eyes suddenly wide and gazing around, "what happened? How did I get here?"

"You slumped over and hit your head," he said, helping Jared to his feet. "You probably have a touch of amnesia. I'll drop you home, Jared, so you can take the rest of the day off. I have to go see Cain at the Q1 building."

Chapter 24 - Wakening

"Shoot its knees!" Elijah shouted as he ran toward the Shadow Lord.

Castiel aimed his Judgement Twins and fired. A barrage of Angel Bullets streamed from the barrels of the Twins, leaving trails of white energy in their wake and piercing the back of the Shadow Lord's knees. Plumes of black smoke spewed out of the wounds, and the Shadow Lord began trembling from the many scores of bullet holes.

Elijah extended his arms above his head and dived headlong onto the floor and glided between the Shadow Lord's legs. Once under the Shadow Lord, he rolled onto his back and swung out his forearm and, like a kite unfolding, his Shield Of Faith expanded from his armlet before him. Elijah came to a stop alongside Sophia. And just as the Shadow Lord's heavy sword, now blazing with Red Energy as if the blade itself was angry, was mere inches from impaling Sophia, Elijah blocked it with his shield. Sparks of white and red energy tangoed in the air. The sword deflected off the surface of the shield and slammed against the floor. Elijah leapt to his feet, grabbed Sophia by the arm, and dragged her away from the Shadow Lord … leaving a trail of blood behind.

Castiel continued firing his Judgement Twins at the back of the Shadow Lord's knees. The Angel Bullets, though mere pinpricks to the Shadow Lord, began to take their toll. Visibly annoyed, the Shadow Lord pivoted and stared at Castiel. The beast's glowing eyes narrowed as it let out a loud furious roar and began trudging towards Castiel. In response, Castiel strode backwards with his arms fully extended in front, a Judgement Twin in each hand, continuing to fire.

"Hold on, Sophia," Elijah said. "I'll get you out of this."

Sophia's face was pale, her eyes dim, as she looked up at Elijah. Their eyes locked and although Sophia's lips parted, mouthing words, no sound followed. Elijah, fearing he might be losing her, said again: "Hold on, Sophia. *Please.*"

Her eyes closed for an instant and then, all of the sudden, a burst of white light erupted from her palm. Startled by the light, Elijah took a few steps backward letting go of her hand. The white light, like a flame consuming paper, trailed up her arm leaving behind nothing but a light puff of White Energy. When the light hit her chest, it spread out in all directions like a raging bush fire and consumed her in a matter of seconds.

Wide-eyed, Elijah stood motionless, gazing at the dispersing white smoke where Sophia used to be, attempting to rationalize what happened. "Castiel!" he shouted. I don't think we're in Kansas anymore!"

After arming his Bow of Sentencing, Elijah sprinted towards Castiel while shooting Angel Light arrows at the Shadow Lord's knees. On striking the beast's knees, his arrows combined with Castiel's bullets to inflict wounds that wept black smoke. The Shadow Lord stumbled, staggered for a bit, and then fell forward as its knees gave way. A resounding thump vibrated through the cavern as the beast slammed the ground.

"What do you mean 'we're not in Kansas anymore'?" Castiel asked.

"It's what Dorothy said to Toto in the *Wizard of Oz*? Didn't you ever see that movie, Cas'?"

Castiel rolled his eyes. "You watch too much TV."

The Shadow Lord let out a series of bellowing screams as it rocked on the floor clutching its knees in its massive hands.

* * *

Gasping for air, in utter darkness, Sophia sat up and patted her stomach feeling for wounds. No wounds. Her eyelids fought with something – *what was it, tape?* – that was keeping them closed. *Am I blind?* She pressed her fingers gently around her eyes, felt the tape, and searched for the edges. In one swift motion, she ripped the tape off both eyelids simultaneously. "Ah," she said, scowling at the stinging sensation.

Her surrounding slowly came into focus. To her right, she saw the sleeping forms of Elijah and Castiel lying on beds. Wires protruded from a small implant in their temples to a central computer above her. She cringed at the idea of having one of those in her own head. Just then she spotted, out of the corner of her eye, a wire dangling to her left. Her stomach flip-flopped. "No, please no," she muttered. She ran her hand up the wire to its destination, which was an implant secured in her temple.

She cringed. She knew she had to remove the piece of metal but wondered how far it penetrated into her head. *Is the implant just surface-mounted or did it go deeper, perhaps embedded in my cerebral cortex?* With the nails of her thumb and index finger, she burrowed under the implant and gently tried to lift the metal disc off her temple. Pain shot through her temple as the skin lifted with the implant. She took a deep breath, closed her eyes, clenched her teeth, and gave the circular disc a hefty tug. That did it. The implant separated from her skin and a trailing glowing red lead attached to it pulled from the resulting small wound like a worm dragged out of a hole. The sensation made her shudder. The incision oozed a little pus and a trickle of blood. Sophia touched the wound with her finger, which glowed bright white, as the hole healed. A moment later she stood up.

The chill of the room suddenly enveloped her in a foul sweep. Until then a rush of adrenalin had shielded her from the frosty air. Goose bumps formed on her arms and legs. She hugged herself tightly and rubbed her arms to warm herself. Her long white silky dress provided precious little warmth against the elements. Teeth chattering, she glanced around the room: four white walls, a grey door, a black metal cabinet, a large window. On the other side of the window the curtains were closed concealing what was beyond. The room itself was dreadfully ordinary. The ceiling, however, was anything but. A large silver computer shaped like a sphere hung from several broad rails on the ceiling. Its surface was dotted with a dozen or so unusual colored flashing lights. The ceiling itself was covered with hundreds of wires and cables of various colors and sizes. It seemed as though the computer was growing. Each cable had a faint glow that flickered red then blue then red. Several wires ran down from the base of the sphere and split into three bundles – one leading to the implant in Elijah's temple, one to the implant in Castiel's temple, and one to the implant that had been in Sophia's temple which was now lying on the floor.

Inside the cabinet, Sophia found the Trio's weapons as well as a computer terminal consisting of an ultra-thin wireless keyboard and a paper-thin display. The back of the display had wires running through to the top of the cabinet and connecting with wires on the ceiling. The wires were of the same color as the wall paint and, from a distance, were hard to detect.

Sophia touched the keyboard. The display faded in showing a live view of Elijah and Castiel. They appeared to be standing around chatting while the humungous Shadow Lord rolled on the floor clutching its knee. Sophia shook her head. "Kill it already."

She knew then that they were in a virtual environment. She knew she had to get them out. *But how?* Elijah was the computer expert. He could shut this thing down in minutes. She stood next to Elijah's sleeping body and contemplated just ripping the implant from his temple but thought better of it because that might be fatal without getting him out of the virtual world first. Thinking back, she wondered how she had managed to get out. *Did I die? No, I was not dead when the white glow flashed around my hand. At least, I don't think I was dead.* She tapped her fingertips on Elijah's forehead. No response. She whispered in his ear, "Elijah, can you hear me?" No response. She was running out of options. She slapped him across the face. No response. She placed one hand on his right temple. With her other hand, she grabbed hold of the implant and, wincing, gave it a quick yank. Once it was detached she immediately positioned her hands over the weeping wound left behind. Her hands glowed. She closed her eyes. The white glow around her hands swirled into streams that ran into Elijah's ears, nostrils, eyes, and mouth. Sophia's whole body began to shake. "Come on, Elijah! Find me."

* * *

Elijah slung his bow over his back. "Right, Castiel," he said, drawing Gunthor from his sheath, "time to finish this Shadow Lord."

Castiel nodded, "Go for it."

"What?" Elijah replied.

"I said 'go for it.'"

"No, no," Elijah said, cocking his head, "what did you say after *that?*"

"I didn't say anything."

"Hmm. I could have sworn I heard something."

Elijah grabbed his cheek, "Ouch!"

"Are you all right?" Castiel asked.

"I'm not sure," Elijah said, rubbing his cheek. "I feel like someone just slapped me."

Castiel raised an eyebrow.

"What the—?" Elijah cupped his hand over his right temple and then, limp as a rag doll, fell to the ground, his eyes staring blankly into space.

Castiel reached for Elijah, shouting his name. Then Elijah just ... *vanished*. Castiel crouched over where Elijah had been and whispered, "I guess we're not in Kansas after all. Just don't leave me behind."

Castiel holstered one of his Judgement Twins. He trained the other directly at the Shadow Lord's eye and strode forward firing as he went.

Chapter 25 - Find Me

"What is your name?"

Elijah looked around, puzzled. He wondered who the man asking him questions was and how he had gotten here – wherever he was. "My name?"

"Yes, your name," the man said. "What is it?"

Elijah looked at the man seated across the small rather old wooden desk from him and said, "Elijah. Elijah Hael. But, wait, how did I get here?"

"*I* will be asking the questions," the man said in a stern but matter-of-fact tone. "*You* will be answering them."

The man's words echoed strangely in Elijah's mind. *Something is not right.* Elijah felt an eerie sense of *deja vu*.

Elijah tilted his head from side to side and scanned the small, well-lit room. It had a single door and a window.

"Your name: What is it?" The man shouted.

This room.… I have been here before. He gazed at the ceiling. Strips of the ceiling began to peel away revealing black empty space beyond. The walls followed, dissolving into blackness. Elijah stood up and took a few steps backwards and as he did both the man and the old desk faded. Then the ground diminished into emptiness.

He was shrouded in total darkness except for a small white light glowing in the distance. The speck of light seemed miles away. Elijah began striding towards the glow. The light drew farther away becoming faint. Elijah broke into a run in an effort to chase down the distant spark. His heart pounded, his lungs burnt, his legs ached. Faster and faster, he ran, until he was staggering from exhaustion. He watched the light, which was now but a distant white speck, fade into a blur as he collapsed to the ground. He lay on his back staring into the blackness.

A whisper in his ears: "Elijah." A pause, then: "Elijah, you must keep going."

Where is the voice coming from? He rolled his head in the direction of the voice. Juliana, his wife and the love of his life when he was human, lay next to him. Her deep green eyes sparkled as she whispered, "You must keep going, Elijah. Don't give up."

I am dreaming, Elijah thought. *This is not real.*

A child's giggle sounded in the distance followed by a young boy saying, "Daddy."

Reece? My son? Elijah struggled to believe what he was seeing. His young son stood next to his sister, Elijah's daughter Kaley. Kaley pirouetted causing her long sunshine yellow dress to swirl outwards as she giggled. Reece motioned for Elijah to follow him as he started walking away. Kaley continued spinning, her outstretched arms parallel with the ground, twirling like a ballerina. Elijah struggled to rise to his feet.

Reece yelled "Come on, Daddy!" as he headed for the distant flicker of white light. Kaley, smiling, let out a final giggle then faded away into the blackness. Elijah glanced back to Juliana. She had vanished.

"Reece, wait." Elijah started to run after Reece who was fading into the distance. He chased Reece as fast as his legs would carry him, but the boy moved too quickly and was soon out of sight. Elijah stopped, put his hands over his eyes, and shook his head screaming, "What's going on?!"

He fell to his knees. Blackness surrounded him in every direction. For a moment, he believed he had been stricken blind, but his own body was visible. His mind was ensnared in the confusion of straddling two worlds – the virtual world and the real world. He was lost in a comatose state.

"Elijah," a soft female voice echoed through the darkness. "Elijah? You must find me." Squinting into the darkness he yelled, "I can't see anything! Everything is black!"

"We live by faith, not by sight. Come find me."

Elijah rose to his feet and spun around searching in all directions. There was nothing – simply *nothing* – to find.

"Focus your eyes on what is unseen."

Focus my eyes on what is unseen. He contemplated the meaning of the phrase and then closed his eyes. A white light then appeared in the distance, glowing in his mind, faint but sparkling. He took a deep breath and focused intently. Like a freight train barreling through a dark tunnel the light grew larger and larger until it fully engulfed him.

* * *

Elijah gasped for air as he sat up. Patches of shadowy darkness clouded his vision.

"Take it easy, Elijah," Sophia said in a soothing voice. "Give me a second."

He felt Sophia's soft hands on his face then around his eyes and then came a sudden stinging pain on his eyelids as Sophia ripped off whatever was holding them sealed shut.

"There you go."

Elijah's vision gradually restored bringing Sophia's face into focus.

"I thought I was going to lose you for a second, Elijah," Sophia said, brushing the side of his face with the back of her hand. "You gave me quite a scare."

Elijah's memories started to flow back: Caught by Cain, the virtual world, and the consuming darkness. He glanced around and knew at once where he was. "We have to get Castiel out."

"We do." Sophia helped Elijah to his feet. "I was hoping you could shut down the virtual world and bring him out a bit easier than what I had to do with you."

Sophia showed him to the terminal, and Elijah went to work. After watching the display showing Castiel finishing off the Shadow Lord, Elijah pressed a few keys to bring up a console interface from which he could hack the system. A few minutes later the system shut down. An alarm, wailing with a high-pitch squeal, started to sound.

Elijah continued his work on the computer, muttering, "There must be a self-destruct command in here somewhere."

Sophia attended to Castiel as he began to come out of the virtual world. "This might hurt a bit, Castiel." Castiel gritted his teeth as she ripped the implant from the side of his head and began healing the wound. "There you go. All done."

Over the sound of the wailing alarm, Elijah shouted, "Is two minutes enough for us to get out of here?"

"That should do us, Elijah," Castiel responded, rubbing his temple, "and give the scientists in the building a chance to escape."

"Right-o, two minutes it is." Elijah's fingers danced furiously on the keyboard so fast that they were but a blur. "There. All done."

A rather friendly female voice echoed loudly throughout the complex. "Self-destruct activated. Detonation in two minutes." Elijah thought it odd how self-destruct voices always sounded friendly rather than frantic. The voice began to count down, repeating the statement every 10 seconds.

The Trio exited the room and scrambled out into the corridor. Several scientists, unaware of the Trio's presence beat a hasty retreat for the exits.

"Self-destruct activated. Detonation in ninety seconds." They upped their pace and followed the scientists back to the main entrance hallway with the security scanners. Two guards wearing sunglasses came charging through the main door into the complex. A faint red glow surrounded their dark lenses. The guards directed their assault rifles towards the Trio.

"They can see us! Move!" Elijah shouted. Castiel and Sophia took cover in the left corner of the corridor while Elijah took shelter in the right. Bullets sprayed down the hallway and chipped away at the walls.

Elijah retrieved the bow from his back and pulled the bowstring, which caused an arrow to appear and nock into place. He slipped around the corner, aimed, and fired. The Angel Light arrow flew through the air gracefully and impaled the guard, who hadn't even seen it coming. He collapsed, jolting, to the ground with the arrow, for a brief moment, until it faded sticking straight out of his chest. Castiel readied one of his Judgement Twins. In concert with Elijah, he leant around the corner, aimed, and shot towards the other guard. His Angel Light bullets struck the guard in the shoulder, chest, and abdomen sending him to the ground in spasms.

The self-destruct voice said, "Fifteen seconds to detonation."

In single file, the Trio sprinted for the front door. Beyond the door, Castiel began creating a portal. Guards began shooting at them from all directions. Elijah opened his Shield of Faith that provided cover for Sophia and Castiel. Bullets sparked and clanged as they bounced off the shield. Other bullets hit the soil around them kicking up little clouds of dust. The portal opened. Sophia dived through, followed by Castiel, and then Elijah who stepped backwards through the portal while using his shield to fend off the furious spray of bullets. Cheekily Elijah waved as he took the final step and passed through the portal.

* * *

A series of underground explosions rocked the compound. Small plumes of smoke rose from the corners and then the complex imploded and fell into the earth as if sucked down into a great chasm. Dust and debris ballooned up into a large mushroom cloud that rose into the sky accompanied by a huge fireball.

When the dust settled all that was left of the compound was a crater filled with rubble where the elaborate complex had once stood. Several scientists and guards helped their fallen comrades, some wounded by flying shrapnel, to their feet.

Chapter 26 - Reveal

"Ah, Seth, you're right on time," Cain said as Seth entered the dimly lit basement of the Q1 tower.

Seth nodded. He rocked back on his heels and watched an eight-ton black semi-trailer with the words **Nanorobotic Organ Development** painted on its side in white backing up to the loading dock, beeping one high-pitched squawk per second. "What's in the semi?"

Cain rubbed his hands together like a cricket in glee. "Patience. You shall see in a moment."

A stocky man with three-day stubble on his bulldog jowls and dressed in shorts and a sweat-soaked singlet got out of the semi. He climbed up to the loading dock and began unlocking the back of the truck.

In a proud voice, Cain said, "Prepare to meet my newest creation, Seth."

Seven well-built bald men in black business suits, complete with ties and shiny shoes, emerged from the depths of the dark trailer. One by one, they lined up facing Cain.

Seth looked them over. They shared identical features and might have been septuplets. Seth knew about the cloning project and the basics of what Cain had been trying to accomplish. He considered it a sci-fi pipe dream and never dreamed he would succeed. "What are they?"

"I call them Hadows – short for Human Shadows." Cain lifted his chin. "Well, almost human. There is quite a bit of nanorobotic technology in them."

Cain's mobile phone's ringtone, the Rolling Stones' "Sympathy for the Devil" sounded: *"Pleased to meet you, Hope you guess my name, But what's puzzling you, Is the nature of my game."* Cain sang along and when the chorus finished he put it to his ear. "What? I'm busy." His face suddenly glowed red, his eyes narrowed, and his jaw pulsed as he listened. He let out a deep breath as if to calm himself and hung up the phone.

"Everything all right?" Seth asked.

After stretching his jaw as if he wanted to scream, Cain replied, "It seems our friends escaped and destroyed the compound." He sighed and then stretched his eyes. "It doesn't matter." He laughed. "Why build only one compound when you can build two?"

Seth's eyebrows rose. He had no idea Cain had more than one compound. "Is it ready?"

"Not quite. But in the meantime, the seven Hadows we have should be enough to keep my New World Order colleagues content."

Seth seized the opportunity to find out who else was involved. "Who are your colleagues in the New World Order, Cain?"

Cain glanced cautiously at Seth. "To be privy to that information," he said, patting Seth on the shoulder, "you would need to be a part of it. Maybe one day you will be if – and only *if*–you stay on my good side."

The Hadows stood motionless – almost like robots, yet they did make subtle movements that you would expect from a human, albeit much stiffer and more mechanical.

"Well, I hope I will, Cain," Seth said, smiling, playing to the man's arrogance. On a roll, Seth figured he would try to press Cain for some more information. "Why do the Shadows work with you, Cain?"

"Old friends. You see, my relationship with the inhabitants of the Underworld goes back to Genesis. My colleagues view Earth as rightfully theirs ... and not just Earth."

Seth nodded.

Cain took a step closer to him and cocked his head. "Now you wouldn't know anything about our friends in the compound escaping, would you?"

Seth turned and stared straight into Cain's eyes. "Why would I?"

Cain, his snake-like eyes narrow as slits, peered at Seth, as if trying to decide if Seth was telling the truth. "Oh, I don't know."

"So," Seth said, turning his attention back to the Hadows, "what are you going to use the Hadows for?"

"Hmm." Cain shrugged. "Fly planes into buildings, carry out assassinations, and execute bombings. Whatever the NWO decide. In the past, it has been a lot more difficult to convince people to do our bidding. Suicide bombers have to be prepped for years. A Hadow doesn't fear death." He laughed manically. "A Hadow is the ultimate warrior."

Seth nodded. "Do they have any special powers?"

Cain winked. "Let me give you a demonstration." Then he shouted, "Hadows Five and Seven, step forward." Two Hadows marched forward. "Fight."

They squared off against each other. Number Five ran, advancing several times faster than a human, towards Number Seven. Seven, anticipating an attack, crouched and flung his legs out in front to try to trip the approaching Five. Five reacted by leaping over the sweep then diving towards Seven. Fist out, Five punched Seven directly in the left cheek. Seven recoiled from the might of the blow. Five recovered from the dive and leapt to his feet. Wasting no time, he strode over to Seven, who was still recovering from the punch, and did not even see Five's boot coming until his reflection in the shiny shoe eclipsed his vision. Seven tumbled backwards grabbing his blood-streaming broken nose. Five followed Seven, grabbed his arm, and wrapped the limb between his legs. With a loud crack, Seven's arm snapped at the elbow like a toothpick as Five twisted his torso.

Cain cheered for Five. Seth observed, both transfixed and intrigued by the merciless display of violence.

Five spotted a rusty iron bar and snatched it up and headed towards Seven.

"This should be good," Cain muttered.

A river of red running from his nose, Seven clutched his elbow and staggered to his feet. Five held the bar over his shoulder and then twisted around and, like a baseball player swinging for the fences, swung towards Seven's head. Seven reached out and grabbed the bar with his good arm. Seven gritted his teeth as Five tried to wrest the bar from his grip. He raised his knee straight into Five's groin. Five smiled. He sensed no pain. But having distracted Five, Seven put his other leg around the back of Five's. Seven pushed forward causing Five to stumble backwards. Five tripped on Seven's leg and, trying to regain balance, released his grip on the bar. Seven aimed the iron bar. Like a pool cue about to hit a ball, he thrust it towards Five's eye. The iron bar passed directly through Five's eye, popping it like a balloon, then proceeded through his head until driving out the back of his skull. Five collapsed.

Cain shouted, "Well done, Seven. Well-played, indeed."

"I appreciate the demonstration, Cain, but wasn't that a bit of a waste of a perfectly good Hadow?"

"Watch on," Cain said. "Here comes the good bit."

Seven grabbed his broken arm and seemingly snapped the bone back into place. Seth was convinced that Hadows do not experience any pain. The blood flowing from Seven's nose stopped and his bruises and contusions healed in seconds. Seven gripped the end of the iron bar impaled through Five's head and withdrew it. To Seth's astonishment, Five started to move. The space where Five's eyeball use to be grew another eye. Seven helped Five to his feet. Other than torn, bloody, dirty suits, they appeared brand new.

"It's a combination of human and Nanorobotic technology," Cain explained. "The Nanos can reconstruct human physiology in real-time when not engaged in other activities. The Shadow inside feels no pain and operates the body as a piece of equipment."

Seth nodded. "Impressive."

Cain shouted to the burly truck driver, "Put the Hadows back in the semi and ready them for deployment."

Cain answered another incoming phone call, which didn't seem to upset him as much as the previous, before he led Seth inside the rear of the semi. The Hadows inside the trailer were housed in seven of the 12 floor-to-ceiling pods that rested against the walls, six on either side. Metal bars wrapped around the Hadows' knees, waist, torso, and neck securing them in place. Their eyes were closed.

At the far end of the trailer, a scientist in a white lab jacket hovered over a computer display built into a desk. He was busy analyzing various readouts and taking notes on a mobile tablet.

"This is one of our mobile Hadow carriers," Cain said while admiring the seven Hadows.

"I see," Seth replied.

"It's difficult to move bodies around. Hence we constructed these transports for when the bodies don't have Shadows in them." Cain screwed up his nose. "Shadows are an impatient lot and don't like being stuck inside a body, waiting around, in transport."

"So why the pods?" Seth asked.

"The *human bodies* – clones, if you will – need to be connected to the pods to enable the Shadows to enter and leave without damaging the body. It's part of the interfacing requirements: sync, desync process."

A voice bellowed from behind the semi. "Time for me to get this rig on the road."

Cain said, "That's our cue to leave unless you want to get locked inside here with the Hadows for the next few hours."

"No, thanks." Seth replied, shaking his head. "I'll pass up that road trip."

Chapter 27 - Step Down

Leigh ran up to Frank's desk. He doubled over and took a moment to catch his breath then said, "Hear the news, Frank? Cain's compound exploded."

"Yeah, I heard," Frank said. "Local police, fire brigade, and ambulances are all on the scene."

"Shouldn't we get out there?"

Frank frowned, shook his head. "No. I've been called into West's office."

"Trouble?"

"I'm not sure," Frank replied. He scratched his head with a lazy hand, wondering what West wanted. "Well, the best way to find out is to go and see the man. I'll be back."

He headed off. A gold plaque on the wooden door to West's office reminded all comers who was behind the door: *Commissioner Jake West*. Frank rapped on the door.

"Come in."

West was seated behind a large pine desk. A built-in wall-to-wall bookcase on the back wall was loaded with books on criminal justice, statistics, and investigative techniques. An old-style white board stood in one corner, the kind that required a duster and marker. Frank decided not to sit but rather stood behind one of two chairs designated for visitors. They were often referred to as the "dress-down" chairs. West, a second-or third-generation Australian by a few generations with some aboriginal blood was well-tanned but heavyset bordering on obesity. Approaching 65, West did not get out of the office much. As commissioner, his job was to ensure everything ran smoothly. He answered directly to the police minister. Frank did not envy West's role, cooped up in a stodgy office. He preferred working the streets and solving crimes.

West put down his pen, the top of which had unmistakable tooth marks from where West had been gnawing on it. "Take a seat, Frank."

"I'd prefer to stand," Frank said. "But thanks all the same."

"Take a seat," West repeated, this time in a stern, commanding voice. It wasn't an invitation but an order.

Frank nodded and took a seat. "What's up?" he asked, out of his comfort zone, sitting in front of the large desk with West's eyes transfixed on him.

West stood up and strode over and pulled the string to close the blinds. "No doubt by now you know about Cain's compound?"

"Yes," Frank replied as he nibbled on the top of his thumbnail.

West returned to his desk and picked up his pen and held it between his hands. "We are releasing the men we apprehended from the hospital and suspending any further investigations into Cain."

Frank squeezed the arms of his chair as anger brewed up inside of him. "They tried to kill me!"

"But you didn't die, Frank." West twirled the end of the pen in his mouth.

"It's still attempted murder," Frank said. His muscles of his upper back tightened sending a dull ache through the back of his neck. He massaged the top of his right shoulder.

"Frank, I've been given a directive," West said. "It's out of my hands."

"From whom?" Frank said, leaning over the desk.

"I can't say." West bit down on the end of the pen. "And I don't want to argue with you over this."

"This is rubbish. What, is some politician in fear of losing Cain's campaign contributions?"

West slammed down the pen. "Frank!"

Frank knew then why West had insisted that he take a seat. If he was standing he would storm out slamming the door behind him. He took a deep breath, trying to control his brewing anger. "So what now?" Frank asked.

West returned the end of the pen to his mouth and gnawed on it lightly. "I want you to resume your normal cases."

"What about Isaac and Nya?"

West looked down at his desk. "We are pulling their protection detail." He picked up a report on his desk and began flipping through the document. "Don't worry. We have asked local police to check in on them once in a while."

Frank clucked his tongue and said, quite sarcastically, "Well that's mighty nice of us. Is that all?"

"Yes, Frank, that is all."

Frank stood up and shoved the chair away from him almost sending it toppling and stormed out of West's office. Back at his desk, he logged into his computer, opened the Cain case, and marked it *closed*.

Leigh placed a cup of steaming black coffee on Frank's desk. "Here you go, Frank."

"Thanks, Leigh."

"So what did West want?"

"To *close* the Cain case."

His voice up an octave, Leigh replied, *"What?"*

Frank tapped his fingers on the desk. "It appears Cain has friends in high places."

Seated back at his desk across from Frank, Leigh said, "So what, we just drop the case?"

"Officially, yes. Unofficially, well, we will see."

Chapter 28 - What's Important

Nya arrived at Isaac's house a few hours before sunset and a little earlier than expected from her chemo and radiotherapy procedure at the Holy Spirit Hospital. Thanks to a cancellation she had an earlier session. She appreciated the support she received during the treatment. The radiologist treated her exceptionally well and made her laugh even though on the inside she was crying.

Her stomach, heavy and bloated, initiated the typical rumblings that would lead to vomiting. She knew that soon the ritual involving kneeling before the toilet, probably for the night, would commence. The struggle through radiotherapy and chemo sessions slowed the cancer, buying her time, but was not a ticket to restore her health. She promised to keep on fighting not just for herself but for Isaac.

Isaac greeted Nya by the door with a broad smile. "I have a surprise for you."

"What is it?" she asked. Her eyebrows raised and a slight smile bloomed.

Isaac took Nya's hand. "Close your eyes."

"Really?"

"Yes, really."

Nya closed her eyes. Isaac took her hand and guided her down the hallway. "Careful, I left my shoes out."

"Don't worry," Nya replied as she shuffled around them. "I can smell them."

"Just a little further. Now we take a right into the lounge."

The fresh aroma of roses filled Nya's senses. "Is that scent roses?"

"Well, not quite roses, it's coming from a fragrance burner." Isaac steered her towards the couch. "Sit down."

Isaac gave her additional instructions and she sat down on the couch.

"OK," he said. "You can open your eyes."

The scene was pure romance as the flickering light of at least 30 candles, set on various flat surfaces like in a chapel, cast a gentle, soothing ambience.

Nya drew in a deep breath and let the scent of roses fill her nostrils. She glanced around the room. In the cabinet under the television she noticed empty space. "Where did your game consoles go, Isaac?"

"Don't worry about that." He took both her hands and knelt down in front of her. "I have something to ask you."

A smile made her lip quiver as her pulse quickened. "Something to ask me?"

"Nya, over the last month, the thought that I might lose you has made me realize how much I really need you." He squeezed her hands gently. "You are my world, and more important to me than anything else." Beads of sweat formed on his forehead. "You are beautiful in every way."

Nya squirmed and repositioned the headscarf she was wearing.

Isaac said, "Your hair loss doesn't worry me, Nya." He blinked rapidly as if to clear his eyes from forming tears. "You look as beautiful to me without hair as you do with."

Nya's broad smile, now fully formed, beamed from cheek to cheek. Her eyes glistened behind the pooling tears. She was not used to Isaac being so charming and affectionate.

Isaac reached into his trouser pocket and pulled out a little pink box covered in velvet. He placed it on his palm and lifted off the top, displaying a beautiful golden ring adorned with a large blue sapphire that matched the shade of Nya's eyes encircled by a cluster of small diamonds. "Nya," he said, his voice breaking, "would you do me the great honor of marrying me?"

A tear coursed down Nya's glowing cheek leaving behind a stream of questions. She tried to rationalize why Isaac would want to marry her in her current condition. She was dying. She closed her eyes overwhelmed with feelings of both great joy and profound sadness. She stuttered, "But…but…but…."

"No *buts*, Nya, just a simple yes or no." He shook his head and placed his hand on her knee and gazed directly into her eyes.

Nya leant forward, embraced Isaac, and whispered, "Yes." In that moment, Nya was certain she was the happiest person on earth. All her worries, all her cares, instantly melted away.

Isaac, slowly and delicately, slid the ring onto Nya's shaking finger. She bent her thin hand back at the wrist and admired its sparkle, wondering how Isaac could have afforded such a stunning piece of jewelry. Then she glanced back at the cabinet with the missing game consoles. "You shouldn't have sold them. Not for me."

"You mean more to me than some silly old game consoles."

A series of medical bills had strained their finances due to the cost of Nya's treatment. Nya's income had stopped when she took an indefinite leave of absence from ASIO, and their savings were rapidly dwindling away. Isaac's income provided enough to cover the mortgage and weekly expenses but not much breathing room for anything else.

Nya embraced Isaac and held him tightly, wishing this moment of joy could last forever. A minute later, though, her stomach convulsed sending burning fluids up into her throat. She darted, holding her hand over her mouth, to her prison for the night. Her knees ground into the cold tiles as she released the fluids from her stomach in a great torrent. The chemo side effects, as usual, claimed her. Doctors had informed her that treatment should get easier after the first few rounds, but it hadn't been the case and Nya was tormented, spending each night at the foot of the toilet on the cold hard bathroom floor.

Outside the bathroom door, Isaac took a seat resting against the wall and settled in for the night. He would do this each time saying that if Nya had to stay captive in the bathroom at the foot of the latrine, the least he could do was be as close to her as possible. He would prefer to be closer, but Nya refused to let him see her at her worst. Between each of her convulsion sessions, they would chat about trivial stuff. Isaac would tell jokes to get a little chuckle out of her. The one-liners were sometimes priceless and other times just downright stupid. But Nya always appreciated the effort and would smile even when they were not so entertaining. Eventually, they would doze off into a short nap before Nya's stomach once again demanded her attention.

In a soft voice, Isaac said, "Nya."

Nya leant back against the firm bathroom wall and tilted her head back. She swallowed to check the coarseness of her throat. "Yes, Isaac."

She heard Isaac tap the back of his head gently against the wall. "When your chemo is finished we should go on a holiday."

"Sounds good, Isaac," she sighed softly. Not wanting to hurt Isaac, she never kept him up to date on her prognosis. He believed, or wanted to believe, that she would come through. So she played along, realizing that the possibility of a holiday was all but a dream, and replied, "Where do you think we should go?"

"I'll let you pick when the time comes, Nya."

Nya eased over to the basin, took a mouth of water, swished it around, and spat out the murky liquid. She took another gulp of water and swallowed it. "Can I pick now?"

"Sure, Nya." She heard the gentle thud of Isaac wedging his head into the corner of the toilet door – his pillow.

"Paris, I want to go to Paris." She imagined the scene. "And look out from the top of the Eiffel Tower."

"Sounds great, Nya," he said. "You're on. Sounds like the perfect romantic place for a honeymoon. The city of love. We'll go right after our wedding."

"That sounds wonderful, Isaac." She imagined standing at the top of the Eiffel Tower at night, wide eyes taking in the dazzling lights of Paris, a chilly breeze brushing her face, in the arms of Isaac. Deep down she knew it would never be a reality, but in that moment the scene in her mind was reality enough. Before closing her eyes, Nya glanced at her striking engagement ring and fixed the image in her mind. "Love you"

"Love you, too," Isaac replied. "Sweet dreams."

Chapter 29 - Patmos

Elijah stood in front of the closed white doors of a Transport point in Elysium. "Where did Araton ask us to meet him, Castiel?"

"Patmos. A place accessible only via the Dolorosa."

Elijah raised an eyebrow and cocked his head toward Castiel. "The Dolorosa? That means 'way of suffering,' right?"

"It's like a train."

With a hissing sound the doors to the Transport Point slid open. Elijah, Castiel, and Sophia stepped into the small white-walled room about the size of an elevator car. Castiel raised his hand up in front of the panel mounted to the side of the door that displayed the word "Waiting...." An instant later, the display updated to "Destination set to Dolorosa Central Station." After the doors slid closed the display once again updated to "Transporting" and a few moments later to "Dolorosa Central Station." The doors opened.

Dolorosa Central Station was a raised stone platform. A single train-width lane covered with a cloud-like white fog ran alongside the platform and ventured into the distance in both directions. The platform was sparse with only a few wooden benches and a high-resolution visual display hovering indicating when the Dolorosa would arrive.

Castiel glanced up at the display. "Not long until the Dolorosa gets here."

Elijah asked, "What's so important about Patmos that Araton wants us to meet there?"

"I've never been there," Castiel replied, scratching his temple. Memories of the implant had him checking the area every so often, just to be sure.... "All I know is it's a secure area. What about you Sophia: Any idea?"

"No idea," Sophia replied from her seat on one of the benches. "This is my first time."

A rather loud medium-pitch tone sounded followed by a pleasant female voice: "Dolorosa is arriving."

Elijah squinted into the distance up the lane in the direction from which the Dolorosa ought to be arriving. Castiel reached out his arm and gave Elijah a gentle push back away from the lane. "Stand back a little." An instant later the Dolorosa appeared in front of them.

Elijah wide-eyed said, "Wow! I didn't even see it coming."

"Of course you wouldn't," Castiel said, patting Elijah on the back. "Dolorosa travels faster than light."

The main body of the Dolorosa was a single shiny-blue tube with identical sharp pointed front and rear, like two bullets end to end with a cylindrical mid-section. Eight dark-tinted rectangular windows with beveled corners ran along both sides.

"You know," Elijah said, "they might want to think about renaming this 'The Blue Bullet.'"

The Dolorosa hovered above the ground, moving slightly up and down, above the white fog. The front and rear of the Dolorosa opened by peeling backwards. Out of each end, a bridge of blue light with rails extending into an L-shape connected the train with the platform.

"Front or back, Elijah?" Castiel asked.

"Back."

The Trio stepped onto the rear bridge and entered the back of the Dolorosa. Inside were 16 cushioned seats, eight on each side facing forward, all vacant. They took a seat, Castiel and Elijah opposite each other and Sophia behind Elijah. Elijah glanced out of the window at the platform. A second later, the window went dark, showing only his reflection. "Are we moving, Castiel?"

"We sure are – faster than light. Nothing to view out the window now until we arrive."

"How long?" Elijah asked while tapping on the window.

"About 36 sectants."

Elijah did some quick calculations in his head. "That makes the distance to Patmos about 170 million miles away."

"Actually it's a bit closer to 200 million."

"Elysium can't be *that* big."

"Who said Patmos was in Elysium?"

Elijah nodded, eyes narrowed and lips pursed.

A wall of translucent green light, spanning the cabin from roof to floor, appeared in the forward section and proceeded to move down the Dolorosa. "What's the light about, Castiel?"

"It's a scan, to ensure we are not carrying weapons and are indeed angels."

The green wall passed through Elijah and Castiel and then through Sophia and continued to the rear of the cabin.

"I guess we passed," Elijah said.

Castiel nodded and then turned to Sophia. "You're awfully quiet, Sophia."

"Sorry, I've been thinking about that Virtual Environment we were trapped in and how I managed to get out. It's nagging me."

Elijah turned and looked at her. "How *did* you get out?"

"That's just it," she said, kicking the back of Elijah's seat. "I really don't know." She paused a moment, glancing around at nothing in particular. "I only remember feeling a strange influence coming from my hand ... as though something was calling me. The sensation is hard to explain." Sophia glanced at the palm of her hand. "And there is this – a small red scar of a crucifix." She held her palm out so Castiel and Elijah could see.

Elijah analyzed her palm, tilting his head from side to side and twisting and turning her hand to view it from different angles. "Odd."

Sophia added, "The cross has faded a little since I first noticed it."

Castiel inspected her palm closely. "Maybe Cain didn't want you to die from your injuries?"

Sophia pulled her hand away from them. "Yeah, maybe."

The windows of the Dolorosa came back to life revealing a scene outside the glass similar to the platform they had left. "We're here," Castiel said.

The platform appeared to be underground, like a subway, with only a single well-lit tunneled walkway leading off into the distance. After a short walk, the Trio came to a sealed entrance guarded by two middle-aged male uniformed angels holding long intricately-engraved golden staffs. Their uniforms consisted of white shirts with the familiar logo of two overlapping feathers embroidered on the right hand side and a pair of ash-grey trousers.

Castiel handed one of the guards a card he retrieved from his trench coat pocket. Without saying a word the guard studied the card, moved aside from the entrance, and gestured for them to proceed.

Elijah shrugged, thinking: *Talkative lot.*

A large silver door imprinted with the feather logo, between the guards, slid upwards revealing a small dimly-lit foyer. Inside the foyer, they waited in front of a waist-high stone pedestal with a sign on the front: "Please wait here." In each corner stood a golden archangel statue in a distinctive gallant pose. Beneath each one was a marble plaque bearing the archangel's name. Elijah recognized one, Zadkeil, the creator of Gunthor, but not the other three whose plaques identified them as Simiel, Lofiel, and Phanuel. Opposite the foyer, two staircases spiraled upwards on either side of a large fountain and met at a balcony leading to a large door. In the fountain, two granite dolphins standing on their tails squirted streams of water from their mouths into the basin below.

A middle-aged man trotting down the stairs dressed in a uniform similar to the guards shouted, "Ahh! The famous Trio."

Elijah glanced over towards the voice and recognized him. "Uriel? Long time no see."

On arriving at the pedestal Uriel said, "It has been a while, Elijah. Araton is expecting you. Follow me."

Uriel led them up the stairs and through the doorway on the balcony that opened into a vast cathedral-like hall with stone walls and no windows. A large theater screen spanned the far wall. The screen displayed a two-dimensional color map of Earth showing every continent and all the oceans. Twelve oak wood lecterns, equally spaced, formed a circle in the position of the hours on a clock, facing the screen. Elijah presumed the lecterns must rotate so that each podium could face the center of the circle for group discussion or to face the screen.

Araton stood behind the forward center lectern, with his back to the screen and said, "Welcome," as the Trio entered the chamber. His voice echoed faintly through the vast chamber.

Elijah, Sophia, and Castiel strolled down and stood in the center of the circle formed by the lecterns. Elijah glanced around at the 12 lecterns. "What is this place?"

Araton replied, "This is where the Council of Twelve Archangels meets."

"Council of Twelve?" Elijah pawed at the stubble on his chin, thinking he needed a shave. Though he did not mind a little facial hair the whiskers were at that stage when they were starting to itch.

"They govern Elysium and the laws of the angels."

Elijah folded his arms across his chest. "Oh, so they are the ones who hand down our punishments when we break the rules."

Araton said, "Sometimes. Other times it's solely my doing where you are concerned, Elijah." He smirked. "Can't be bothering them every five minutes."

Elijah laughed.

Araton turned to face the screen. "There is also sophisticated equipment in this place that allows us to oversee all the doings of humanity." The lectern began emitting a pale blue vaporous color as he positioned his hand on its polished surface. "Let me show you."

The chandeliers suspended from the chamber's ceiling high above them dimmed. Distinctive colored dots began emerging on the screen all over the map of the earth. They appeared incredibly fast, forming large clusters in the densely populated cities.

Araton explained. "The dots you see represent souls." The map zoomed in to Australia, then to Brisbane, then to a church building, and then displayed the floor plan of the church with several white dots. "White ones represent souls who have accepted Jesus into their life." The screen zoomed out a bit to show a larger view of Brisbane. "Yellow ones represent souls who believe in God. Green ones indicate souls who have no opinion on whether God exists or doesn't – agnostics. Blue ones are souls who don't believe in anything higher than themselves – atheists. Red ones represent souls who have aligned with the underworld. Gold ones represent angels."

Castiel walked over and stood beside Araton. "Can this dot graph show us Shadows?"

"Unfortunately not." The map zoomed back out to show the whole world. "But Shadows do tend to congregate around red clusters."

Elijah was totally mesmerized by the various clusters of color. "How does the system track the souls?"

"Every soul has SNA, sometimes referred to as the light within," Araton said. The map on the screen faded into a picture of a rotating translucent blue sphere. Inside the sphere were many bright white lines, like lightning bolts, weaving around. "Similar to human DNA, SNA is unique. It is an energy that can be detected by a special device, if you could call it that, deep in Patmos."

Elijah stared wide-eyed at the image of the SNA. "How come Shadows don't have them?"

"Because they lose their SNA when they become part of the underworld." The screen faded back to the map and zoomed in on a cluster of red dots in the Kings Cross district in Sydney. "As a souls drifts away from God their SNA shrinks until they lose it completely when becoming an inhabitant of the underworld." Some red dots flickered on the map as if the signal was shorting in and out. "Some red souls are extremely difficult to follow as a result. A soul's SNA is the way a person experiences and communicates with God. Humans often experience a sense of emptiness as they stray from God as their SNA shrinks. Everyone feels their SNA, but some choose to ignore the sensation and some run from it while others turn to God and allow the Holy Spirit to energize their SNA. The larger their SNA the closer to God their soul becomes in many ways."

Castiel stuffed his hands deep into his trench coat pockets. "So why show us this?"

"Before you destroyed Cain's compound, he managed to get seven of his new creations out." Araton removed his hand from the lectern and turned around to face Elijah, Castiel, and Sophia. Congratulations on taking the facility out, by the way."

Elijah smiled. "It was nothing. All in a day's work."

Araton continued. "We have received information that Cain calls them Hadows.'"

"Hmm," Elijah said, pondering the abbreviation. "Human Shadows?"

"You're a quick study, Elijah. Because they are Shadows we cannot trace them, so we will have to rely on physical methods of discovery."

"Old-fashioned detective work?" Elijah said, puckering his lips.

"Precisely." Araton pointed over his shoulder towards the map. "With the aid of the Spiritual Realm and this map, you should be able to actively pursue them. I added the ability for you to access this map – minus the capacity to track angels – on your EVE."

"I guess you removed the angel-tracking capability so that, in the event we get captured, the Shadows will not be able to see where angels are." Elijah looked downwards and mumbled, "Of course it's not like we ever get captured."

"Right," Araton said, nodding. He chuckled. "Castiel and Elijah, I want you both to track down the seven Hadows and eliminate them."

"And me?" Sophia asked.

"Your task is a bit different. I want you to provide support for Isaac and Nya as needed. They have been through a lot and got caught in the cross-fire of a battle that was not their own." Araton paused for a moment and then made direct eye contact with Elijah, Sophia, and Castiel by turns. "As angels, we cannot forget our primary purpose, which is to change the hearts of mankind so that we will see more white and yellow on the map."

The Trio nodded.

Castiel asked, "If the map doesn't show Shadows, how does it help?"

"If you see a Hadow in the physical realm we can tag them. Because Hadows are part human physiology, they should send off a little energy reading. The reading is so tiny that unless we have a precise location to scan we will never pick the signal up. Once you sight them, EVE scans the area, then tracks the Hadow by continuing to scan within ten meters of its last known location. Your EVE is only good at tracking while the Hadow stays within 100 miles of your location. Beyond that distance the Hadow will be out of your EVE's scanning range and we'll lose them."

"Nifty," Elijah said.

"Right, you three have work to do," Araton said, then added, "Godspeed."

Chapter 30 - A Summer Day

The sun loomed high in the clear blue sky on a sultry blazing-hot summer afternoon. Isaac sat on a tired old bench in Seventh Brigade Park, Chermside, overlooking the Kidspace play area while chewing on another hot greasy chip.

Kidspace was a wonderland for youngsters. It had a Rocket Tower, Fairy Tower, slides, ramps, swings, and a large balance beam. Constructed primarily from timber the attractions drew children and their parents like a magnet from all over north Brisbane. The gleeful sounds of laughter and the sight of children just having fun, carefree without a worry in the world, filled Isaac with joy, a feeling that was harder to find with each passing day.

"Do you mind if I sit here?"

Caught a little off guard, Isaac turned in the direction of the voice. A tall lady with long raven-black hair fluttering in the wind and wearing a full-length dress with big orange and white flowers on it stood before him. Isaac locked onto her emerald-green eyes that exuded pure peacefulness and an instant sense of comfort that Isaac was at a loss to explain. "Certainly," Isaac told her, as he slid to his right to make room for her.

The lady glanced towards Kidspace. "Are your children playing over in Kidspace?"

"No." Isaac shook his head. "I don't have children. How about you?"

"No," she said, scrunching her nose, eyes glistening. "I just love coming here. Watching children play always fills me with a cool sensation of tranquility. It reminds me of my own childhood."

As she leant forward and reached for her shoe her gold cross necklace slipped out of the neckline of her dress. Isaac watched the cross swinging back and forth glistening in the sunrays as she brushed some dirt of the tip of her shoe. As she returned upright, the cross dangled between her breasts. Isaac quickly glanced away from the cross so as not be taken for a lecher.

"I'm Sophia by the way."

"And I'm Isaac." He smiled.

"Nice to meet you, Isaac," she replied accompanied with a gentle smile that could warm the coldest of hearts.

Isaac tilted the white butcher paper with the chips towards Sophia. "Care for a chip?"

"No, thank you," she said with a gentle wave of her hand. "That's very kind."

Isaac dug into the grease-soaked paper, pulled out another oily hot chip, and worked it into his mouth.

"What brings you here, Isaac?"

"I come here while I'm waiting for my fiancé."

"Oh, she lives nearby?"

"No," he said, "she is at the Holy Spirit Hospital."

The woman frowned. "Is she OK?"

Isaac could feel his countenance darken. "No, not really. She has cancer and is undergoing treatment. I'm afraid the chemotherapy has been especially hard on her."

With deep empathy in her voice, Sophia said, "I'm very sorry to hear that, Isaac."

"Me, too. Sometimes life doesn't seem fair." Isaac kicked at the dirt under the park bench. "She is such a good person and so faithful, believes in God and all that, yet she ended up so sick."

Sophia scratched at the crumbling paintwork on the park bench with her well-manicured nails. "It can be difficult to understand at times. That's for sure."

"I see you wear a cross." He turned and looked her square in the eye. "Do you mind if I ask how you can believe in God when there is so much suffering in the world?"

Sophia nodded for a moment and said nothing, then: "You see that little girl over there?" She pointed over towards Kidspace. "The one crying off to the side of the balance beam?"

Isaac turned and looked in the direction where she pointed. A child with tears rolling down her cheeks sat on the ground clutching her leg crying out for her mum. Just then the child's mother ran over to the little girl and inspected the leg the girl was clasping.

"Yes," Isaac replied.

"She is suffering, right?" Sophia swatted away a fly that had landed on her knee.

"Yes." Isaac sized up the scene. "Looks like she took a tumble off the balance beam and hurt her leg."

"Do you think the designers of Kidspace want the children who play there to hurt themselves?"

Isaac took a moment to think. "No, I can't imagine they do." He glanced at the numerous youngsters laughing, playing, and thoroughly enjoying themselves. "Most kids have a lot of fun playing in the park."

She nodded. "I see Earth the same way." Her eyes sparkled, the way a person's eyes twinkle when she is talking about something she is passionate about. "I believe God created this wonderful planet for us to enjoy." She paused. An expression of sadness came over her face as she continued. "Unfortunately, sometimes we fall over and suffer." She stared directly into Isaac's eyes. "Then we have a choice. We can continue to dwell on it and blame the One who made the Earth and us or we can call on our Parent, the way that dear little girl just did, and stand back up and enjoy our surroundings."

Isaac turned his attention back to the little girl. Her mother helped her to her feet, wiped the tears away from her eyes, and kissed her. The little girl smiled, ran to the end of the balance beam, climbed up, and began once again to walk across the narrow piece of wood with a renewed expression of determination.

"What happens to the ones who die?" Isaac took a deep breath. "They can't get back up?"

"A saying I once heard, which gives me great comfort is, 'If we live, we live for the Lord, and if we die, we die for the Lord. So, whether we live or die, we belong to the Lord.'"

Isaac chewed on another chip as he stared out into the distance thinking about what Sophia said.

A jogger was passing by the bench as Isaac said, "So you're saying that we don't live for ourselves, but for God?"

The jogger stopped and faced Isaac. "Sorry, buddy, but what did you say?"

"Sorry," Isaac said. "I was talking to my friend here."

"What friend?" The jogger raised an eyebrow and cocked his head. "Are you nuts?" He resumed jogging, shaking his head.

Isaac turned and … Sophia was gone. He lay down his chips, stood up, cupped his hands over his eyes, and scanned in all directions. She was nowhere in sight. "I wonder where she went," he mumbled as he sat back down. On the ground in the dirt below where Sophia was seated he noticed a little smiley face. He closed his eyes and smiled.

Chapter 31 - Into the Spiritual Realm

Elijah had not been in the Spiritual Realm for some time. He often wondered why he struggled to enjoy it and in fact dreaded it for the most part. After all, it allowed instantaneous travel to any event at any point in history. OK, so being able to view Shadows feeding on the Red Energy spawned by humans' harmful ways, such as sexual immorality, quarrelling, jealousy, outbursts of anger, selfish ambition, dissension, division, envy, drunkenness, wild parties, and the like, was a little disturbing. But seeing the White Energy flow from people experiencing love, joy, peace, forbearance, kindness, goodness, and faithfulness was a truly remarkable sight. The Red Energy bothered Elijah the most because it brought back ugly memories of how his parents' negative behaviors had produced Red Energy that attracted the Shadows and eventually allowed the Shadows to exert more influence in their lives. The more Red Energy a person produces the greater the number of cracks appear in the protective energy shield around their body. Once enough fractures form, Shadows are able to wrap their spawn around the person's soul.

So the Red Energy was a bit of a bummer, but the main reason Elijah was not fond of the Spiritual Realm was that true interaction with the Human Realm from within the Spiritual Realm was impossible. Thus Elijah felt more akin to a ghost than an angel. The Spiritual Realm was a space for lost souls, an intermediary place for the dead before reaching their final destination. Given their nature, Shadows romped through the domain. The Underworld provided many leaks into the Spiritual Realm that enabled Shadows to come and go. Entering the Human Realm proved much more difficult for Shadows and rightfully so. Shadows had had their chance at life and blown it. So partly out of revenge and partly as a means to survive, they stalked the Human

Realm, causing trouble so as to generate as much Red Energy as possible so they could gorge themselves.

Therefore, Elijah seldom entered the Spiritual Realm, preferring to port directly to the Human Realm and work among the humans in a physical capacity. Although the Red and White Energy are generated in the Human Realm, they are only visible in the Spiritual Realm. While in the Human Realm angels have the capacity to view into the Spiritual Realm whenever they choose. Elijah only used that skill when he sensed a strong Red Energy source that he needed to pursue. Some humans develop the ability to glimpse into the Spiritual Realm for short periods. Hence people sometimes report seeing a spirit or a ghost. What they are actually observing are Shadows, sometimes angels, and deceased human souls travelling to their destination.

Castiel gave Elijah a light tap on the shoulder. "Elijah, you with us?"

Elijah blinked hard and snapped out of the daydream. "Sorry, I was just pondering the Spiritual Realm."

"Have you been back, here, inside the Spiritual Realm, since our journey together through your life?"

"A few times, but not often." Elijah didn't want to get into details and quickly changed the subject. "Where are we anyway?"

"We're at the last known time and location reported of the seven Hadows, which is outside the basement of the Q1 tower at about the same time we destroyed Cain's compound." Castiel pointed towards a black semi-trailer backing into the loading dock." He nodded toward the truck. "It's that semi there that we're interested in."

Elijah focused on the truck and nodded.

Castiel continued. "We can't view inside Q1 through the Spiritual Realm thanks to the barriers Cain established. I have to give credit to old Cain: He certainly knows a lot about our abilities, the Spiritual Realm and such."

"Why is that?" Elijah crossed his arms over his chest. "How does he know so much?"

"Hmm. We've pondered this question before." Castiel squinted as if he was thinking it over. "Must have something to do with his Shadow friends."

"So we just wait until the semi starts to move?"

"Yes. The semi carrying the seven Hadows should be leaving momentarily."

The driver of the semi hopped into the cab and fired the engine. Moments later, the truck pulled away from the loading dock and out onto the road leading away from the Q1.

"Now we follow, Elijah." Castiel and Elijah tailed the semi, floating above the ground like ghosts.

Elijah showed off his Spiritual Realm skills by floating backwards while talking to Castiel. "Can't we just zip forward in time to wherever they are going to be next?"

Castiel shook his head. "That's the problem. We don't *know* where they are going to be."

"What about the truck driver?" Elijah spun around and floated forwards. "We would know where *he* is going to be."

Castiel raced ahead a little. "We would, but he may no longer be with the Hadows." Castiel and Elijah were competitive in most things. If an opportunity to race presented itself, they would compete.

"Wouldn't the driver hold a manifest showing where to deliver the Seven?"

"You might be right, Elijah. Good point."

"Indeed," Elijah said, with a wink.

Castiel rolled his eyes. "Let's take a look."

Elijah and Castiel, each racing to be first, floated into the cab of the semi and searched around for any type of manifesto. "Castiel, look here on this clipboard. He has a scheduled delivery at a warehouse on Link Drive, in Yatala."

"Right, then let's jump forward to around the time of delivery at the warehouse."

Elijah and Castiel appeared inside the warehouse. No signs of life were about. In the center of the sparse cinderblock warehouse sat a foldout fiberglass table with seven manila folders on it. On one wall seven 9mm pistols with holsters hung on hooks beside a metal wall rack housing several complete sets of clothes, including footwear.

"This looks like the place they came to," Elijah said, whizzing about the warehouse, "or *are* coming to, depending on how you look at it."

Castiel inspected the closed folders on the table. "It does indeed, Elijah." Each had a number, scrawled in black pen, on it from 1 to 7. "It seems by these folders the Hadows identify themselves by a number."

"What's in them, Cas'?" Elijah said, then added, "Never mind." He remembered, in the Spiritual Realm they cannot physically, pick up, or open the folders.

Elijah glanced around at the clothes. Some of the outfits consisted of dresses and skirts, including women's dress shoes. "Hey, Castiel, I thought all the Hadows were male."

"Right. As far as I know they are."

Elijah's eyebrows drew tight as he pondered the female clothes. "How far behind them are we on the timeline to their current positions?"

"About eighteen Earth hours and increasing," Castiel said as they heard the warehouse door opening. "Here they come."

And in walked the Seven.

Elijah floated back over and stood beside Castiel. "Attractive bunch."

Each Hadow marched up to the table and picked up a folder.

Castiel positioned himself behind one of them. "As they flip through the documents in those folders see if they provide any information. I'll take this one; you take the one next to me, Elijah."

"OK." Elijah floated over behind the Hadow who had picked up the folder marked "2." He hovered above so he had a clear view as the Hadow flipped through the sheets in the folder.

Elijah shook his head, frustrated at not being able to interact with objects. "I don't see anything but a bunch of names, phone numbers, and addresses."

"Same here, Elijah." Castiel retrieved his EVE from eSpace. "Looks like a list of contacts for the Hadow to become familiar with. If we cross-reference the names they may give us some insight into the Hadow's assignment. For now, I guess all we can do is get them all down on our EVEs."

Elijah retrieved his EVE from eSpace and photographed the pages as the Hadow flipped through them.

They repeated the procedure three more times, skipping back in time, inside the Spiritual Realm, to just before each Hadow picked up its folder. Castiel stood by and took broader photos as Elijah photographed the folder marked "7."

After placing their folders on the table, open to a page full of photos showing a front, back, left, and right profile view of a person, the Hadows started to undress.

"What are they doing?" Castiel said.

"Getting naked?" Elijah said, wide-eyed and wondering what was going on. "Seriously? I have no idea."

Undressed the Hadows stood motionless. Their skin began bulging in various places as their bone structure transformed. Each one began growing hair with a unique texture and color. The sexual organs of some morphed from male to female and their pubic hair, once grown, in most cases, changed to match their hair color.

Castiel looked on dazed as the Seven transformed. This was a first. He knew that angels could change appearance – in fact he had altered his own appearance, but that process took a bit of time. This was real-time morphing.

Castiel shook his head. "Elijah, take a picture of each transformed Hadow with your EVE. We'll need to determine who they are."

"We don't need to." Elijah compared the photos on the table with the Hadows. "They now appear the same as the profile photos in their corresponding folders we already recorded." Elijah floated around the Hadows, viewing them from all angles. "How are they able to morph like this?"

"They are part human and part Nanomite," Castiel said, relying on his knowledge of Cain's technology and the information Araton had shared in his brief on the project. "My guess is that Nanos can restructure their bodies in real-time. Their ordinary appearance is nothing more than a blank canvas for them to work with."

The Hadows approached the clothes rack and began dressing.

"Well, you don't see that every day," Elijah said, floating above the clothes rack.

After they finished dressing, the Hadows huddled up in a circular formation in an empty corner of the warehouse. One Hadow proceeded to chant words in a strange dialect that neither Elijah nor Castiel understood.

Castiel said, "Record this, Elijah." Elijah hovered above the circle and recorded the scene on his EVE.

"What are they doing, Cas'?"

"I'm not sure," Castiel said, and just then a shimmering black oval portal opened in the center of the circle. One after the other, the Hadows stepped through the portal.

"They can create portals, Cas'?"

Castiel floated over and circled the portal. "Well, they are Shadows. But I've never seen them port human flesh, or physical objects, through them. It's certainly going to make finding them very, *very* difficult."

"Can't say Araton didn't warn us when he said it's likely going to take some good old-fashioned detective work." Elijah hovered above the portal with his hands clasped behind his neck. "We'll need to go review the information we've collected and the personas they took on and try to piece together where they may be headed and why."

The portal vanished.

"I agree, Elijah," Castiel replied, nodding. "We might even need Frank's assistance on this one."

Chapter 32 - Plots

After a short Ancar ride from a Transport Point, Elijah and Castiel entered the Jabin Building in Elysium. Glancing around Elijah asked, "What is this place, Castiel?"

"I guess you could say that Jabin is where angel detectives work to analyze data. The main function is planning assignments based on review of the information we angels collect. So that data we collected with our EVEs is being processed here."

Several groups of angels were working away in teams of four, two male and two female, sat on smooth black swivel stools around square black metal tables. The tabletop itself was a display screen from corner to corner, which allowed the angels to simultaneously access, manipulate, and review information. The various teams appeared to be collaborating, sharing data and analysis with each other. On the edge of each table's display was a bank of thumbnail images showing what the other tables were reviewing. Clicking a thumbnail enabled a team to work with the other angels' information, extending the collaborative effort. The teams appeared to be working together as one giant think-tank.

A large oak wood conference table surrounded by 18 chairs – eight to a side and one on each end – occupied the far center of the room. Araton sat by his lonesome at one end of the table. That table top, too, was a screen that displayed all sorts of information, from videos, to maps, to folders, to photographs. Araton appeared to be reviewing various sets of data before noticing Elijah and Castiel. "Come, fellows, take a seat."

Elijah approached the chair to Araton's left. The chair silently slid out by itself, allowing him to walk in front, and then slid inwards allowing Elijah to sit. "Nice! Invisible butlers."

Castiel chuckled and took a seat across the table from Elijah.

Araton moved his hands over the table's surface, manipulating folders and files on the display. After a few moments, seven holographic images projected above the table forming three-dimensional constructs of seven individuals. "These are the identities the seven Hadows changed into."

The holographic displays of the Hadows slowly rotated providing a 360-degree view. As they turned, they moved like miniature versions of themselves standing on the table, wearing the clothes they had changed into at the warehouse. One was even smoking a cigarette and another was applying lipstick. Each Hadow continued to exhibit regular actions that formed part of its unique assigned personality.

Araton said, "We determined that six are unique creations that do not match the appearance any person living or deceased."

"Any idea why?" Elijah asked. He squinted as he studied the rotating holographic images.

"Yes." Araton manipulated the display surface, turning off three of the holograms." These four were placed into government roles, each in a different country – one in the UK, one in the USA, one in Australia, and one, oddly enough, in New Zealand."

Castiel retrieved his EVE from eSpace and began taking notes. "Why those countries?"

"Well, one possibility the think tank here came up with is that Cain's largest establishments are in those countries."

Puzzled, Elijah said, "How can the Hadows just be placed?"

"Well, in government there are already quite a few Shumans and many Shadow-inflicted people. They use their influence to introduce the Hadows." The surface of the table in front of Elijah and Castiel displayed four sets of names, each with a profile image, arranged beneath the corresponding Hadow. "The names in the folders you provided us with show how the different Shadow-inflicted people are connected."

Elijah cocked his head at Araton. "What do you mean Shumans are already in government?" He fidgeted on his chair at the thought. "Can't you stop them?"

"In democratic countries, it is the people who ultimately maintain the right to vote for those who lead them. We let the people be the judges. Comes back to free will."

As Elijah read the names associated with the Hadows, his eyebrows raised as he recognized some of them from when he was a human. "I know some of these people." He pointed to one, then another. "They're in the Australian government."

Araton nodded. "Indeed, they are."

Castiel synchronized the surface display with his EVE, transferring the groups of names to a file on his EVE. "What about the histories of the Hadows: Will it not be strange they have none?"

"Ahh, good question." Araton clasped his hands. "This is the interesting part. The Hadows were all placed in situations where they are the only child, no brothers or sisters, and don't have any children themselves." He opened up a few extra files, and additional holograms appeared next to two of the Hadows. "Their parents," Araton pointed to the new holograms, "if still living are either Shumans or strongly

Shadow-influenced. The host of the Shadow is made to believe the Hadow is their son or daughter."

Castiel interrupted. "Pretty elaborate scheme."

Araton continued. "History-wise, most of the information for a person comes from digital records, which in these situations was forged to give them an academic pedigree, news reports, Internet records, and employment histories that support the roles they are now in."

Elijah rubbed his forehead. The heady information was causing his muscles to tense up. "What sorts of roles?"

"Elected members of parliament, senators, council men, that sort of thing. It's possible they may even become prime minister or president."

"It sounds prophetic." Castiel paused before continuing. "Like Daniel's vision in the Bible regarding the Four Beasts."

Elijah nodded, massaging his aching neck, and glanced towards Castiel then to Araton and mumbled, "Can't we just take them out?"

"Wish it were that easy," Araton said. "But, see, in just the past 24 hours they have already obtained high profiles and lofty posts. The Angel Council thinks observing them is best for now." Araton tapped a few icons on the corner of the display surface and a glass of clear sparkling water appeared. He took a sip. "The information we gather from surveillance may give us a better idea as to Cain's and the Underworld's greater plans."

"I guess an advantage we currently have is that they don't know that we know who the Hadows are," Elijah said.

Castiel said, "And what about the other three Hadows?"

"Well, two were placed in large corporations – one in the oil industry, the other in the software industry."

Elijah played with the icons on the surface display in front of him. A glass of milk appeared. He shrugged. Not quite what he was after.

Castiel must have sensed that Elijah's mind was wandering because he gave him a funny look and kicked him in the shin under the table. Elijah jolted and smiled as he returned his attention to the discussion. Elijah had always struggled with meetings because his attention span was rather short. He was the hands-on type and preferred leaving the details to Castiel.

"And the seventh Hadow?" Castiel said.

Araton made a few gestures across the surface of the table. All of the holograms on the table vanished leaving just one. "Well. The final Hadow, which we know about, appears to have taken on the identity of Leigh Mansfield, Frank Mercer's partner in the AFP."

Elijah's applied his full attention to the hologram of Leigh Mansfield: slim body, brown eyes, black hair with a side part, about 5'8" tall, in his mid-thirties, wearing the usual AFP black suit. "Wait a second. What about the current Leigh – was he eliminated?"

"No," Araton said, "oddly not. I guess killing Leigh wouldn't serve their purpose. When someone dies we know about the death right away and investigate." Araton updated the surface display to show a live video of Leigh and Frank. "As you can see Leigh and Frank are busily working away at the AFP headquarters."

"So what is the Hadow up to? Is it—"

Castiel interrupted, eyes wide. "Isaac? He's probably after Isaac."

Araton nodded. "I agree. We came to the same conclusion. Our video sensors cannot view inside his house, but we are presuming the interference is due to a perimeter setup by Sophia to keep Shadows out. That said, I think it's best if you two go and check it out."

With a puzzled expression Elijah said, "Wait, why would he be after Isaac?"

"Well, a few of the angel teams here came up with a theory." Araton shutdown the hologram. "They suggested that when you destroyed the compound you may have also destroyed Cain's copy of Nya's software. Cain is going to want to get his hands on another copy if he is going to create more Hadows."

"Wouldn't Cain have backed the software up?"

Araton took another mouthful of water. "That is why it's a suggestion. We would presume that he would have redundancy, but maybe he never got the opportunity, or just believed his copy was perfectly safe in his 'fail-safe' compound."

Castiel stood up. "Right then, we better be off."

Chapter 33 - Leigh

"Coming," Isaac said as he rushed across the lounge to see who was knocking – more like pounding – on the front door.

The man flashed his badge at Isaac who was standing in the half-open doorway. "Detective Sergeant Leigh from the AFP."

"Yes, of course, I remember," he said, glancing at the man's ID, going through the motions somewhat distracted. "You were with Sergeant Mercer – Frank – when you found me in the bush."

"That's right." Leigh slipped his credentials into the interior pocket of his suit jacket. "May I come in?"

"Sorry." Isaac swung the door open. "Of course. I'm making a coffee. Would you care for one?"

"That would be great, thank you."

Isaac led Leigh into the lounge and motioned towards the couch. "Take a seat." He went to the kitchen and pulled another mug from the cupboard. "How do you have your coffee, Sergeant?"

"White with one, thanks. And 'Leigh' works fine…. Nice place you have here, Isaac."

"Thanks. So what brings you by, Leigh?" Isaac poured the boiling water into the two mugs and inhaled deeply to draw in the pleasing aroma of the melting instant coffee. "Just checking up?"

"Yes." Leigh swiped his tongue over his dry lips. "You could say that."

"Or I could say… something else?"

"Well," Leigh said, looking down at the floor.

"Where's Frank?" Isaac added milk and sugar to Leigh's coffee.

"He is stuck doing paperwork, office detail. He sent me to see if I could obtain any additional evidence in regards to the Cain affair."

"Ah, I see." Isaac carried the coffees to the lounge and set them on coasters on the coffee table. He sat down on the opposite end of the couch. "Not sure how I can help, but I'll do my best."

Leigh scratched the side of his nose and gazed around as if searching for something. "Well, actually, we were wondering if Nya's Ultrabook is here?"

Isaac thought for a moment. "Yes, it is probably in the bedroom." Isaac's eyes narrowed. "Do you mind if I ask *why?*" Of course he wanted to help, but Isaac was a private person and had never been keen on how the police occasionally invaded people's privacy. He knew Nya considered her Ultrabook a highly personal asset.

"We would like to take it in and examine it for evidence." Leigh took a sip from his mug. "She'll get it back, of course, once we're finished."

"I don't see it as a problem, but of course you'll have to ask Nya."

Leigh set the mug down on the coaster. "Is she here?"

"No," Isaac said, shaking his head. "She is in Brisbane shopping for a wedding dress."

"For herself?"

"Well, certainly not for me," Isaac said, smiling.

"I suppose not," Leigh responded with his own smile.

"Yes, for her. We are getting married."

"Well, congratulations are certainly in order then."

"Thank you."

"Would you mind calling her and asking if it would be OK?" Leigh weaved his fingers together, stretched his arms out, and bent his hands backwards cracking his knuckles. "It's rather important and time is of the essence."

"Sure." Isaac pulled his mobile phone from his pocket and dialed Nya. The call went straight to voicemail. "She must have it turned off. She will call me back when she notices the missed call."

"I see." Leigh leant back into the couch. "How is she doing with the cancer treatment?"

"It's a struggle, but I think she is improving." Isaac picked up his coffee, steam still rising, and took a cautious sip. The bitter dark liquid burned his tongue. *A struggle,* he thought, staring into the swirling hot coffee.

"Is she working?"

"No." Isaac blew gently across the surface of the coffee. "She is putting all her effort into her recovery and the wedding."

"I see." Leigh crossed his arms over his chest.

Several moments passed in silence before Leigh said, "Any idea how long it might be until Nya returns your call or gets home?"

"It's hard to say." Isaac glanced up at the clock on the wall. "She is due back in a couple of hours. But she will likely return my call before then *if* she checks her phone."

"I see. Do you mind if I use the bathroom, Isaac?"

245

"No, go ahead. It's down the hall, second door on the left."

* * *

Leigh walked briskly down the hallway, entered the bathroom, and slid the silver sliding bolt to lock the door. He pulled his 9mm side arm out of the shoulder holster, clicked the safety off, released the ammunition clip, checked it, slammed it back into place, and put the pistol back in the holster – without snapping the cuff. After a minute, he flushed the toilet, returned to the lounge, and took his seat on the couch.

"To save time, Isaac," Leigh said, staring directly at him. "How about you just give me the Ultrabook and you can sort it out with Nya later?"

"I can't do that." Isaac shook his head. "It wouldn't be right."

"I see." Leigh slipped his hand inside his jacket and gripped the butt of his 9mm. "That's very unfortunate."

"What's that supposed to m—?" Just then a loud incessant thumping came from the front door, interrupting Isaac mid-sentence.

Leigh withdrew his hand from his jacket.

"I'll go see who it is. It can't be Nya. She has her own key." Isaac dashed to the front door. Leigh withdrew his 9mm, placed it behind his back, and followed Isaac.

"Hang on a second," Isaac shouted, as he opened the door a crack. Isaac took a step back as though he had seen a ghost. "Sophia?"

She barged forward, wedging Isaac between the door and the wall and drew two long other worldly-looking swords.

Leigh, pistol at the ready, aimed his 9mm at Sophia and fired.

Isaac stood frozen, pinned between the open door and the wall as the bullets hissed through the air towards Sophia.

Chapter 34 - The Chase

Golden sparks flew into the air coinciding with a loud twang as Sophia deflected the spray of bullets from Leigh's 9mm with her Sister of Light blades. The swords moved so fast they were but a blur to Isaac. His eyes simply couldn't process the rapid movements.

Leigh continued tapping the trigger, sending bullet after bullet hurtling towards Sophia until only a clicking echoed through the air: the magazine was empty. He cursed, tossed the gun aside, and stormed towards Sophia with a dark scowl on his face.

Sophia lifted her right Sister of Light over her shoulder and held the other across her waist. The instant Leigh came into range, she swung towards his left side. Before the blade hit flesh, though, Leigh's incredible reflexes shifted and he caught her wrist in his right hand. Sophia reacted by drawing back her other Sister and thrusting the blade full-bore towards his abdomen. Once again, though, quick as a cat, Leigh intercepted her wrist with his other hand. Sophia struggled to free herself from Leigh's grip. Sophia was no match for his strength. Her forte lay in her speed and dexterity not in her brawn. With a rapid motion, she kicked him in the side. He jolted slightly at the impact of each strike.

With a smug grin, he taunted her: "Is that all you got?"

In a classic Judo move, Leigh pulled both her wrists up towards his shoulder, rotated, placing her at his back, then lunged forward throwing Sophia over his shoulder onto the floor with lethal force. Sophia's back slammed into the ground, hard, so hard that she dropped both Sisters.

Seeing Sophia in trouble, Isaac scurried up behind Leigh and double-thumped him as hard as he could in the kidneys. Leigh spun around so fast Isaac didn't even see him move. With little effort, Leigh shoved Isaac as if he was a balloon. Isaac stumbled backwards through the front door and into the yard and tripped over his own feet. He fell flat on his back and knocked his head on the concrete walkway.

Leigh turned his attention back to Sophia. She scrambled towards her Sisters, only to be interrupted by Leigh's foot that connected with the underside of her belly and sent her flying through the air and into the far wall. There she lay, dazed, as Leigh approached. Before she gathered her bearings, Leigh reached down and grabbed her with both hands and flung her across the kitchen bench. She slid from one end to the other knocking off a knifeblock full of knives, salt and pepper shakers, a bottle of tomato sauce, and a large mug waiting to be washed. She dropped off the far end of the bench and fell onto the kitchen tiles with a thud.

Sophia scanned the floor for something to use as a weapon: Nothing. Leigh strode over to where she lay, grabbed her by the neck, lifted her up against the white fibro wall, and tightened his grip. He whispered, "Enough games." Her eyes bulged. Her face turned red. She struggled to breathe. She thrashed with all her might, but to no avail. Leigh was simply too powerful.

Just as her vision started to cloud, to her surprise, Leigh released his grip and let her drop dead-weight onto the floor. Glancing upwards, she saw Isaac standing behind Leigh with his hand on the hilt of a kitchen knife protruding from Leigh's side. Isaac let go the knife before staggering backwards a few steps. Leigh turned to confront Isaac. Emotionless, Leigh withdrew the knife in a slow methodical manner. With each beat of his heart, blood spurted like a fountain from the wound. He stared at Isaac with deadly contempt and then turned his attention to his geyser-like wound. Leigh roared in anger and started to shake violently. Isaac, jaw wide open, watched in a state of disbelief as Leigh's skin bulged and contorted. His features morphed into a well-built bald man … and his injury healed. Once the transformation was complete he landed a hard looping blow to Isaac's right cheek. Isaac toppled like a boxer receiving the knock-out blow.

The Hadow glared towards Sophia and, seeing her open-eyed but incapacitated, raced into the bedroom, grabbed the Ultrabook, and ran out the front door.

Defeated and disappointed, Sophia rested to regain her strength.

Moments later Castiel and Elijah entered through the front door. Elijah spotted Sophia and sprinted straight to her. "Are you all right?"

"I'll be fine," she mumbled in a despondent tone.

Castiel lifted Isaac from the floor and laid him on the couch.

"What happened?" Elijah asked.

Sophia rose to her feet with Elijah's help. "I had a small disagreement with what I presume is a working human shadow."

"That would be a *Hadow*," Elijah said. "What about Isaac?"

"He was extremely brave. You should have seen him, Elijah." Her eyes glowed with admiration. "You would have been proud."

Castiel paced around the room. "Let me guess. The Hadow made off with Nya's Ultrabook?"

"Yes. I'm sorry," Sophia said, her head bowed. "I tried to stop him."

Elijah patted Sophia on the shoulder. "No doubt."

"Can you clean up here, Sophia?" Castiel glanced around. "We should pursue the Hadow before he gets too far."

"Yes, go. I'll heal Isaac's wounds the Hadow inflicted and clean up the house. When I'm finished Isaac will simply wake up on the couch believing he just fell asleep watching TV."

"Shame you have to wipe the event from his memory." Elijah walked over to Isaac. A nasty shiner had begun to appear on the right side of Isaac's face. "Sounds like he really rose to the occasion."

"We'll know his courage," Sophia responded.

Elijah peered into the Spiritual Realm. White Energy flowed all around Isaac's house. Like ocean waves, the energy gushed through the hallways, into the lounge, and all around the kitchen. "Wow, there is a lot of White Energy here. With Nya's illness and current events, I would have expected to see some red."

"Love, Elijah!" Castiel said. "The love Isaac and Nya have for each other. It conquers all Red Energy even amongst all the trials of the hardest times. Jesus made that clear when he said *You must love the Lord your God with all your heart, all your soul, and all your mind. This is the first and greatest commandment. A second is equally important: Love your neighbor as yourself.*"

Elijah watched in awe at how the White Energy flowed so freely in and out of the open spaces. "If only everyone followed those basic commandments there would be no Red Energy. The Shadows would find no place on earth and be banished to the Underworld."

"Indeed," Castiel said.

"You sure you'll be OK, Sophia," Elijah asked.

"I'm sure. Now go on! Go and stop that Hadow."

With that, Elijah and Castiel raced out the front door.

"How do we find him, Castiel?"

"He'll be headed for Cain, probably to the Q1."

"Wouldn't he have just ported there already?"

"Well, *he* could have but he couldn't take the Ultrabook with him through a portal. The electromagnetic fields in a portal would wipe the drive of all that precious data he fought so hard to get." Castiel noticed a fresh set of dark skid marks on the street and pointed towards them. "My guess is he has taken a car."

"Well it's about a two-hour drive from here to the Q1. That'll give us some time to prepare for him if we port."

"Let me call Frank first. We may need his backup."

Castiel retrieved his EVE from eSpace and placed a call to Frank. He informed the officer that something was going down in Cain's office and advised him to assemble a SWAT team to assist. Frank agreed without hesitation, for over the years they had built up a lot of trust.

"Right, Elijah, Frank organized," Castiel said. "It will take him about two hours to assemble the SWAT team. He should arrive around the same time as the Hadow, or shortly after."

"So, Castiel, how are we going to stop the Hadow?" Elijah glanced back towards Isaac's house. "If Sophia couldn't take him out, well, to be honest I'm a little bit worried."

"Well there are two of us. Let's hope that will be enough. Keep in mind that our main objective is the software on the Ultrabook. Destroy it if we have to."

Elijah nodded as he opened a portal with the destination set to the Q1.

* * *

After he was convinced that nobody was following, the Hadow pulled the sedan off to the side of the Bruce Highway and opened the Ultrabook. The picture login screen, which happened to be a photo of Isaac, prompted him to authenticate by touching different parts of the image in a particular order while, in some instances, drawing various shapes, like lines and circles, around various parts of the photograph. The number of possibilities was endless. One option allowed him to switch to a password entry mode. But considering that Nya was an expert cryptologist, he realized that trying to guess her password, which was most likely more than 20 random characters long, would be pointless. He forced a hard operating system shutdown and then attempted to access the hard drive through a back door only to find it had been bit-locked, meaning it, too, was encrypted using a password. He resumed driving, but not until he sent an SMS to Cain: *"Nya took precautions, the hard drive is encrypted, wireless transfer not possible."*

Chapter 35 - Q1

Elijah surveyed the road approaching the Q1 basement. "What if we're wrong, Castiel, and the Hadow isn't headed here or, worse, transfers the software to Cain?"

"It wouldn't be good," Castiel said. "But Nya encrypted the hard drive and password-protected the computer with a secure login. It will take some pretty sophisticated resources to breach that. Of course, Cain has the technology to do so, but he would need to have the computer physically present to hack into it. Since the compound is gone, this is the most logical choice."

Elijah nodded and then turned his head slowly towards Castiel. "How do you know about the encryption and password protection on the Ultrabook?"

"In her assignment update Sophia reported that Isaac complained when he tried to access Nya's Ultrabook to play Minesweeper and couldn't. Nya told him she added the security measures to keep the data safe and thought it best that not even he know the password. Isaac understood."

"How did I miss that bit from the assignment update?" Elijah shielded his eyes from the midday sun and squinted towards the top of the Q1.

Castiel patted him on the back. "Maybe you were not paying attention."

"All right," Elijah said, smirking, "fair point." He appreciated the humor but at the same time knew he had to work on his attention skills.

Castiel retrieved his EVE from eSpace.

"What are you doing, Castiel?"

"Placing an order for something I think we are likely to need."

"A large pizza pie and couple of soft drinks?"

"What?"

"Just a bad joke from my days on Earth. I'll get serious now."

"Right." After a few moments of operating his EVE Castiel continued. "Right all done. Let's go check out the basement."

They headed through the open loading dock. Nobody was around, and the basement was sparse with only a half dozen cars, one parked in the building manager's designated place and the others in the maintenance crew spaces. Several empty parking spaces were marked *"Reserved."* Towards the center of the basement was a rectangular brick structure that housed the elevators. Dim lighting filtered through the darkness from overhead fluorescent tubes spaced evenly across the ceiling. A sign on the western wall above a sturdy closed wood door glowed red: *"PRIVATE."* The door had no handle, only a keyhole. Elijah and Castiel scoured the environment for potential ambush positions. Elijah said, "I can't see any particular advantage spots. He may not even come through the basement."

"Oh, I think he will. I doubt he would want to walk past reception, and from this level he can call the private elevator." Their inspection of the basement complete, Castiel said, "I think we will be best off watching from outside and follow him in when he gets here."

Elijah agreed. They returned to survey the basement entrance from across the street.

* * *

Nya arrived home to Isaac's house 30 minutes earlier than expected. She cut her shopping trip a bit short and rushed home after Isaac did not answer his mobile on several occasions when she tried to return his call. She unlocked the door and ventured in to find Isaac asleep on the couch, remote control in hand, and the plasma TV blaring in the background. Nya presumed he had fallen asleep watching TV. She headed for the bedroom. After putting away her new clothes – a pair of shoes, slacks, and a top – in the closet, she returned to the lounge and turned off the TV. She knelt down and gave him a light tender kiss on the cheek.

She made a coffee and took it to the bedroom and set it on the bedside table. "Hmm," she murmured as she searched around for her Ultrabook in all the usual bedroom locations – under the bed and on the dresser. Then she headed back to the lounge and explored the typical places there. Several minutes of fruitless searching passed before she considered the possibility that she had left it at the hospital during her last procedure. She would sometimes work on software, browse the Web, or read a novel on her Ultrabook while sitting in the waiting room. She called the oncology section of the hospital on her mobile. A recorded voice thanked her for calling and explained the operating hours. They were closed. *Well, I'll phone them in the morning,* she thought. *I can live without it tonight.*

* * *

"There he is, Elijah," Castiel said, pointing to a late model indigo Audi pulling into the basement of the Q1. Together they hurried across the street.

The Hadow parked in one of the reserved spaces and stepped out, Ultrabook in hand, and began heading toward the elevators. Hearing footsteps, he glanced over his shoulder and saw Elijah and Castiel approaching. He smiled and whispered, "This ought to be fun." He placed the Ultrabook on the driver's seat and turned to face his rivals.

Elijah drew Gunthor from his sheath while Castiel readied his Judgement Twins and aimed them directly at the Hadow. In a stern tone Castiel said, "We only want the Ultrabook."

Apparently unfazed, the Hadow replied, "Come and get it."

"Cas'," Elijah said, giving Castiel a nudge with his elbow, "you can't open fire here. The noise will draw too much attention."

"I know, right. I thought he might be courteous and hand over the Ultrabook." Castiel holstered his Judgement Twins. Elijah, with Gunthor held out to his side at waist level, approached the Hadow head-on while Castiel made a wider birth.

Elijah charged. The Hadow grasped the Audi's door and, with a mighty roar, tore it off the hinges and hurled the hefty door towards Castiel. Castiel sidestepped, but the door was faster and slammed him in the chest. The intensity of the impact propelled him backwards where he collided brutally with concrete wall. The Hadow said, "One down, one to go."

Full-force Elijah swung Gunthor towards the Hadow. The Hadow leapt to his side, somersaulted over Elijah, and landed behind him. Elijah spun around and was greeted by a stiff punch to his gut. Elijah staggered backwards, gasping for air. With a swift kick, the Hadow knocked Gunthor out of Elijah's hand.

"Wait," Elijah said, fighting for breath. "Can't we be friends?"

The Hadow growled like a wild beast as he leapt into a double sidekick that connected with Elijah's rib cage and sent him plummeting into a nearby-parked sedan. Glass shattered, an alarm sounded, and metal crumpled as Elijah left his imprint in the side of the vehicle. And then he collapsed. So much for not wanting to be seen or draw attention.

The Hadow seized the Ultrabook and headed to the elevators. A moment later the elevator arrived with a muted ding. Before Elijah could get back on his feet he watched helpless as the Hadow got in the elevator and used his pass card, no doubt heading up to Cain's office.

Just before the door closed the Hadow smiled at Elijah and waved. "See ya."

Elijah dusted off shards of shattered glass, struggled to his feet, and stumbled over to Castiel. "You all right, Cas'?"

"I will be shortly. Maybe that pizza would have been a better idea." Castiel winced as he pushed the car door off himself. "If the stakes weren't so high." He groaned. "I'll be just fine as soon as I finish healing."

"That Hadow packs a punch." Elijah pulled up his shirt, inspected where the Hadow had punched him, and watched the purplish bruise slowly vanish.

"Indeed," Castiel replied as he stood up.

The car alarm, designed to ward off a potential thief, ceased blaring away after hitting the four-minute limit.

Now on his feet but still a little shaky Castiel straightened his trench coat. "Good to see lots of people came running to see if someone was stealing the car."

Elijah laughed. "It's the Gold Coast. People probably ran the other way."

A small portal, half the size of a typical one, appeared near Castiel. Elijah, startled, leapt back a few steps. "What the—?"

"Don't be alarmed, Elijah, it's only my goods coming through."

Castiel retrieved his EVE, pulled up the order he had placed, and accepted the prompt asking if the delivery was satisfactory. Seconds later, a medium-sized rectangular cardboard carton passed out of the portal before closing.

"The pizza? Thank heavens," Elijah said, rubbing his hands together and licking his lips. "Took them long enough."

"You wish," Castiel said with a smirk. He opened the carton, retrieved a set of Ares's, and handed them to Elijah. "Here you go. You wanted these to try out, now is your chance." Elijah gleefully accepted and secured them to his wings while Castiel did the same with a pair of his own.

Elijah said, "So we are not taking the elevator then?"

"No. We are going express."

Castiel and Elijah raced over to the elevator. Once at the lift, they pulled the elevator doors open. "You ready, Elijah?"

"Oh, yeah."

"On three: One, Two—"

A voice echoed from the distance, "Don't forget about me!"

"Oops." Elijah concentrated. Over on the other side of the basement Gunthor started to flutter before raising from the floor. Gunthor careered through the air up above the cars and into Elijah's waiting hand. He sheathed Gunthor. "Sorry about that Gunth'."

Gunthor grunted.

Castiel started again. "On three: One, Two, *Three*."

Together they leapt into the elevator shaft and activated their Ares's. Restricted by the narrow space, they spread their wings just enough to provide steering as the thrust from the Ares's propelled them. "Woo-hooo!" Elijah shouted as he soared upward.

An elevator was descending the shaft. They veered into the lift's counter weight space, passed the elevator, and then swerved back into the main shaft. As Cain's floor approached Elijah adjusted his bearing to head right through the doors leading onto the floor. At speed, using his physics ability, he passed through the doors as if they were made of water. On the other side, he disabled his Ares's, a little later than he ought to have, and crashed into the ceiling of Cain's office. Castiel followed close behind making the same mistake. They both fell to the floor. Slightly dazed, they scrambled to their feet and heard a vaguely familiar voice.

"Ahh, nice of you two to join us."

They turned to see Seth, the Hadow, and Cain standing in the office like some sinister greeting committee. Nya's Ultrabook lay on Cain's desk connected by a cable to his desktop computer.

Cain turned to the Hadow and said, "Finish them."

Castiel drew his Judgement Twins, one in each hand, aimed them at the Hadow and, wasted no time in pulling the triggers.

A single Angel Bullet glanced the side of the Hadow's arm as he sidestepped out of the line of fire. The Hadow made a small arc and raced towards Castiel. Castiel aimed slightly ahead of the Hadow with his Twins in a hope his Angel Bullets would collect him. The Hadow moved fast, leapt onto the windowed wall, defying gravity as he bounded around the room. Glass shattered behind him as the trailing Angel Bullets ruptured the windows. Within striking distance, the Hadow lunged and punched Castiel on the forehead. Castiel's world went black.

"Oh crap," Elijah muttered as the Hadow turned his attention towards him. Elijah drew Gunthor.

Gunthor said, "Didn't we try this last time?"

Elijah squeezed Gunthor's hilt tightly. "Shhhhh."

Before Elijah could even swing, the Hadow knocked Gunthor from his hand with a fast right kick. The Hadow grabbed Elijah by the throat and raised him off the ground so that his feet were dangled and his arms flailing. He struggled to get out the words, "Are you *sure* we can't be friends?"

The Hadow tightened his grip. Elijah's throat made gurgling noises as his windpipe labored to get air. And just as he felt the world begin to fade to black a loud cracking noise echoed through the room. As his eyes were closing, the thought came: *Gunshot.* Then, gunshot after gunshot, in quick succession, resonated through the office. With each sound, the pressure of the Hadow's grip grew weaker.

Elijah heard a shout, "Now's your chance, Elijah!" Given the opportunity, Elijah willed Gunthor to his hand. Without hesitation Gunthor soared to his waiting palm. With quick forward momentum, Elijah plunged Gunthor through the Hadow's ribs and into his heart. The Hadow let out a guttural moan that morphed into a piercing scream. He released Elijah and staggered backwards as torrents of black smoke erupted from his nose, eyes, and ears. Elijah, still holding the hilt of Gunthor, placed a foot on the Hadow's stomach and pushed, and the Hadow, like a string puppet with severed cords, collapsed.

Elijah glanced towards Seth who was still holding his pistol pointed in his direction.

The elevator chimed.

Cain, with blazing fury in his eyes, yelled, "Seth, what did you do?!"

Seth cut his eyes around at Cain and tossed his 9mm towards him. "Catch."

Cain caught the butt and aimed the gun towards Elijah. He gritted his teeth and grimaced as he squeezed the trigger with his shaky hand. Nothing but a clicking noise sounded.

The elevator doors opened. Two men stormed in dressed in SWAT gear and trained their assault rifles on Cain. Towards the back of the elevator, wearing a flak jacket and pointing his Glock 22, stood Frank Mercer.

One of the SWAT members shouted, "Drop your weapon and get on your knees! Now!"

Cain looked down. Several red laser dots danced on his chest. He released his grip on the 9mm and let it fall to the floor. He gazed around. Elijah traced his line of sight through the window and saw other SWAT team members dangling on rappel ropes with their assault rifles trained on Cain. Game over.

"Get on your knees!" the SWAT team member said again, his boomy voice echoing through the room.

Cain pleaded as he knelt, "Wait, I assure you it's not what it looks like."

"What it looks like," Frank said as he entered the office, "is one dead man full of bullets and you holding a gun."

Cain replied. "No, the angels: *They* shot him." Cain pointed towards Elijah, then Seth. "They're here now, honest. I have glasses in my office desk I can show you."

"I'm sure you can, Cain. I'm sure you can." Frank moved around behind Cain and cuffed his hands behind his back. "You can tell us all about your hallucinations down at the station after you do your perp walk." Frank jerked Cain forcefully to his feet. "For now you're under arrest for murder. You are not obliged to say or do anything unless you wish to do—."

"It wasn't me," Cain interrupted. "I didn't do it."

Frank yanked Cain's wrists up high behind his back, causing his shoulders to roll, as he pushed him towards the elevator. "But whatever you say or do may be used in evidence. Do you understand?"

"Whatever," Cain responded.

The two SWAT members followed close behind Frank. One of them asked Frank, "Shall I secure the room?"

Frank shook his head. "I'll have crime scene investigations and the coroner take care of that. In the meantime, get reception to lock out this floor."

The SWAT member nodded.

As the elevator doors began to close, Cain, glaring at Elijah, yelled, "This is not the end! It's only just—."

"The beginning," Frank completed his sentence, as Cain broke into hysterical laughing.

Elijah watched as the SWAT team members outside of the window used their rappelling gear to ascend toward the roof. Then he turned his attention towards Castiel who was starting to come to.

Castiel mumbled, "What did I miss?"

"I'll fill you in later."

Elijah turned to Seth. "So you're an angel?"

"Yes. Undercover – well, I was undercover until now." He smiled. "Not much chance of Cain letting me back into his organization after this."

"I don't guess," Elijah said. "Sorry your cover got blown."

"I'm not," he said with a shrug. "It's been a long decade. We could have done with more information on Cain's ultimate plans. He'll only be out of the way for a short time until his lawyers and mates get him off this murder charge."

Castiel walked over to Cain's desk, disconnected Nya's Ultrabook, and placed it under his arm.

Elijah looked at the Hadow laying on the floor. "Is it dead?"

Seth squinted. "It's never been actually alive. But, yes, you could say that. Unless another Shadow enters the body, it is as good as a corpse. For a Shadow to re-enter, Cain would require the software, and from the looks of things you have prevented that for now. The coroner will have the unclaimed corpse cremated after autopsy."

Elijah gave the corpse a gentle nudge with his foot to reassure himself that no life remained. "Will the autopsy show anything?"

Steve Goodwin

"Only the bullets that came from the gun Cain was left holding. The inactive Nanomites will not show on the coroner's technology." Seth leant down over the Hadow. "I'll fix the damage Gunthor did."

Castiel said, "Elijah, can you check to see how much Cain transferred from Nya's Ultrabook?"

Elijah sat down at Cain's desk and ran some diagnostics on the desktop computer, then said, "It's hard to say. It appears as if he was still trying to decrypt the hard drive."

Castiel handed the Ultrabook to Elijah. "I'll entrust you to get this back to Nya."

"Shouldn't we destroy it, Castiel?"

"Only if it's in unsafe hands. Seems safe enough for now."

"But won't Cain just go after the Ultrabook again?"

"It is possible, but we cannot simply destroy Nya's work without a direct threat or imminent danger. That would be up to her."

Elijah turned to Seth. "So where do you go now?"

"Home to Elysium for some much-needed rest." Seth extended his arm towards Elijah.

Elijah took his hand and shook it with a tip of his head. "We should catch up in Elysium, share some stories."

"I would like that, Elijah. You take care."

"Will do."

Seth opened a portal.

Castiel said, "Hold the portal for me, Seth. Elijah, I'll see you back in Elysium after you return the Ultrabook. Let Nya know Cain may be after her software again someday – perhaps sooner than later."

Seth and Castiel entered the portal.

Elijah strode over to one of the shattered windows and gave the glass a boot to knock the fragments free. He extended his wings and leapt out of the Q1. With occasional afterburner speed boosts from the Ares's he flew to Isaac's house.

Chapter 36 - Graveyard

Nya pulled a blooming dandelion, roots and all, out of the compacted acidic soil surrounding the gravesite, adding the captured intruder to the assortment of weeds in her hand. Two weather-beaten marble headstones sat side by side at the head of the graves Nya was weeding between.

"Do you come here often?"

Recognizing the voice, Nya dropped the weeds, wiped the dirt from her hands on her jeans, and managed somehow – as weak as she was from her treatments – to spring to her feet. Eyes gleaming she spun around and wrapped her arms around Elijah. "Where have you been? It's been too long."

Elijah hugged her gently as he replied, "It has. I'm sorry. I wish I could have been around more often."

"How did you find me here?"

Cheekily Elijah replied, "We have an App for that."

Nya rolled her eyes and grinned. She broke their embrace and, beaming with delight, took a step backwards. "I was starting to think I had imagined you. Oh, it's so lovely to see you again."

"Let me help." Elijah knelt down and started tugging weeds from the clayish soil around the two gravesites. "By the way, I've put your Ultrabook back on your bedside table."

Her eyebrows raised. "You had it? I thought I may have left it at the hospital."

"One of Cain's goons took it." Elijah yanked on a stubborn weed, the roots of which dug deep into the dirt. He gave it a more spirited tug, and the green leafy stalk ripped from the ground with a bunch of earth. "Cain is in custody at the moment, but he may be after your software again."

"They're not going to find it on the Ultrabook. I deleted the software a while back and ensured the deletion was unrecoverable."

Elijah tossed the mass of different varieties of weeds he was holding into a half-full red plastic bucket that Nya handed to him. "Why all the Ultrabook security?"

"I haven't gotten around to removing it yet." She smiled. "Plus the security keeps Isaac from hogging my Ultrabook playing Minesweeper or Solitaire."

Elijah let out a little chuckle.

"Don't pull that one!" Nya said. Elijah released the thin long leafy reddish plant from his grip. "It's not a weed, but a flower."

"Oops," he said, looking sheepish. "I confess, I was never good at gardening."

Nya glanced towards the headstones. "I miss them, Elijah – my Mum and Dad."

Elijah pulled up a few remaining weeds, tossed them in the bucket, and then went and sat next to Nya who was resting on the grass hugging her knees. "I'm not sure if it's the same, Nya, but I miss my wife and children, too. They are still alive."

"Can't you go and see them?"

"Yes, but I'm not allowed to let *them* see me. It hurts when I see them. I think of the song 'Iris' from the movie *City of Angels* whenever I'm around them."

With a sense of his pain, Nya sang the lyrics. *"And I'd give up forever to touch you. Cause I know that you feel me somehow. You're the closest to heaven that I'll ever be. And I don't want to go home right now."*

His eyes welled with tears as he listened to her enchanting, rather angelic singing voice. "That's beautiful, Nya."

Elijah pulled a seeding dandelion stem out of the ground, complete with a budding flower head made up of dozens of smaller florets attached to their seed heads. "As a child I used to pick these, make a wish, then blow, and watch the dazzling white florets glide through the air carrying the seed to a new destination. When a good wind blows and there is a lot around it almost looks as if it is snowing." Elijah held the white snowy summit of the dandelion in front of Nya. "Make a wish and blow."

After a moment, Nya took a deep breath and blew. White florets, like parachutes, streamed through the air, each one carrying its seed as a passenger. She watched the light breeze carry them some distance before they landed, scattered, in amongst the grass.

Nya pointed to the empty patch of grass next to the gravesites. "That's where I'll be buried."

"Not for some time, I hope," Elijah replied.

"I don't know, Elijah. I'm struggling. I'm fighting, but I'm struggling."

"You can make it through this."

"But I'm so tired of fighting, Elijah." Nya tugged at the grass by her side. "I'm at peace with life. I've had a blessed life, and I'm truly grateful for what I've had."

Elijah pushed Nya on the shoulder. "Don't talk like that. You'll be OK."

"The pain never stops, Elijah."

"Let's go for a walk." Elijah grabbed her hand, stood up, and lifted her onto her feet.

"Around a graveyard?" Nya replied.

"Why not? We might even see a ghost."

Nya laughed before her mood dimmed and she started to sing *In the Arms of an Angel* as they walked hand in hand.

> *There's always some reason*
> *To feel not good enough,*
> *And it's hard, at the end of the day.*
> *I need some distraction*

Elijah squeezed her hand tightly as her voice echoed around the tombstones like an angelic choir.

> *Oh, beautiful release.*
> *Memories seep from my veins.*
> *Let me be empty,*
> *Oh, and weightless,*
> *And maybe I'll find some peace tonight.*
> *In the arms of the angel, Fly away from here.*

"When it's time, Elijah, will you fly me away from here?"

"It would be hard to say no to you, Nya. I'd be happy to if it's possible." They walked together in silence, admiring the golden glow the setting sun cast over the graveyard. "How about I take you for a fly now, anywhere you wish to go?"

"Really? I would love to see the Glass House Mountains from the air."

"All right." Elijah placed his arms around Nya's waist, his belly to her back, and spread his wings. "Ready?"

"Yes!"

After a dramatic downward movement of his angelic wings they rose into the air.

"Won't we need the belt?"

As they continued to climb, Elijah said, "Not this time." When they reached around 5,000 feet, Elijah released one arm from around her waist and took her hand. Then he released the other arm from around her waist.

"How are you holding onto me, Elijah?"

"It's a new trick I've learnt, hard to explain exactly how it works."

Flying parallel to the ground, he pushed Nya away from his body so that he was holding her at arms' length. "Spread your other arm out at your side."

Nya did so, and side-by-side they flew.

"This is incredible, Elijah! I'm flying."

They soared towards the Glass House Mountains. Once there, Elijah circled around their magnificent spires. "Amazing, isn't it."

Nya studied the craggy brown volcanic peaks that had spewed great waves of lava from the earth at some distant time in the past. Now, quiet and stately, they towered like the pointed tips of brown icebergs above an ocean of trees. The mountain ranges were like a family, each standing alone, yet together, separated by tree-lined plains.

"It is breath-taking, Elijah."

Stars began twinkling in the early night sky as the sun set low in the west. Nya gazed in awe at the beauty of the landscape. In that moment, she felt as though she was in Heaven. Free as a bird, gliding on the wind. The endorphins coursing through her blood released all her pain and worries. "Thank you, Elijah."

Elijah flashed her a gentle crooked smile and cast his eyes down as if to say *I wish there was more I could do for you.*

He continued to taking her on the ride of her life. They coasted a few feet above the surface of the salty waters of Moreton Bay, where dolphins leapt alongside them. They glided low through the valleys between the great mountain peaks, skimming the treetops, alongside flocks of birds. They soared down the windy waterways of Stanley River and circled Lake Somerset, admiring the stars and moonlight reflecting off the glassy still water.

After an hour of scenic flight they landed gracefully back at the graveyard.

Nya checked her watch. "I should be getting home, Elijah. Isaac is probably awake by now. I left him a note, but he might get worried."

Elijah nodded, gave her a hug, and whispered, "Take care." He turned to face the moon, unfolded his wings, and readied for flight.

"Wait!" Nya shouted.

Elijah faced her, "Yes?"

"One last thing, Elijah: How did you become an angel?"

He smiled and cast his eye heavenward as if recalling some great adventure, then shrugged. "It would take a novel to explain that."

Nya kept her eyes on Elijah as he took flight and sailed off into the distance. She wondered where he would be going before thinking that he was possibly off to be with his family.

Chapter 37 - Wedding

Nya's heartbeat quickened as Frank opened the rear passenger door of the white limousine parked outside of the church. Frank leant in, gave her his hand, and helped her out of the vehicle.

Over the preceding few weeks Nya and Frank had built up quite a rapport that advanced their friendship. Nya had invited him to over for dinner regularly, and he and Isaac had hit it off quite well. She enjoyed hearing him laugh and have a good time with Frank because although he was a friendly chap Isaac did not have many friends. They had all gotten along so well, in fact, that the previous week Nya had asked Frank if he would lead her down the aisle at her wedding. Frank accepted, saying it would be his privilege.

The small white wooden church on the Northern edge of Caboolture, close to Nya's parents' graves, was located about 15 minutes from Isaac's house by car. Nya had little difficulty in talking Isaac into being married in a church. Isaac, not being the religious type, was at first none too fond of having to stand in front of a pastor. He was keener on a civil celebrant. After some gentle persuasion, however, he had come to realize that it did not matter to him either way. *Who* married them mattered quite a bit to Nya, and so she chose the little church. They had a small circle of friends, which made the size of the church perfect for the occasion. A short pathway led to the rectangular bay-gabled front of the wood church with a fresh coat of white paint. The interior itself was a single hall, and the simple old-fashioned design at once carried a sense of history and created an intensely personal and friendly atmosphere.

As they stood before the large wooden front doors, Frank said, "Are you ready, Nya?"

"I am," she replied. Nya took Frank's hand as she planted her walking stick onto the ground with the other. The last several weeks of battling the cancer had taken their toll on her body. Her legs had become weak. The walking stick provided her the added support necessary to trundle forwards.

Frank pushed open the doors and the music of John Denver's *Annie's Song* began playing through the church's sound system. Nya and Isaac had chosen that song together. The traditional bridal march simply did not appeal to either of them.

Down front, Isaac stood next to the altar at the right side of the aisle that ran down the center of the church. Nya could see him fidgeting his hands, which were no doubt sweating from nervousness. Not because he was anxious over the idea of being married but rather from the stress of stuffing up the vows he had been practicing. The notion of becoming tongue-tied had worried him all week.

"Don't worry, love," he had told her. "All those worries will melt away when I see you walking down the aisle in your dress. Then the only thing on my mind will be that I am the luckiest man on earth."

From the look on his face, he had not lied. Nya's ice blue modern wedding dress, made of thin satin, flowed gracefully down her slender figure and into a full-length skirt. Hand-beaded detail around the front and back of the bodice traced the gentle lines of her torso. A short train with embroidered accents streamed behind. And the hand-crafted scarf cut from the same cloth emphasized her sparkling blue eyes. She looked beautiful in every respect.

Frank walked her slowly down the aisle, timing her approach at the altar with the end of the song. Nya beamed as she fixed her gaze on Isaac's bald head. He had said that he was going to shave his head before they got married in support of her losing her hair. Isaac wanted the wedding photos to show them both with no hair. God love him. Her heart was overflowing. At the altar, she handed her walking stick to Frank, faced Isaac, and grasped his hands. Frank bowed his head and took a seat beside his colleague Leigh on the front row.

The small audience made up of their close friends watched on. Many people in the crowd had tears welling in their eyes, the women dabbing at them with tissues while the men sniffled as if from pollen and dragged their shirt sleeves over their eyes. Nya knew why. Before the service one of her friends had spoken for all of them in sharing how they felt. They all knew the struggles that Nya and Isaac were facing together and greatly admired them for their courage. She said the wedding reinforced her own love for her cherished ones and reminded her that life was short but love carries us through difficult times.

As Nya and Isaac gazed into each other's eyes, Pastor Nathaniel started to speak. "I welcome you all to the marriage of Nya and Isaac. You have been invited here to share in their very special, once-in-a-lifetime, moment."

Nya and Isaac were in their own kind of heaven. They were so in sync that Nya knew he was feeling the same powerful emotions she was feeling. This time meant more to them than they had even imagined. Nya squeezed Isaac's sweaty hands, and he squeezed hers back. Their heads tilted toward each other, just a little, as they could hardly wait for the kiss.

Isaac said, "Nya, I think it's safe I can skip the in sickness and health part." Nya let out a small chuckle before Isaac continued. "You are my fire, which melts my icy heart and allows my love to flow. You are my lighthouse, which guides me during the darkness. You are the wind, which lifts me up when I'm down." He paused for a few seconds and just stared at her radiant smile. Nya knew that he had taken some time on his vows. She appreciated the effort he had taken to come up with his own original vows. He continued. "Let me join us, to be as one in this life, today, tomorrow, and forever. I pledge to be a husband you will respect, admire, and trust."

Nya cleared her throat and then said, "When you asked me to marry me after my diagnosis, it didn't seem real. I could not understand why anyone would want to be with someone going through cancer. Then I thought back to how I wanted to be with my mother during her cancer and *why*. I loved, and still do love, my mother. For you to love me the same, I felt blessed to have someone in my life who would care as deeply for me. I'm not sure I can ever prove my love for you in the same way, Isaac. I can only say that I do. I give myself to you as your wife, and I promise to *always* be grateful for the times we spend together. Let us unite as one."

"Nya," Pastor Nathaniel said, "will you take Isaac as your husband, in happiness and with patience and understanding, through conflict and tranquility?"

"Gladly." Nya took a ring resting on the altar and slid the golden band onto Isaac's shaking finger.

"Isaac, will you take Nya as your wife, in happiness and with patience and understanding, through conflict and tranquility?"

Without hesitation, he replied, "You betcha."

Isaac slipped the remaining ring off the altar and carefully, slowly, slid the diamond-studded gold band onto Nya's waiting finger.

Pastor Nathaniel said, "For years to come we hope Nya's and Isaac's love for each other continues to grow abundantly. May the vows they have made to each other be a constant reminder on their commitment and keep them strong in moments of despair and hardship. For their lives are now lives shared as one, together they shall course through time joyously enjoying the fruits of life on earth, their current home."

After a few seconds of silence, Pastor Nathaniel continued. "In a show of that true love Isaac and Nya have shown before their family and friends, and God, they wish to spend their lives together. I now pronounce them husband and wife. Isaac, you may now kiss your bride."

The small crowd clapped as Isaac touched his soft lips against Nya's. Jolts of electricity shot through them as their lips touched. They had kissed many times before, but this kiss was different. As their mouths slowly opened, they experienced a deeper love for each other than they had before. Endorphins ran akimbo as the passion of their kiss increased before subsiding into a release. They took a moment to gaze into each other's eyes, open windows to each other's souls, and then embraced in a hug, Nya's legs lifting momentarily off the floor.

A sudden dizziness came over Nya, something different, something she had never experienced before. She whispered to Isaac, "This is not the end." She closed her eyes as her legs went limp.

* * *

Sensing the sudden weight of her body, Isaac tightened his grip around her to keep her from falling to the floor. Then he collapsed to his knees holding her, cradling her in his arms as if she were a newborn. His faced turned white. His eyebrows lowered and his jaw dropped. He looked into empty space as he screamed, "Nooooooo!"

The shriek sent shockwaves of anguish through the audience, most of whom stood up, in shock. Several reached for their mobile phones.

Isaac shouted, "Someone, please." His voice went softer knowing his time with Nya was over. "Call an ambulance." He held her tightly, rocking her gently back and forth, sobbing.

* * *

Nya had told him when her time came her death would be probably quick. Like her mother, an aneurism had claimed her. Isaac gave her a gentle kiss on her lips then whispered, "Be at peace."

Chapter 38 - Paris

Isaac stood inside the third-level observation platform of the Eiffel Tower, 279 meters up, overlooking the lights of Paris on a star-filled moonlit night.

In his hand was Nya's cross attached to a golden chain. He had brought the necklace with him knowing how much it had meant to her. She had left Isaac an envelope with the inscription on the front in her own handwriting in blue pen: "Open at the top of the Eiffel Tower."

She had written the letter when it became clear to her that she was not going to make it to Paris for their honeymoon. Nya's solicitor, obeying the instructions given to him, passed the letter onto Isaac on her death. The solicitor informed Isaac that Nya very much wanted him to go on the honeymoon in the event that she was not able to be with him. At first, Isaac balked at the idea, but after contemplating it for some time he decided to take the trip. He was going mad sitting around at home, by himself, moping about. Frank and Leigh would come by regularly, but the visits did not do much to lift his spirits.

Isaac retrieved the envelope from his pocket, used his fingernail to slit open the top, and read the note inside.

Isaac, if you are reading these words then my solicitor has decided, due to my passing or becoming too unwell to handle my own affairs, to give this letter to you. I wanted to ensure you would still go on our honeymoon if I couldn't be with you – in body. I hope you did.

Isaac smiled and whispered, "Of course I did. I would do anything for you."

Thank you for everything, Isaac. You have made the final moments of my life worth living. Even during the times of extreme pain, you made every second worthwhile. You kept me fighting even when the fight was lost. Whatever happened, never believe your efforts were in vain, they helped me tremendously.

A lump formed in his throat as he struggled to read through the tears blurring his vision.

Angels are around us. They are real, and help us when were in need. I hope one day you find God and experience the warmth and comfort a relationship with God can provide during the hardest and best of times.

A man named Zac who passed from bowel cancer, left a video, and at the end he said, "If God heals me, God is good. If I die, God is still good." I believe this, Isaac, so please, don't blame God for my passing.

Love forever, Nya

But Isaac did blame God. He never understood why a loving God would take her. If he existed, why not heal her? It would be so easy for Him. The concept of a loving God taking Nya made no sense to him. At the same time, he struggled to believe that God even existed, which caused him to battle with the idea of how he could blame God.

P.S. In case I never had the chance to say this to you, "This is not the end."

There was a chill in the dark air of Paris and he could see his breath. The coldness comforted him in a kind way. It seemed fitting, for his heart had frozen from pain. Being numb to emotions made getting through each day a little easier.

"Beautiful night," a voice spoke from beside him.

Isaac directed his attention to the source of the voice. A man in a long trench coat with short brownish hair, fair skin, and blue eyes stood next to him. Isaac gazed out over Paris as he shoved the note into his jeans pocket. Ordered lights of different colors scattered the landscape of the City of Lights. Isaac had seen many night scenes before, but none as magnificent as the one he could see tonight. "Yes, it is…. I guess."

The man asked, "What brings you up here on this rather coolish night?"

Isaac clenched his jaw. "I'm on my honeymoon."

"Oh, and where is your wife?"

Isaac dangled the chain and rocked the cross back and forth in front of him. "She passed away."

"I'm sorry to hear that." The man glanced at Isaac's necklace. "Are you a believer?"

"No, no I'm not," Isaac said. "This is her necklace. I can't believe in a God who would take someone as good as my Nya."

Staring out at the lights of Paris the man said in a sincere, comforting voice filled with empathy. "God doesn't always heal a person. He simply brings them home."

Isaac watched the cross dangling from his fingers, swaying back and forth, mesmerizing. He had never considered the possibility of a different home from the one he had, here, on earth.

The man turned to Isaac, put out his hand, "I'm Elijah, Elijah Hael."

Isaac took his hand and shook it. "Isaac."

"Good to meet you, Isaac."

After placing Nya's necklace in his jacket pocket, he asked, "What brings you up here, Elijah?"

"Oh, just flying around."

Isaac nodded. He was not sure what the man meant, much less how to reply.

After a few moments, Isaac asked, "Do you think she is out there, out there somewhere?"

* * *

Elijah peered into the Spiritual Realm. Castiel gave him a wink while Nya pain-free and fully healed, with a radiant smile full on her face, stood next to Isaac and gazed out at the beauty of Paris.

"I'm sure she is," Elijah said. "Probably closer than you realize."

The End

Song Lyric Credits

"In the Arms of an Angel"

Lyrics: Sarah McLaughin

"This is not the End"

Lyrics: Gungor

"Iris"

Lyrics: Goo Goo Dolls

"Annie's Song"

Lyrics: John Denver

Book Blurb

Nya struggled to believe her accomplishment. Nearly a decade's work was all coming together. This was her moment. The Nobel Prize would be hers for the taking. Her work was going to change the very face of bio-science forever.

The only problem was, someone with a very dark desire wanted to twist her work for very sinister purposes that would change the very face of life on earth forever. And he was prepared to go to any lengths to get it.

Thus began a chain of startling events that would force Nya to place her trust in an unknown man whom she discovered from archived news reports … had died years ago.

Keep up to date with Elijah Hael at

Facebook

www.facebook.com/ElijahHaelTheGeneticCode

Official Web Site

www.ElijahHael.com

Official Blog

blog.ElijahHael.com

Authors Facebook Page

www.facebook.com/SteveGoodwinAuthor

Authors Blog

www.stevegoodwin.org

Elijah Hael & The Last Judgement

"What is your name?"

Elijah looked around, puzzled. He wondered who the man who was asking him questions was and how he had gotten here—wherever he was. "My name?"

"Yes, your name," the man said. "What is it?"

Elijah looked at the man seated across the small rather old wooden desk from him and said, "Elijah. Elijah Hael. But, wait, how did I get here?"

"*I* will be asking the questions," the man said in a stern but matter-of-fact tone. "You will be answering them."

Elijah nodded.

Thus began the merciless interrogation. Confused and disoriented, Elijah Hael scrambled to defend himself for various crimes he was not even aware he had committed. It seemed that all would be lost ... until a mysterious stranger bearing an envelope entered the room. And in that instant *everything* changed, in ways that Elijah Hael and those who read his story could never anticipate or imagine.

Join Elijah Hael on his spellbinding and unforgettable journey and discover, with him, the answers to a host of questions: Where is Elijah Hael? Is he innocent, guilty, pardoned? Who is the mysterious stranger? What is in the envelope? Why has Elijah been set free and at what cost?

www.ingramcontent.com/pod-product-compliance
Lightning Source LLC
Chambersburg PA
CBHW062125170626
46813CB00002B/575